HITTING HOME

by

ROBERT WILKINSON.

CHAPTER 1

'Marcellus'

"Marcellus," the hiss of breath, boasted stale tobacco and bygone garlic-laced meals along with its strong undercurrent of threats. "Marcellus, tell us what we want. Tell us and it will all be over."

Marcellus, once powerfully built, grinned pathetically at his captors. He was now a battered, bruised, cut and drugged shell before them. All that sustained him against the ordeal was his resolve. Metternic returned his grim smile and pulled back his arm in a wide arc striking Marcellus' shattered cheekbone, causing him to slump forward in his chair. He showed no pain, even though he felt it. By now it was only the pain that sustained him. He could feel the pain, therefore he was alive. It was as simple as that.

Metternic stood back in the concrete room, rubbed the stubble on his chin, and contemplated the next step. The upright guard by the iron door looked across as another man walked in. A tall man, thin to the point of emaciation entered, and removed his hat. Unlike Metternic, he wore a sharp suit, crisply starched shirt and discreet striped tie. He nodded his welcome to Metternic who lit a cigarette and retired to the rear of the plain cell, beneath the air vent and spoke to the new man in hushed tones. "Still no names?"

Metternic shook his head.

"Tough bastard this one. Any more punishment and it will probably kill him."

"Not before we have the name!"

The command in Radagadz voice was unmistakable. Metternic exhaled cheap smoke through his clenched teeth. He would not gainsay his boss. He had attended too many funerals of his colleagues who had.

"What next? Why is this one more important than the others?" Radagadz put his face near that of the other mans, and stared at him, grey cold eyes issuing dark threats and innuendo. He pulled back and lit his own cigarette. American, not the cheap Albanian state imports which Metternic was poisoning himself with. He spoke to his subordinate in a conspiratorial tone. "My friend, I will tell you this. I expect it not to be repeated."

He nodded. It would not be.

"Marcellus here is a spy. American, British, who knows. I am sure he has a contact in our military command. A traitor who is passing on information to him. Information which, in the right hands, would allow the fucking Moslem hordes to overwhelm us. Meddling westerners are getting vital information from a high source of power. Needless to say, the Minister is fairly keen to know the source of the leak.

Marcellus here knows the man. Knows the name. We must not fail in this. I have promised the minister personally."

Metternic knew what that meant. He lit another vile cigarette and nodded over to their captive. He was falling asleep. The guard by the door walked over and kicked him, to keep him awake, then returned to his sentinel pose.

Metternic continued.

"He is very tough. He has been branded, beaten. Treated with electricity, had cuts infected with shit on his back, chest and balls, and has had three fingers chopped off. Toughest bastard I've ever known. Like I said, any more and he'll die."

Radagadz looked over to him.

"OK. Treat his wounds, let him sleep- for a couple of hours- I'll bring my doctor friend. He has some interesting drugs which should loosen his tongue. We must not fail Metternic. You must not fail."

He left, and Metternic carried out his orders, releasing Marcellus from his chair and allowing him to rest on a camp bed, after a nurse had given him a wash and treated the worst of the cuts and infections with stinging antiseptic. He would return later. A couple of hours rest would serve him well too.

The small, wiry man leaned against the broken wall and pulled a bent cigarette from its battered pack and tried vainly to light it with a book of damp matches. It was wet. He was wet. Everywhere was wet. The rains had been long and persistent that autumn, soon eclipsing the memories of the hot summer. Now the mountain villages were slippery with mud. Curcic trudged though the mini torrent which was once the main street, his battered holed shoes offering little protection against the cold muddy waters. He neared the uniformed militia guard who was huddling away from the rain in a guardhouse, ostensibly protecting the building behind him, which was the local military headquarters. Curcic shuffled inside the six by four corrugated hut.

"Excuse me. Sorry to trouble, but could you spare a light? I have managed to get some cigarettes after doing without for two months and all my matches are wet."

The guard looked at him suspiciously. He was scruffy, wore oversized trousers secured to his waist by a belt, an old collarless shirt and patched cardigan, topped by a pin striped suit jacket. His shoes were inadequate. He decided that he looked harmless, and he could begrudge no one shelter from this weather. He nodded his agreement, and his conditions.

"I will trade a light for a cigarette." Curcic nodded reluctantly and offered him a twisted smoke. At least the tobacco was dry.

The guard inhaled appreciatively and looked at the cigarette in his hand. "French." He nodded appreciatively. "Where did you get.."

Curcic offered a nervous laugh. "You know you can get anything for a price."

The guard nodded. Curcic knew that he would have no interest in tracking down black marketeers, but would be more interested in being able to get some scarce commodities. That was how life was now. The normality of law and order had been superseded by a different order, a different rule. Rule by fear, rule by reaction to ethnic hysteria, rule by brutal repression and retribution. Petty matters such as theft, smuggling, and muggings were all given no priority. Few seemed to care. In a few short years the country had become uncaring and brutal.

"French cigarettes. A pretty price too I bet?"

Curcic nodded. "I have more. I have the best commodity in trade." The guard looked back at him. Curcic held his gaze for only a second and returned to his cigarette. He looked back at the guard.

"I would buy your lighter. How much?"

The guard laughed. He had had the lighter only a few days. Had taken it from one of the poor 'visitors' to the building he was ostensibly guarding. It was nice. Zippo. Good stuff.

"What makes you think I want to sell?"

"Money. Dollars. American dollars."

The guard stopped his smoking. Here was a sudden interest. With American dollars you could get anything. He would see just what the man had.

"Fifty dollars. You can have it for fifty dollars." Curcic laughed out loud and finished his smoke, flicking the end into the stream which ran in front of the hut. The guard looked out, doing his duty. When he stopped laughing, Curcic looked at the much taller man.

"OK. Fifty. Here."

He handed across five bills, creased but whole to the man who examined them carefully before stuffing them into his pocket and tossing the lighter to Curcic. He looked out into the rain again, to make sure no one was looking.

"Want to earn some more?"

The guard bared his teeth.

"What is your game? Are you trying to trap me? Get me into trouble?"

"No, no. Look, my friend I will be honest with you. I have to find someone, I need help. I am willing to pay for that help."

The guard looked down once again, scrutinised him closely, and tried to glean more information from his appearance. He was as eccentrically normal as the rest. Worse than some, better than many. He seemed harmless enough, could be easily overpowered if needs be. He nodded slowly.

"What do you want to know? Who do you need to find?" Curcic nodded. "Look, not here. Your bosses may start getting suspicious if they see me in here talking to you. What time do you finish?"

"In two hours. I'll meet you at the top end of town. There are two trees at the end of the road. Behind the one on the right there is a ruined house see me there. We can talk then."

Curcic watched from the shelter of some bushes a little was up the hill from his rendezvous. He needed to be sure that the guard would come alone, and that there was to be no trap. He saw the man trudge up the hill, rifle slung over his shoulder and hat at a tired angle. His army issue boots were giving him plenty of protection against the muddy wet streets. The rain had stopped and twilight was whispering her goodbyes to the day as the other man entered the shell of the house. Nicolai waited five minutes, scrutinised all ways to the house then deciding it safe slipped down the hill and into the house. He called out a welcome to the guard.

"Ssh fool. Come."

He led Curcic to the cellar door and descended into the blackness, squelching through some water until they stepped up onto a raised brick plinth which had three battered chairs and a table. The guard lit candles with a (different) lighter and fished a bottle from under some dusty sheets and poured stale wine into two filthy tumblers. He pushed one to his guest. "What are you called?"

"Curcic."

He frowned slightly tossing the name around his memory looking for a connection. He could find none. "Where are you from? I haven't seen you around here before."

"Nis. I originate from Nis. My mother still lives there." He nodded. He knew the place. It was about eighty kilometres away. Curcic was a name from those parts, and his accent fitted. He seemed satisfied. He had to be careful. Everybody had to be careful.

"How shall I call you?"

"Me? Oh just call me Rad. But tell me what you want?" Nicolai kept the wince from his face as he sipped some of the wine. He offered a cigarette to Rad.

"How do you know this place?"

"Family home. Was. Talk."

Nicolai exhaled smoke and held the man's stare easily, but kept the sense of intrusion skilfully away.

"I have a friend, or rather, a business associate who is in the building which you are guarding."

"How do you know that?"

Curcic smiled. "I just know. I have made it my business to know. But I need to get a message to this person, and for him to give a reply. I need to see him for a brief period of time."

Rad laughed. Poured more wine and laughed again. "Very funny. Do you know what the building is?"

Nic nodded slowly. "I believe it is where suspects are er questioned."

"Yes it is. How long has your friend been there?"

"Three days."

"I should not waste your time. He is probably dead already."

"I must find out."

"Why is this so important to you? What is in it for me?"

Curcic sipped more wine and spoke.

"I shall tell you. If you can get me to see my associate for a few minutes I will give you six hundred dollars. Just a few moments face to face, or at least in hearing distance, deliver my message, get my reply and then out. You'll never see me again, and you get your money."

"You're telling me, that you want to get in to the building, talk to a prisoner then casually get out. You are off your fucking head. There are a lot of soldiers in there. No. It cannot be done. I may consider taking a note but that is all." Nicolai shook his head.

"No. I must see him personally. It is vital."

"What is so important? Why not send a note?"

"Let me say this to you. My associate has knowledge of the whereabouts of certain er goods. I need to ask him, and get the reply. He will tell me, I have no doubt about that. I also have no doubt that he will not tell anyone else. If I send a note, two things happen. One he will not write the reply on it. Two, even if he did, it is safer for you and me that no-one else knows the contents of the note. The trust would be gone. It could get complicated."

Rad knew what words like 'complicated' meant in these times. They were the new words of threat, the new language of disappearance and torture. He did not feel threatened by Curcic, but any one with access to large amounts of dollars obviously had useful contacts. He felt in a curious dilemma. First was his duty, not that he cared much for that, he was doing it through self-preservation, rather than devotion. He was sorely tempted by the money, it would smooth the way quite nicely. Well, very nicely. It would give his children clothes and good food. The third part of his predicament was the fear of entrapment, double-crossing and being caught. If he was caught, well the prospects were unthinkable. He turned to the other man. "I am not happy about this. What information is it?"

"I cannot tell you."

"I am not asking you to tell me exact details. I need to know if it is about black market, or is it to help betray.." He was cut short by Curcic.

"Don't even think of betrayal. I am a patriot. But I am a pragmatic patriot. Suffice it to say that it is knowledge of the whereabouts of certain goods- and they are not guns."

Rad nodded slowly. It was one thing being caught making money. It was another being caught smuggling guns to Muslims. "OK. Two thousand dollars. My price is two thousand dollars."

Curcic looked at the man with a frown on his face.

"Before I agree to your price, I need to know how you will do it.

How you will get me there."

"If your friend is being questioned, he will be in the cells. The dungeons as we call them. In some ways it is better he is there, than in the ground floor cells. More activity there. More guards. The underground cells are all separate. I know a way into the boiler house, and around the back into the ventilation system. You are small enough to crawl into the vent and can go to the grid in the room. You should be able to see him and speak to him through that."

"Will it be wide enough. Wide enough for him to see my face? He will have to be sure it is me."

"Yes. There are fans with three to four centimetre wide flaps, which open when the fan is on. Just need to make sure we disconnect the fan, so that you can lift the flap, and not get your nose chopped off."

Curcic nodded. It seemed ideal. "OK. I agree to your price. You get it on completion."

"Five hundred now. The rest when the job is done. With respect my friend, you don't exactly look like you are flush with cash." "How could I wear a suit? I need to blend. OK When?"

Rad smiled and poured more wine.

"Soonest is best. For one, your friend has a limit of time. I will need your friends' name. Find out his cell."

"Marcellus."

"Meet me tomorrow. Here. Same time. I'll get the key. Do it at night. Bring the five hundred."

"Fine. See you then."

The next evening Curcic saw Rad hurry up the hill to the house. He slipped over to see him, and they descended once more into the cellar. When Rad had lit the candles he turned quickly and grabbed Nicolai by the neck slamming against the damp wall, taking his breath momentarily from him.

"You mad fucker! Marcellus! Nearly shit myself when I found out who was looking after him. Fucking Radagadz, that's all. Head sadist. No fucking chance."

"Look, look. What is the problem? I don't know who this Radagadz is. All I need is a few minutes..."

"You can have one minute. And the price is double. I must be mad even thinking about it."

Rad released him, and sat in a chair. When he had found out that Radagadz was in charge he had been consumed with guilt and panic. Fortunately for him, he knew the building intimately, and most of the militia. They were from the same town, from the same race, had the same friends, and were troubled less by the civil war than most. He got his information without the slightest suspicion. He had wondered if he had blushed when the gossip turned to Radagadz and the mysterious Marcellus. It was assumed that he was some kind of spy. It had to be someone important for Radagadz to be involved.

He wondered about Curcic, wondered if he was a spy, thought he was, and it gave him fresh doubts, but offered him fresh solutions. He would go along with the plan, collect the money, and then turn Curcic in. Might even shoot him, to save his own neck. He would decide that later. He looked back at Curcic. He was pacing the room.

"I don't have that kind of money. Not yet anyway. Not until I know where..." His voice tailed off. "Tell you what. I can get about three thousand for you, and can make the rest up in goods."

"Goods? What kind of goods,"

"Cigarettes. Maybe some scotch whiskey, maybe some cocaine."

"I have no need for drugs. "

"It has value. A commodity to trade. Nothing more."

"Ok. Forget the whiskey- too heavy to carry- no make it one bottle."

"Here."

Curcic tossed a bundle of dollars to the other man. Five hundred as arranged. He looked at it, did not count it and stuffed it in his pocket.

"What about the rest?"

"As we said. Later, when I have seen Marcellus."

"Meet me at midnight, about two hundred metres to the left of the guard hut, there is a telegraph pole. Meet me there. Don't trick me or..."

"Don't worry. This time in a few hours you will have what you asked for. Then you'll never see me again and nobody will be any the wiser."

Rad nodded.

"Curcic. Tell me one thing. This Marcellus is already a dead man. Why should he want to share the whereabouts of his wealth with you?"

"It is a family matter. He is in the family business. It is a question of honour. "

They met as arranged and scurried around the back of the building. It was unguarded, there was little need. The war was raging well to the south, the storm had left them, for the moment at least. They descended to the cellar, Rad showing the way to the ventilation shaft, and pointed upwards where the grill had been removed. It was barely big enough for Rad, but Nicolai was small and wiry and would be able to crawl easily down it. Rad looked around.

"All the fans are off, so no worries there. Your friend's cell is straight down. It is either the third or fourth grill. Just be quick. You have one minute."

He lifted Curcic into the aperture and he scrambled down the shaft. At the third grill he lifted the flap and saw a woman sleeping fitfully on a makeshift bed. He moved to the next. Carefully lifting the flap he noted a guard by the door, smoking and pacing around. To his front, sitting in a chair, arms fastened down head slumped forward was the unmistakable form of Marcellus.

Curcic reached down into the front of his trousers and pulled out his pistol, and then carefully screwed on the long silencer. He peered through the flap and inched the silencer barrel through the small aperture. There was just enough room for him to aim accurately. He squeezed the trigger, the 'pop' disturbing Marcellus as the guard tumbled forward, a neat hole in his forehead, a wide gaping wound at the back of his head and red stained wall behind.

Marcellus looked around, and grinned inanely.

"Marcellus! Marcellus: It is Mercury. Can you hear me?" Curcic half whispered, half shouted to the man. Marcellus knew why he was here. He needed no prompting to deliver his message. With half closed eyes he called out.

"It is OK. Everything is safe. I have kept my silence. They do not know. Thank you."

Curcic nodded to himself and squeezed the trigger twice.

Marcellus twitched to his death. His secret safe. Curcic unscrewed the silencer and felt the wince of pain as the hot gun barrel burnt his thigh as he re secreted the weapon then quickly scrambled back down the vent to Rad.

"OK?" He hissed.

Nicolai nodded. "Yes. Got what I wanted. Now let's get out of here. Your money and goods are at the house."

Rad replaced the grill and retraced their steps to the house they went unchallenged, only stepping into the shadows as a black Mercedes swept down the street.

In the cellar Rad was lighting the candles and turned round to face Curcic who was pointing the barrel of a silenced pistol at him.

"What?"

"Yes, sorry old boy. All fair in love and all that stuff. Thanks for the help, couldn't have done it without you. Couldn't let Marcellus talk to Radagadz. Sorry."

As he left the house alone, Curcic looked down the street. They would have found Marcellus' body by now. He looked up the mountains. Quickest way was to climb and go over. He looked forward to putting his boots on; they were about two kilometres up and across the mountains. He wondered whether they would ever find Rads body. He shrugged. He did not care.

CHAPTER 2

'Different Lives'

Tim eased gently into his well-worn armchair. It was almost as if he was a naughty boy hiding away from his parents whilst they were out looking for him. He was in a way, hiding. Well avoiding anyway. He pressed the appropriate button on the remote and watched the television warm to life.

Nancy was out. It was from her that he was 'hiding'. He released a beer from its home, listening to the hiss with smug satisfaction. She hated that. Hated him slothing about, sinking into lethargy and watching football on the box.

To Tim it was as close to his ideal as possible. England playing live, cold beer, bag of smoky bacon, and more importantly- no her. No Nancy. No wife to nag, to ridicule or berate him for his simple pleasure. If he loved football, she hated it more. He could never understand that even if there was nothing of interest to her on the television that she couldn't bear it if a match was on. It was as if she wished to rid the world of the beautiful game. He had tried a few times to comprehend her loathing for soccer, but never got near her motivation. He once thought that because she was so active, enjoyed playing sports, certain sports anyway, and he was an inactive voyeur for all forms of sporting activity, that she felt a kind of superiority to him, felt that playing was good, watching was bad.

He had long since given up worrying about her opprobrium, and became quite secretive about his slavish devotions to the endless diet of sport served to him on his satellite dish. He had become like an alcoholic- a sportaholic- sneaking in, watching the games in secret, like hiding evidence of his empty bottle of sportahol. Now was nice. She was in a tennis competition, or squash, or something, and would be home later, around eleven. After the game, highlights, post match comments and reruns had finished. He could enjoy the match, beer, and crisps without interruption. Very nice.

In many ways they led very different lives, were very different people. Not that they had always been like that. They had grown into other people, had different, ideas, ideals, and goals now. He didn't care that much, having become much more self-oriented and hedonistic. So was Nancy. Her pleasures were different to his. That was all.

Twenty four years of wedded bliss were behind them, and here he was, forty seven years old, overweight and underpaid, with a fit energetic wife who constantly nagged him to get up and get in shape, to lose weight before his arteries hardened completely. She blackmailed him by telling him that Anthony, their only child, now away at university, needed a father, and his future children would need a grandfather. She was right, of course, but the thought of pounding the streets was foreign to him, and the idea of working out under the sadistic eye of a trainer at some gymnasium just turned him cold. He would do something about his weight, his fitness, but not just now. The match was about to start.

She was late that night and he was already in bed. He didn't worry about her staying out late, after all she had told him she could be late, if the match went well, they would stay behind and celebrate. How they could celebrate with mineral water was a strange notion to Tim. She crept in around midnight. He was not asleep, but pretended to be. He didn't want to be regaled by the re-run of her night with her toffee-nosed friends from the squash club. Or was it the tennis club? Who cared? He didn't.

Next morning he buttered his toast as she breezed down. Even at seven thirty she looked good. Even Tim had to admit to it. She had a beautiful tanned trim figure, short blonde hair, and had well cut clothes. She had always had excellent taste in fashion, and now, well she looked around thirty, having cheated nature by some fifteen years. She poured juice and pecked him somewhere on the ever-broadening bald patch on top of his head.

"Morning sweetie. Sorry I was late. The game went on rather late.

All the excitement I suppose."

Tim knew he should ask about the excitement, but deliberately chose not to. She would tell him anyway. Besides it infuriated her. He stuffed more toast in his mouth.

"We won! Made it to the finals. Went right to the last match.

Doubles. Tanya and Joe. Tie breaker in the end."

"Great."

"I won my singles."

"Great."

"Aren't you interested?"

"Interested? Of course. I'm pleased for you. I'll come and watch you in the finals if you like."

She heaved her breasts slightly, reigning in her temper. He always did this to her. Always. She slammed the glass on the worktop and took her tennis clothes from her bag and stuffed them forcibly into the washer muttering " don't bloody bother". in the process.

He sighed too. He had over stepped the mark. Maybe he could have shown a little more interest. It was important to her. But then he shrugged. Why should he? She was good at this, good at making him feel guilty, making him be the one to relent. Well he wouldn't apologise. Balls to her. Let her play with her own toys, he was taking his ball away.

"Better get to work. New boss starts today."

He waved at her and grabbed his coat before stepping out into the bright sunlight.

"Bitch!" He cursed to himself seeing her car hemming his in the driveway. He had told her about this before. Leave a gap for him to get out in the morning. A few minutes the wrong side and he could get fouled up in the morning rush, make him late. Well make him so he would have to start work straight away, rather than enjoying a coffee and secret cigarette in the canteen, and chewing over the remains of the indifferent football match the previous evening. He unlocked the door.

"Nance? Nancy? NANCY!"

"What?"

She half entered the hallway, rubber gloved hands indicated she was washing the pots. She always wore rubber gloves to wash the pots; they kept her hands smooth. "What?"

"Your car. It's in the way. Again."

"Oh. Be a sweetie and move it for me. The keys are hanging up.

I'm in the middle of.."

"Can't you..? Oh never mind."

He grabbed the keys and stormed out, outrageously revving her engine as he parked it carelessly across his neighbours' drive. He moved his vehicle out and drove hers back across the front of the lawn running over some plants in the process, then chucked the keys on the hall table before roaring off to catch the dual carriageway into town and to work.

Work was dull. Dull and dreary. It always was. He had been there twenty years. Twenty years of the same routine. Piles of invoices passed through to him, in the past few years that had altered by the arrival of an office computer, it had been a welcome change at the time, but now it was routine once more. In some ways he didn't mind, it taxed him not, and he could enjoy the office banter without losing out on his efficiency. It was all so different from his early promise. He had a good degree from Sheffield, and early on, early in his marriage he seemed the man most likely to succeed. He was bright, bright but lazy. He accepted it now. lived with the stigma. Knuckled down to the reality of having to earn a crust.

Nancy had often goaded him to seek promotion. Early at Fenners, she had encouraged him to leave when promotion passed him by, but now, twenty years of service, twenty years of pension contributions anchored him firmly to the cause. Today, well, another new start. Yet another new boss. He considered whether to suck up to this new one like he had done to countless others, wondered whether to retread those worn out boards once more. Could not decide. He smiled as he drove into the car park.

"I used to be decisive, but now..."

Same tired old jokes. Same tired old routine. He decided to be spontaneous. To go with the flow. See how this new boss was, what his attitude was. Decide on the spur. He'd see. Probably a new whippersnapper, college boy arriving with great ambitions, ready to change the world, to climb the corporate ladders. Just like he had done really. Those twenty years ago. Came as assistant accountant, ready for big things. He could do the job his new boss had, could do it standing on his head, but getting it was another matter. He had been passed over time and again. His personnel file was probably filed under 'L' for 'loser'. Trouble was, nobody wanted a forty seven-year old boy wonder.

"Morning Tom. See the match? Yeah, pretty dire eh? I still say Lewis is the man to shore up the defence, not that prima donna Madison. Wants to prance about.. yeah. See you in a bit."

Most of his conversations were like that. Shallow, meaningless drivel. He could have held a conversation with a plant and still come away with the essence of the usual standard of his chat. He had few friends. Knew plenty of people, casually. Had only one close friend, one real confidante, some one on whom he could hang the dubiously meritorious title of 'best friend'. Most of the people he and Nancy mixed with socially, went out with, invited over and the rest were friends' of Nancy. He was like an accessory to her on such occasions. It was a duty he reluctantly fulfilled. He entered his vast office and grimaced at the pile of invoices waiting for him.

"Bloody Thursdays." Always the busiest day and month end to boost activity levels. Funny day for a new boss to start. He mentioned it to Craig who sat opposite him.

"Naw, not really Tim. Started on Monday apparently. Been doing the company indoctrination programme. You know, lobotomy, personality transplant. Humour bypass, that sort of thing. Bright young thing or so I understand and.."

He was cut short by the arrival of Morris. Director and Chief Bastard. Everybody fell silent in his presence. Well almost everybody. Tim didn't. The rebellious streak in him surfaced in that mans' presence. He found him to be odious. It was probably the main reason he had never earned promotion at Fenners, stemming back to the time when, shortly after his arrival there, he had been on a working party with Morris, who was then the ascending star of the company, not yet bestowed with the title of director, when Tim had called him

George. Not in itself a major gaffe, but when Tim had been corrected by being told that his correct title was "Mr Morris, thank you Oakes." It just seemed to summon up the red mists for Tim.

"In that case, my correct title is Mr Oakes, thank you Morris." He could still recall the deafening silence in the room at the time, and recalled the boiling staring eyes of the other man. Shortly after he had been taken off the working party and the two men rarely spoke since. When they did, Tim still insisted on calling him Morris, and received an unsmiling response of 'Oakes'. It seemed to be petty revenge to hold a man down for a spot of trivial name calling. But then, it had been petty and naive of Tim to do it in the first instance. He had not relented, nor ever would. It was typical of him, standing up hard and fast for something so meaningless, and yet caving in easily when important things happened.

His new boss approached, shaking hands carefully with each member of staff, and diligently repeating each name when offered, as if trying to commit it to memory. The big surprise, to Tim, was that his new boss was a she. He had never had a female boss before, save for Nancy.

"Ah hello Mr Oakes. I understand you are the father of the house as it were. I shall lean heavily on your experience."

She was medium height, had short bobbed dark hair, pale skin, plum coloured lipstick, piercing deep blue eyes, all neatly packaged in a trim dark suit. She was maybe twenty four. No older. Similar age to his son. She was pretty.

"If you want to lean on me. Lean away. Sorry I didn't catch your name..?"

Morris leaned forward. "Miss Woodward. Oakes."

"Nice to meet you Miss Woodward-Oakes. I see we share something of the same surname, maybe we're related?"

Morris glared the famous glare. Miss Woodward blushed, blood pumped through her pale cheeks giving her an alluring new hue. Oakes, reddened slightly at his stupid joke. His new boss defused the moment.

"Actually it's just Woodward. Joanne Woodward. I shall see you later."

She glanced a smile at him, then looked past him and continued the rounds. Craig leaned over and whispered to him.

"Cracking start Tim my boy. Old Morris didn't seem full of the joys did he? Did you do it on purpose?"

Tim didn't bother to answer. He couldn't answer. He didn't know why he did it. Didn't matter really. He picked up the pile of papers and breathed in deeply. He would bury himself in the delights of his mind-expanding work. Joy oh joy.

Joanne Woodward seemed to be quite pleasant after all. She held a staff meeting on the Friday, and on Monday called Tim in to her office. He wondered whether her first task was to deliver the poisoned chalice. He considered apologising for his crassness, or crassitude as he liked to call it. He didn't know whether it was a real word.

"Sit down Mr.. can I call you Tim? I prefer Joanne."

Tim smiled to himself, thought to say that he didn't feel he looked like a Joanne, but decided against it. He nodded to her, indicating his consent.

"Right Tim, I know you have been around here for a long time, know everybody, know all the ins and outs and all the short cuts etc. Mr Morris tells me you are a very capable man. Capable of more."

"More? More what?"

"Bear with me, Tim." She stood and walked to the coffeepot pouring them both a cup, before returning to her seat. He looked closely at her. His first estimate may have been wrong. He noticed for the first time slight lines under her eyes, a slight veining around the neck, and judicious use of make up covering other minor blemishes. He pushed her age to thirty. She interrupted his thoughts.

"Times change. Fenners must change. I have been brought in to make those changes. We must move on or die. It is as simple as that."

Here it comes, he thought. The bullet. The chop. The sack. The boot. Hang any name on it, it accounted to the same thing. He tried to quickly calculate what twenty years redundancy was worth. She was talking still, but talking on a different topic to the one along which his mind now wandered.

"..and as a result we will split the operation in two. Input and output. Simplify what we earn and what we spend. This will also mean investing in more new technology to stream in the new plans, the equipment is to be delivered in seven weeks. To implement the strategy I will need two trusty, dependable and loyal team leaders. It will mean downsizing the liveware and these team leaders must be up to the task of assisting in that process. What do you think?"

Tim looked puzzled. It was no pathetic joke. He was puzzled. What on earth was she talking about? He shook his head and spoke slowly.

"Sorry, but I don't understand. What exactly are you proposing?"

"Which part don't you understand?"

"All of it? No, sorry I understand that you are going to split the operation. Credit and debit. Understand that new equipment is coming, scanners, read-feeders, that kind of thing, yes?"

She nodded. He sipped his coffee and continued. "Liveware? What's that?"

"Operators. Input manipulators."

"People, you mean?"

"Yes."

"Oh."

"Is there a problem, Tim?"

"Where do I fit in? Why are you telling me this?"

"Team leaders Tim. I'm talking team leaders."

"Me? A team leader?"

She nodded, and stood up, walking to the window, revealing her shapely legs through the split in her skirt. His mind wandered again. She brought him back.

"It isn't definite you understand. Not cast in stone. I just want to sound you out. Get your thoughts on the scheme that sort of thing. Well?"

He leaned back in the chair. Looked back to her, pushed intrusive thoughts to the background and played a straight bat.

"I've got to say I'm interested in what you say. It makes sense.

I've been saying it for years. We are an inefficient bunch.

Fenners has been slow to embrace the computer age."

"That is changing."

"Yes, of course. I would like know more. Know why you are asking me. After all you don't know me at all."

"Your record speaks for itself. Intelligent, unfulfilled. Grasp new ideas quickly. Rebellious. Basically Tim, you are a real pain in the arse, but there is no more well qualified man or woman on the staff. I don't know why you haven't been promoted before now."

"Wait till you know me better."

"Very well. I will."

He felt stung by that remark. Surely his reply hadn't been so bad had it? So bad to dash the job away from him? She laughed at him playfully enjoying his squirming discomfort.

She was better than he had originally thought, had better perception than he had first expected. He smiled back. She leaned forward arms on the desk and looked him in the eye. He couldn't help but notice her cleavage. He knew she knew. Knew it was part of her strategy to disarm, to control and gently seduce him into her web of corporate ambition.

"Look Tim. No bullshit. If you can keep your stupid comments to yourself, if you can keep your mouth shut when you feel the urge to make a merry quip, if you can fire the corporate bullet on our behalf.."

"..you'll be a man my son."

She rolled her eyes upwards, lit a cigarette and stared at him, shaking her head slightly.

"See what I mean. Can't keep it buttoned can you?"

"Sorry, er Joanne. I hear what you are saying. You are giving me a chance yes?"

"I'm sounding you out. That is all. I am not 100% convinced. I want you to think about what I've said. I want your total secrecy for now. I want you to draw me up a thumbnail sketch of what priorities you think we have. I want you to short list twelve people who would be your first choice in your team. Bring it with you on Thursday. Eight o'clock. Here. We'll talk of offers and the like when we've had a full conversation."

"Eight o'clock? Evening or morning?"

"Morning."

He returned to his desk. Craig leaned over.

"What was that all about?"

"Bollocking."

"Oh the Woodward-Oakes thing?"

"Yeah. Woodward. Oakes. That's the thing. Canny wee lass is our Miss Woodward. Anyway, numbers to crunch, brain cells to kill. Tally-ho."

Oakes. That's the thing. Canny wee lass is our Miss Woodward. Anyway, numbers to crunch, brain cells to kill.

Tally-ho.

CHAPTER 3

'Promises'

Tim and Nancy spoke to each other often. They communicated in real conversation on a less regular basis. Occasionally the tides of their oration overlapped to give the semblance of intelligent utterance, but in reality were random bites of sound intended for personal consumption, rather than the ebbing and flowing of real intercourse.

"Interesting developments at work, Nance."

"Changes at the club. Big developments. I mean big."

"I have a new boss now. I don't know if I told you before. Her names Jo."

"Joe is in charge now."

"Anyway she is reorganising the entire operation, and about bloody time too."

"Hatchet job."

"Yes. She is talking about team leaders. Asked me if I was interested."

"Team is breaking up, despite the other night. Need a ladies captain."

"What do you think? I think I'll go for it."

"Go for it? Glad we are of the same mind. I will." She leaned over and gave Tim and unexpected kiss.

"Hey, thanks Tim. Glad we agree on something."

He looked back at her and smiled.

"Yeah. Makes a change. Thank you."

Nancy was out at her aerobics class, and for once Tim left the TV firmly in the off position. He was due to see Jo, Joanne next day, and hadn't yet got round to doing his list. He fetched out a note pad and scribbled the reorganisation plan down. That was easy. He knew everything about the operation. Knew where the crap was, knew the important tasks, knew the flow of work to its critical path. He had prepared such things before for interviews, had thought them through carefully, but had never had the real opportunity to air them properly.

The next part was more troublesome. He had no problem in picking out the best workers, those who were most proficient and efficient. The tea lady could do that. What concerned him most were the consequences of his selection. Would those not on the list be given the chop, and whets more, would he be the one to do it? He agonised for a while. Stood and fetched a can of beer, but left it unopened. He finally decided.

"Sod it!"

If he didn't do it someone else would. If he gave her a list of the people he liked the best, rather than worked the best would have two outcomes. One, he wouldn't get the job, and two, he might find himself on the other list. The list for the condemned. Actually, he secretly longed for that, but his financial obligations were quite onerous. He had a large mortgage. A son on extended university education, and had only in the past few years escaped the onerous debts he had incurred through investing in a dubious business opportunity with his beloved brother-in-law. He had ended up by being saddled with enormous debts and liabilities, whilst dear Graham had gone abroad, ostensibly to work, but in reality to avoid Tim, and Nancy. But that was a different story. Suffice it to say that at a point in his life when his contemporaries had paid off their mortgages, were contemplating early retirement and topping up pension funds to the full, taking two or three holidays a year, he was in the mire. As it was he would have to work to the age of sixty eight to pay off the mortgage. He had borrowed on it to pay off the debts from the business. It had been, and still was a source of much anger and bitterness between Nancy and him. She had warned him about Graham.

She reminded him often.

He returned to the list. He would pick out the good ones, see how many there were, then trim down to the twelve she had asked for. Craig, Sonya, Helen B, and Helen W, Terry, Josie, Susie, Jane, Pete Marsh, Corinne, Kathy, Mags, Bob and Tony Jones. They were the obvious ones. He counted back. Fourteen. Two to get the red line through their names.

Another thought struck him. Two team leaders were the requirement. Who was in contention? He frowned. Pete Marsh was an obvious choice, Helen B a possibility, but then again she might bring in someone from outside. From a different department. There were endless possibilities. In the end he crossed out Corinne (too emotional) and Bob (too old- he was only eighteen months away from retirement. May as well put him out to grass early.) He neatly typed the names down, along with the salient points of his plan and popped them into a brown envelope. He was ready for her.

Eight o'clock! He would have to take an early night and set the alarm. He was unused to such early starts.

He felt a little bleary eyed the next morning. Nancy had got in late and disturbed him when trying to do the decent thing by putting his car at the top of the drive so he could drive straight away the next morning without having recourse to shouting and moaning at her. In her so doing she had set off his alarm which had catapulted him out of a deep restful sleep. He was suffering that interruption now.

He felt a bit of a twinge as he drove to work, and made a mental note to heed Nancy's constant nagging to get fit. He would start that night. Jog around the park lake, cut down on the beer, leave off the crisps, and eat some of Nancy's rabbit food.

A new job, a new way of life.

He laughed at the thought, and played his chances down. He had been caught out by the euphoria of false expectation before, and had been badly depressed at the outturn of events.

"Morning Joanne."

"Ah Tim. Come in. Pour coffee will you? Mines black, no sugar."

He heaped his customary three sugars in and stirred in the cream. That might have to be reconsidered. He grimaced at the notion, but put the thoughts behind him and focussed on the mornings meeting. He sat down and straightened his tie, smoothed the creases in his trousers, set the brown envelope at a precise angle, whilst Joanne retrieved some files from the cabinet. "Sorry to keep you. Right. Did you have chance to put some ideas together?"

He nodded. Feebly waved the envelope at her and uttered a weak 'yes'.

"Not much use in there. May I?"

She took them from him and read through them. She looked at the operational plans first, and asked him questions around the headings on the paper. She seemed satisfied with his answers. "So these are just sort of bullet points, rather than a full explanation then?"

"Yes. You did ask for a thumbnail sketch only."

"Yes I did, didn't I?"

She gave a contrived smile. He didn't quite know how to take it, but her examining the other list interrupted his thoughts.

"Good. They seem to be tied in with others thoughts. All seem solid enough. Tell me, tell me Tim. If you didn't get the job, who would you give to?"

"Interesting question Joanne. Like asking a drowning man who he would sacrifice to save himself."

"I suppose it is."

She cocked her head to one side, awaiting his answer.

"I suppose it would be between Pete Marsh and Helen Beresford."

"Choose one."

"One? Depends what you are looking for?"

"I'm not looking for anything. You're the one deciding."

"OK. In that case I think I would probably choose Helen."

"Why?"

The real answer was that she was a woman, and he had a new woman boss, so he wanted to be seen as non-sexist, progressive and even handed. He sipped some coffee and gave her an alternative explanation.

"She grasps new ideas well, works on her own initiative and is well respected."

"Why not Peter Marsh?"

"You asked me to choose one."

"Yes I did, but I just wondered why not Peter. Is he not ready for a step up yet?"

"Yes. But you asked..."

"Tim. Cut the crap. Why is Helen a better choice than Peter?" She was making him uncomfortable. That was usually a difficult task to achieve. He usually breezed through such things, totally unfazed by hard questioning. He felt the temptation to slip into flippancy, but resisted the urge.

"Look Joanne. They are both good choices. Pete has more experience, is a good, dependable man, ready for a step up. It is just that I think Helen has better potential. I would choose both, ideally, but you asked me to choose one only. So I did." She lit a cigarette and nodded slowly.

"You said you'd choose them both ideally. Are they better choices than you?"

He felt stung by the implications of the question but answered immediately, giving her no time to think he was contriving an answer.

"I think I have the mixture of experience, potential, and progressive knowledge. I have both their qualities. What did you think of my proposals?"

He tried to control the questions and the direction the interview was taking. She would have none of it. Morris had chosen well. "What would you feel like if you didn't get the job?"

"Like shit- sorry."

She waved her hand dismissively. "I have asked these same questions to the other candidates. You are the last I am interviewing. Who do you think was the most popular choice?" Candidates? He hadn't really considered he was one of a number of candidates being interviewed. He had arrogantly assumed that he was the obvious choice, and that she just needed the reassurance of the correct responses to the appropriate questions. "Me?" He said unconvincingly.

She leaned back in her chair and smiled. The deep blue of her eyes twinkled at him, gave off an easy warmth. "Actually yes. You have the respect of all your contemporaries. Also, interestingly enough, you were the only one to nominate Helen. It either makes you very perceptive, or very rebellious. I wonder which one it is?"

She eyed him coyly, trying to peer through his veil of secrecy. He was a difficult man to know intimately. Several of the other 'candidates' had said as much. He didn't allow the veneer to crack, felt boosted by her admission of the esteem in which he was held by his peers. He wondered what her decision would be. He wondered if she was waiting for an answer to her question, which he had assumed to be rhetorical.

She stood and poured them both more coffee. He tried it without the sugar, but kept the cream. It tasted bitter. He hoped her decision wouldn't be as difficult to swallow. "Well, to answer your question, yes, your proposals are sound. Along the lines of mine, minor alterations, here and there. I expected nothing less than a comprehensive set of proposals from you. You would have to be pretty brain-dead to have worked here as long as you have without seeing how to improve things. Mind you, some of your colleagues would have seemed to have achieved that dubious distinction. How would you feel about having to fire someone? Someone you knew and worked with for years?" He shrugged. In truth he would hate the confrontational situation, it was obviously a task he would have to perform. He decided to answer honestly.

"I wouldn't relish it, I admit, but it is a necessary evil, then it is something I would have to do."

She nodded. "Yes you would. Have to do it. We will be running with two teams, input and output. Input will run with a team of fourteen, output with ten. Including the two team leaders there will be a total staff of twenty six, as opposed to the thirty seven we currently have. I assume you can work out the numbers?" He still hadn't had the answer to his unasked question burning a hole in his consciousness. She lit another cigarette. It was eight fifty two, staff were arriving, taking off jackets, switching on screens, making coffee. Joanne was not to be disturbed. Trudy, her secretary had had instructions the previous evening. She smiled.

"Well, the decision has been made. I want you to look after Output."

"Output?"

"Yes. Is there a problem?"

He shook his head. He was relieved and surprised. "Output is fine. I assumed, or rather that is I thought that Input would be the obvious choice."

"I believe in change, Tim. A fresh pair of eyes often sees things which blinkers cannot reveal. I would like to offer my congratulations, that is if you accept the offer."

"Yes, well rather, in principal, yes. Is there any.."

"Any what"

She knew well what he meant, but she was not a person to offer easy rides to anyone.

"P-pay." He spat out the word.

"An extra three grand, plus performance related bonus, healthcare as well. You'll get the full details in a formal letter of offer."

He nodded in satisfaction. She raised her eyebrows at him.

"Oh, sorry. Yes. I'd be delighted to accept. Thank you."

She stood and shook his hand and then motioned him to resume his seat. She waved through the glass to Trudy who disappeared into the main office.

"You're about to meet the new Team Leader for Input."

"Good." He wondered who it was, and resisted the temptation to turn round. There was a short tap and the door and he heard the door open and close, as someone entered. Helen Beresford sat next to him. She smiled at him, and they nervously shook hands. He whispered 'congratulations' to her.

He felt great. For the first time in years he felt good about himself, apart from the indigestion, which he had had all morning. He blushed as Joanne gave a short speech about teamwork, pulling together, goal setting and all the rest of her plans to transform Fenners accounts section. He nodded at appropriate moments of her oratory, then she came to its end.

"First things first. Tongues will be wagging already, wondering what we three are doing in here. I will have to inform those not successful. I want you two to pick the twenty four staff. You have a common pool of about fifteen or sixteen from your lists. The sooner you draw up the lists, the sooner you can fire the rest. I'll bring in the unlucky losers, then I'll call a staff meeting for twelve. Announce the new set up, stop wagging tongues, then we can get on. You two can use my office for your lists after that. I have a meeting all afternoon. Two points of direction for you on picking your teams. One eventually they will all be multi-skilled, i.e. interchangeable, so no need to be competitive between you both. Second, pick on merit first. The remainder will be the unlucky ones, although they may be considered for two new vacancies in tele-sales. Congratulations to you both. You both picked each other as team leaders. I think that is a great start for the creation of a successful team, so well done. I'll see you both later, but a quick word Tim before you get back to work."

They waited until Helen had returned to the body of the main office. She half whispered in his ear.

"I ought to say that there were certain objections from certain quarters regarding your appointment. But I have good feelings about you. I am sure you won't let me down will you?"

"Oh, Morris, you mean."

"Will you?"

"Let you down? Look, Joanne, if I just concentrate on not letting myself down, everything will be fine. Don't worry. And thanks."

He rubbed his chest as the indigestion gripped probably the pasta he had last the previous evening. He sucked on a mint and sat back in his seat, switching the screen into reluctant action. Craig leaned over.

"What's going on Tim? Not more bollockings surely?"

Tim shook his head, but stayed quiet.

"Come on mate, let us in on it."

Tim had a broad grin on his face, but was sworn to temporary secrecy. Craig stopped his questions as Joanne announced the staff meeting for noon, then turned back to Tim, enlightenment and pleasure spreading across his face.

"You dog. You've got a new job haven't you? The one which you, Helen, Marshie, Josie,Terry and Mags were in for. Well done mate well done."

He offered his hand but Tim waved it away. "Not now, Craig, I've been sworn to secrecy. Speak later."

The announcement went down fairly well. Both Helen and Tim were popular members of the department. Joanne made no announcement about job losses. That would be announced next week. She spoke with a quiet authority which impressed Tim, spoke with enthusiasm about reorganisation, and promised new technology, allied to extra and necessary training. She emphasised Helen and Tim's importance to the role, laid the foundation to committed teamwork and promised regular staff updates and impromptu meetings such as this. She would manage in an open manner with the support of the workforce, rather than the grudging wage-slave mentality, which tended to pervade at present. Good times were round the corner.

Tim excused himself from Helen early, so that he could nip to the chemists for some antacids to quell the disquiet rumbling beneath his shirt front, then he returned and started the job of selecting their new teams. They elected to pick the twenty four first, then select their teams from that. That way they would get the best staff, and select those for their teams who they would get on best with. The first eighteen were straightforward. Their first lists and the also-rans provided the core. Helen had an idea.

"Why don't we pick two extra each, then one etc until we get the right number?"

"OK fellow team leader. Let's do it."

He picked Shirley and Jim Sedgwick. Helen picked Shirley and Bob.

"Don't forget Bob only has eighteen months or so till he retires Helen."

"Oh, yes. Better think on then. Well Shirley and Jim are in. Four to go. Two each again."

The last four were surprisingly difficult to pick. Had they started the process in reverse, getting rid of the wasters first and keeping the rest, it would have been even harder. There were about four people who merely went through the motions, then there were the top fifteen or so who always did their best, but the rest, in the middle were difficult to separate. Helen argued points pro and con all the remaining staff, having written off the bottom four, plus another three who were near retiring age. Tim had mumbled something about casting them adrift in life's stormy waters, he felt a little guilty about having to play the part of some minor deity, doling out life or death to these peoples livelihoods, but he had to swallow his feelings for the sake of his new job.

In the end they were two short, and totally unable to choose between the rest.

"Let's draw lots. A kind of job lottery. Winners get the huge reward of keeping their jobs, their homes, dignity, whilst the losers are consigned to the scrap heap. Why can't our dear Joanne pick them?"

Helen rounded on Tim. "Because she has delegated that task to us Tim. To us. We're starting to play the big boys game now, we need to toughen up. You need to get a ruthless streak."

"The trouble with me is I have too much ruth. Far too much ruth." Helen made a funny face at him. She wanted to keep this discussion entirely cool and professional, he was slipping back to his old ways. She didn't like his attempt at wit. They had been locked in discussion for nearly three hours and could not reach agreement.

Tim spoke out. "Wendy Turner. She'll do."

"Wendy Turner. She's a bit dim isn't she for this?"

"Nice tits though."

"Tim!"

He stood up and stretched his legs, popping another indigestion tablet into his mouth. They seemed to make it worse rather than better.

"Tell you what Helen. You choose. I've had enough of all this crap. I know you fancy little Peter Hardy. Have him. He'll be ever so grateful."

"Tim, I find that entirely insulting to suggest.."

"Keep your knickers on Helen. Just bloody choose. I don't care any more."

She blushed slightly as she spoke. "Actually Pete Hardy isn't a bad idea. Why not him and Karen Jessop?"

"Fine."

"But you said earlier that Karen was an air head?"

"I was wrong. I was thinking of a different Karen Jessop. That'll do. We have our list."

Helen sighed and wrote the last two names on a piece of paper.

"Well, Tim. All we have to do is pick our teams from this lot."

"Tell you what Helen. Since they will all be 'multi-skilled' as Joanne put it, then you choose yours, I'll have the rest."

"Tim. It isn't really team work if we do it like that..."

"Fuck team work. Look, I've done nothing all day but sit and agonise about who gets the bullet and who doesn't. I have headache, guts ache and have been here since eight. I am quite happy to work with anybody from the final list. You choose. Please."

She nodded and started to look at the list once more. Tim glanced at his watch. It was ten past five. The office was all but clear. He smiled and patted Helen on the shoulder. "Sorry for swearing flower, but well. Just give me my list in the morning will you? I'm shagged- sorry- tired out."

CHAPTER 4

'Graham. Bastard.'

Nancy finished washing the dishes and peeled away the latex from her hands, dispatching the gloves neatly into the under sink cupboard. She poured herself a black decaffeinated coffee and sat on the patio enjoying the early morning sun. She was in a reflective mood, was at a kind of emotional cusp in her life, she was undecided. To say she was undecided was in itself not a very decisive statement. She knew what she wanted, was sure of that at least, but how to get it? That was a different matter. Her life had changed over the past few years, or more accurately, she had changed.

Her thoughts started with Tim. Married for years, a lifetime in fact. They had met at a party in the sixties, she wore a cheesecloth dress and he had his hair tied back with a leather band and wore violet sunshades. They had courted over a few years and he had always been spontaneous, witty and attentive to her. She had been in love. She had no doubt about that, but now that love had gone. Slipped away, dissolved, evaporated. She could not pinpoint the exact moment. She had been in love when she gave birth to Anthony, their only child and for some time after that as well. Their life together seemed to be developing nicely along traditional lines. He had got a good job with prospects at Fenners, and they had moved into what was still their present home- a nice detached four bedroomed house with the right postcode. They had planned to have more children and raise them there. It wasn't to be. If she could have made a best guess at the point at which their love started to fade it would be somewhere near the point she had her miscarriage. In Churchill's words it was if not the end, then the beginning of the end.

Tim was enthused by his job at Fenners, superficially at least. She was active at the mother and toddler group and had made friends with several of the neighbours and had generally been enjoying life. She had left work when Anthony was born and had no ambitions to return to her secretarial duties. She would rather clean up after her baby than clean up the messes left behind by her former bosses.

Sally, her next door neighbour, had introduced her to tennis, which she had never played before, and she became an enthusiastic participant. Tim had reckoned another interest was good for her, and positively encouraged her. He had played a couple of times with her or with Richard and Sally as a foursome, but was not very able at the sport and soon found appropriate excuses not to take part. Besides which he and Richard just couldn't get on. There was no actual animosity between them, but neither was there a spark of mutual interest. If Tim liked beer, Richard liked wine, if Tim wanted to eat Chinese, Richard wanted Italia and so on. Nancy could manage that, since she and Sally became, and still were, best of friends.

Three years after Anthony entered their lives, she discovered that she was pregnant and they were both delighted. Nancy had a clean bill of health from the doctors, and since she was naturally very fit, he advised that tennis, in moderation would not harm her, or the baby in any way. She carried on, as advised, and the unthinkable happened. Ironically. it was not the playing of the game which caused her miscarriage, but she had taken a shower afterwards and had slipped, falling awkwardly, and lost consciousness for a few minutes. When she awoke, she was being gingerly lifted into an ambulance, and wrapped in several white towels. Sally was beside her as the ambulance took them to St Luke's, and as she was taken into surgery. She was still under the knife as Tim arrived on the scene, asking Sally exactly what had happened, nervously waiting for her to emerge from theatre.

When she did she was still unconscious, had a drip into her arm

and was in a private room. Over the next week she had two

more operations to rectify internal damage.

She had lost the baby-she had called it Lucy and had the name engraved on her fathers grave, and still put a small posy of flowers on the stone when she could- but worst of all she had damaged her womb so badly that she had to have it removed. Anthony was to be an only child after all.

As she remembered the accident, she wiped a small tear from her eye. If she had been writing her autobiography she accepted to herself that that point was probably the beginning of the end. The end of the end came later. It was Tim's attitude to her, and the accident, which had started the decline, or so she reasoned. He had naturally been upset, but only showed it through tense, pursed lips. Superficially at least he accepted the doctors' verdict of a freak accident when she fell in the shower. Internally she always thought that he blamed her for taking exercise whilst pregnant. If she had dutifully stayed at home this would never have happened. The problem with Tim was that he would never openly admit that that was his problem. He would never stand up and confront her or the situation. Sure they had had fights, stand up rows, but they were always about fairly trivial things. What she had spent on a new dress, what he had or more commonly hadn't done. Things, which in the great story of their lives would never get a mention.

When it came to important matters,. serious matters, matters which were life changing, then he kept his thoughts beneath his patina of sarcasm and barbed wit. He often made fun of her, and in public, despite her repeatedly asking him not to he continued. It was as if he either had no self-control or that he enjoyed ridiculing her. It was his only participant sport. That, in truth, had hurt her, had kept her anger simmering and had stung her into retaliation and retribution. Retaliation and retribution in its' most mild form, but sweet to her for all that. She would forget to iron him a clean shirt for work. Would park her car in front of his so he had to move it before going out. Would be deliberately late when they went out. Tim absolutely hated being late. Detested and loathed it. She had turned away from his sexual advances for quite a while after little Lucy's' loss, but still had a healthy sex drive herself, and as such had never used that as a weapon against him, he had accused her of it on several occasions, but it was never true. He had not enjoyed her leading an active life, not enjoyed it at all, and as she became more active, he seemed to become less so. Promotion had passed him by a couple of times, and he had become more introverted, more lazy and apart from TV and novels, seemed to lose all interest in just about everything.

Except Anthony.

He was good with Anthony, and had happily looked after him whilst she went out to play tennis, badminton, or went to various night classes or club meetings over the years. As a result, and to Nancy's secret chagrin, he and Anthony had become the very best of friends. Even now, when he called from university, she would get a few words of such things as 'everything's fine, how are you? etc' whilst he would talk to Tim for an age, and Tim would laugh, speak in lowered tones at some secret shared and generally have a good chinwag. When she had asked Tim what they had been talking about, he had infuriatingly answered 'the usual'. She was secretly envious of their relationship.

But that was now. Then, if she were to admit to a fault, she would admit that she ought to have spent more time with her son.

She may have thrown herself into all her myriad activities as some

kind of penance over her unsubstantiated guilt over Lucy, but it had never been a conscious decision, and she lacked the moral strength to find out if it had been subconscious by enlisting psychiatric help. Her father had always said 'if it ain't broke, don't fix it'. Well she wasn't broken, she needed no mending. If she were to sum up the decisive split in their lives, the pivotal moment, it would have been Lucy's loss, she decided that for certain now. She had busied herself in diverting pastimes, whilst Tim had closed in on himself and had had the ambition driven from him, which was why he was still in the same job at Fenners, having been overlooked for promotion more times than she could recall.

To say it was his ambition which had gone would perhaps fog the issue. He no longer had the energy or drive to want to achieve his dreams. Sure he craved for financial security and had ambitions in being his own boss, but could never quite take the plunge.

That was where Graham came in. Her brother, dreamer. Graham and Tim had always got on famously. When he had come round, he had often stayed the night as he and Tim dipped into the pool of mirth, alcohol and chess in which they happily swam and splashed. Again, Nancy had been excluded from this cosy little world, but in this case she minded not. She had always distrusted Graham, had seen him cheat, lie and in some cases steal to get what he had wanted when they had been children. She had blamed him, partially for driving her father into an early grave, when Graham had got into some trouble and ended up in court, narrowly missing a custodial sentence. She was convinced that the shock and shame had put the extra strain on her fathers' heart to send him early from this world. She could never prove it. Didn't have to.

She had liked Wendy, Graham's temporary wife, and still kept in touch with her, now re-married with two children, but she still kept herself distant from Graham, not that she had seen him for some time. He now lived abroad.

Graham was an ideas man, full of grand schemes to make him rich and famous, always tried to live a life of elegance and sophistication before he had the means to support it. He would turn up with a bottle of champagne and leave having borrowed a hundred pounds. He was that kind of person.

Full of shit. Tim and Graham had often gone down the route of ' when I am rich, I'll leave that job- by helicopter! give two fingers to the boss, then buy him out, make him grovel and squirm'.

It never materialised into anything substantial, until one day when Graham was, as usual, between jobs. He had got some casual work with an acquaintance doing markets etc selling garden ornaments, gnomes, rabbits, badgers, that kind of thing, all cast in concrete and sold on. He was enthused by how quickly the items were sold out. There was a ready market for such things. He thought of new ways to improve them, spray paint and finish the job, cast personalised name tags to each one, so that a black cat could have the name 'Sooty' neatly painted on to the cast frame at its' feet. He kept these ideas from his boss and when, out of the blue he was asked to take over both the manufacturing and selling whilst the owner went on holiday, he jumped at the chance to try out his ideas. They went down a storm. Whilst the cat was away, the mouse did play. He schemed, and talked over his plan with Tim.

By the time Nancy found out it was a fait accomplis. Using their garage, they started making a few concrete foxes, cats, dogs etc, which they sprayed, painted and finished off. Graham had learned how to make copies of the moulds and had systematically raided Kevin's stores to make his own venture as profitable as possible. Tim and Graham worked over two weeks getting up a good stock of goods, and hired a van and market stall one Sunday and set off early to see how they would do. They sold out. It was a tremendous success, and they were to repeat the process several times over the next few months.

She was relatively happy at this time to let them carry on. Tim seemed to have another interest, not that it meant she saw any more of him, but she was content, that at last he was actually doing something. She had little idea that Grahams dream would have grown from the part time pin money operation into a corporation. They had decided that, if they or rather Graham at least sold the stuff at four or five markets a week, they could make some real money.

She had urged caution when Tim stumped up the cash for a van, and deposit on a small unit on a run down industrial estate. They rented the premises, and he bought a stack of raw materials, whilst Graham organised the markets. So far, Tim had invested just over twelve hundred pounds. She repeatedly warned him about doing business with her brother. He shrugged her criticisms off.

"Purely a business venture. We need the van to shift the gear, hiring is too dear, and the raw materials and premises are essential. Nancy, don't worry. It's like printing money." Another five hundred pounds from Tim bought a second hand cement mixer, and over the next three months he and Graham worked at weekends and in the evenings, casting, sealing and painting the animals, and added wishing wells, bird baths and cast fountains to their range. During the day, whilst Tim worked, Graham sold them on markets. Dutifully, they balanced the books each week, and at least half of Tim's initial investment was repaid. Despite this, Nancy still warned against Graham, but the cash kept if not exactly rolling in, kept trickling in.

It was not enough to sustain two families, but the way things were going, there were distinct possibilities. Graham as ever, had his ideas, and they bore sweet fruit. He made contact with the buyer of a large chain of garden centres, who was impressed with the goods on offer. She recalled Tim and Graham's excitement at the prospects, as they celebrated the big order with champagne. She still had doubts.

Graham and Tim had experimented with cast iron, through an out of work welder friend called John Field. He made nice wrought iron pieces quickly and expertly, and the buyer soon issued a contract for those. All this was posing a few operational headaches. Tim was going to leave Fenners to work full time at the job, but had been persuaded by Nancy to stay on a few more months until he was sure that everything would be sustained. The trouble came when they needed to move premises. Not only had they obtained the big order from Costains, but also Graham had secured two equally large orders from two other groups.

They needed large premises, equipment, staff, delivery vehicles and the like to fill the orders on time. Tim worked the cash flow forecasts, borrowing requirements and investment capital necessary and took two weeks off work and went to the bank to support their proposals. Graham had about five thousand pounds to invest, mainly the remains of his fathers legacy, whilst Tim could put in nearly twenty thousand in hard earned savings and the beneficence of Nancy's father. They needed another sixty thousand to go big.

The figures all added up, were well presented, and they walked

from the meeting with business account set up, overdraft

facility and sixty thousand-pound loan to launch their business

into orbit.

The drawback was that the loan needed security. Tim

had used their house as necessary collateral. Nancy was incensed, pleaded with Tim to undo what he had done, but he accused her of trying to kill off his one real chance of making it. She remembered warning him about Grahams hair brained schemes, but he had countered with the argument that it was Graham who had got them the lucrative contracts in the first place. In a blur of activity they installed the equipment, hired staff and started to churn out the goods. Fieldy had brought in some welders to do the welding work, and became increasingly lost to the activity. He was an alcoholic, and frequently went missing, despite prodigious talent in his sphere. Problems with quality of the goods began to materialise as the workforce was rushed into action with woefully inadequate training. Costains had already made noises about slowness of supply, and Graham had persuaded Tim to let the substandard work through, just to keep the order. As they caught up, they could replace any defective merchandise.

Nancy saw Tim work and work at the business, but could not sustain it full time, because of his commitment to Fenners. He had put his notice in, but was contracted to three months notice period, which he had to work out. Graham therefore took the major part in running the business. At first the money rolled in, justifying Tim's predictions, and Graham rationalised that a classy car would help obtain more orders from other companies. He leased a Mercedes in the company's name and true to his word obtained more business. They seemed to be on a roller coaster. Then the problems started in earnest. Because Fieldy had been entrusted with the wrought iron side of the business, and was so unreliable, there were often no raw materials for the welders to weld. Graham sent them home unpaid when this happened, and two out of the five left, feeling hard done to. The result was they could not keep up and failed to fulfil deadline dates. The concrete castings were being returned as being unsuitable and substandard, and almost overnight they were hit by a succession of penalty clauses, cancelled orders and cash flow suffered. They missed a couple of payments to suppliers and raw materials began to be delivered on a cash-on-delivery basis. Graham's idea was to be aggressive. The goods coming off the line had improved dramatically in quality; due largely to Tim's efforts, and Graham had loaded a van with samples and taken the short trip to France where he obtained high value orders. The last time Tim or Nancy saw him was eight years ago as he headed off overseas in search of bigger, better contracts.

The business fell apart rapidly at that point. Orders were not met, goods were returned, and the queue of creditors lengthened. Tim had taken two weeks off unpaid, to try and salvage something from the wreckage, and had, at Nancy's prompting managed to withdraw his resignation from Fenners. It was a wise move. The business collapsed, as the accounts showed that Graham had withdrawn large sums of money, ostensibly billed as expenses, samples, and entertaining overseas customers. Had that money stayed in the business, they could have at least kept the continuity of raw material supply going, and concentrated on good quality control and deadline meeting rather than expanding too rapidly in chasing new business. On his accountant's advice, Tim called in the receiver and the business wound up. The stocks, equipment vans and tools were sold off at a fraction of their cost and the leases paid up.

The final debts amounted to eighty thousand pounds, give or take a few pence, and Tim, in Graham's absence, and lack of collateral became liable. He mortgaged the house to the hilt, and drained every penny from his savings in the process. He had become sullen and reclusive after that. Nancy had decided against carping on about her warnings concerning her brother. It was all too painfully obvious that she had been right to be suspicious of him. He was currently somewhere abroad. Away and out of reach. Tim had ranted that he would personally kill him when he caught up with him, but she doubted he had it in him. She was different. She could do it to him.

The resulting years proved to be difficult, if not nigh on impossible for her. She absolutely refused to seek work herself, knowing that it merely let Tim off the hook, and the burden of debt hung round Tim's neck like a yoke of repression. If he had lacked ambition before, he dashed all hope away now. She was bitter, very bitter, and still was. That point had finally cut the chord for her, had finally given her real determination to live her own life, to make her own way, to become independent. She enrolled in an Open University course and began making long term plans for herself.

Whilst Anthony was still young, until he was away and settled in both home and career, she would stay. She would and could never hurt the only fruit of her womb. She knew she had to go. Knew she no longer loved Tim. He never talked properly to her about the collapse of the business, but then he probably knew what she was going to say. It didn't take much imagination to fore guess her. He became more isolated and withdrawn, and enjoyed his own, and a bottles company more than her.

Now, she knew what she wanted. Knew was about the time to part. Anthony was in his last year at university, taking a Masters degree. He had already been offered a research post at university, so he was settled. His home was no longer with them. She had also met someone new. In the past few years she had had one or two secret affaires, had kept herself in good shape and was enjoying the kind of intimate attention which Tim had only managed a long time ago.

This was different. She was nearly in love. Alive like she had not been for a long time. Ricky was nearly twenty years younger than she, and they had been introduced through Sally. He was a lifeguard at the local sports centre, and was handsome athletic and charming. She knew this was no casual thing, and they had been together for over a year now, sneaking off to his flat for the evening, ostensibly to some committee meeting or match. Tim never questioned her, and Sally was always a willing alibi. They had even managed a holiday together in Spain. That was not difficult to arrange. Over the past six years or so they had not taken a holiday together. Tim was not really interested, and besides, they couldn't really afford them, so she had taken to holidaying with Sally, who was financially secure, and helped her out with the costs.

Now, well, she needed to get away from Tim. To set up with Ricky

and to have her share of the family home. She had invested twenty

four years in her marriage, twenty four hard bloody years. The

trouble was, that if she divorced him, and they split up the

assets, then she would get sweet nothing. The bank had first

charge on the house, there was still about twenty years to pay

off the mortgage. Nancy needed to fathom a way to obtain a share

of what was rightfully hers. If only she could lay her hands on

Graham

CHAPTER 5

'To Bacchus - a son.'

Tim awoke early that morning, and held his side. The brief introduction to a workout was taking its toll. Nancy was staying over with Sally that night. She had arranged it a week ago, and so he had taken the opportunity to start on his new regime. Nancy would mock him if he had started in her watchful gaze, and he would be accused of not doing this or that in the right way, but so what? New job, new way of life. He felt that he was on the change, on the move.

It was half past six and Tim donned some old trainers, jogging suit and picked up his newly acquired stopwatch. He drove the short distance to the park, and gently jogged his way around the lake in the centre, staring ahead, being sure not to catch the gaze of those similarly inclined at such a time in the morning. The very last thing he wanted was to have a jogging 'buddy'. It was hard enough for him to put himself out by having to push himself into the tedium of taking exercise, but he felt empowered, felt charged with life, and in charge of his life. He sincerely hoped it would last this time. Previously such attempts had fizzled out into inaction.

When he returned to the car, he had the pain of stitch in his side. It was only to be expected. He took his pulse and waited two minutes to determine his recovery time. He took a swig of bottled water and felt the acid in his throat. This bout of indigestion had seemed to last for several days. He would take something for it when he got home for breakfast.

Nancy still hadn't returned home, no doubt she had got her customary hangover when she had sampled Bacchus's liquid delights. He showered and left for work, reminding himself to actually tell Nancy that he had got a new job. He wondered what her reaction would be. No doubt she would make the extra cash welcome, but would probably tarnish the news with some caustic barb about it being about time.

He started work with some enthusiasm, ploughing through the pile of papers in front of him with vigour. In his in tray was the formal offer for the position. He looked at the sentence 'subject to medical'. He worried slightly about that, but knew Bob Jeffries the company doctor, and gave him a call.

"Hello Tim. I hear congratulations are in order."

"Yes, thanks Bob. Look, just a quickie really, but I know I have to have a medical. What does it entail?"

"What, the medical? Well just blood pressure, height, weight, eyes teeth, heart lungs, testicles..you know the routine."

"Yes, sorry Bob, I'm not making myself clear. What can you, er fail on."

"Tim, don't worry. It's just routine. All it is, is that you will be joining the healthcare scheme. It's a kind of insurance. All the insurers want to know is if you are a really high risk- you know, are you HIV, do you indulge in any hazardous sports etc. You don't actually fail, but I will make recommendations over certain health related matters."

"Such as?"

"The usual. Weight. Teeth. You know. Is their something worrying you?"

"No, it's just that, well I know I carry a little too much weight. Just didn't want to jeopardise my new job by failing the medical, particularly since I've just started an exercise routine."

"Look Tim. Come and have your medical this afternoon at two. I'll advise you on fitness if you like."

"Sure. Thanks Bob."

He duly attended the medical and Bob gave him a thorough examination. "Anything, apart from too much weight worrying you Tim?"

He shook his head.

"Not really. Just the usual aches and pains."

"What sort?"

"Oh. Stitch. I woke up with it, now it won't go. Oh, yes, and I've had horrible indigestion for about a week now."

"Really?" Bob looked back at Tim's chart. "Despite your weight, your heart is quite healthy. Slow, steady beat blood pressure normal, surprisingly healthy for your size. Now, show me where this stitch is."

He pointed to his right side, and Bob got him to lie down whilst he prodded at his side. Tim shot up with pain as Bob prodded. "Jesus, that hurt."

He noticed the look of concentration in Bob's eyes as he gently this time touched and prodded at Tim's side. He allowed him to get up.

"No problem with the water works?"

Tim shook his head.

"Bowels?"

"Bit loose, but not bad."

"How do you mean?"

"Well always been a once in the morning man you know. Occasionally went for seconds in the evening, but recently it's been twice, maybe three times a day, and loose. Not diahorrea, but loose."

"Indigestion? How long have you had that?"

"Like I said a week. Why? Is there something wrong?" Bob smiled and indicated that Tim put his clothes back on and scribbled on his notes.

"You seem to have a bit of a swelling around the liver, pancreas area. Could be a minor infection, it's causing the looseness and indigestion you describe. I'll prescribe you some anti-biotics, and send you to the hospital for a few tests, just to be on the safe side."

"Bob. What is it?"

"Like I said, no need to worry. Just a precaution."

Tim walked back to his desk. When a doctor tells you there is no need to worry, it's like a pilot telling you there is no need to panic. Obviously there is something wrong, but what? It would be typical of his luck, not to get the job, because of his health. He resolved to get fitter quickly, to run the bug out of his system.

Over the next six weeks, until his hospital appointment, he embarked on a quite rigorous fitness routine. Morning and evening he jogged around the park. Extending the circuit and quickening the pace in the process. He went to the gym three times a week and pushed and strained at the weights and exercises set for him. At the same time he eschewed alcohol, drank water only, and cut right down on fats, ate salads, fruit and took vitamin supplements. In that time he lost a stone and a half, and started to regain a waistline.

Nancy half smiled at his efforts. She had been as anticipated by Tim, fairly non-committal about his work news, and shook her head as he scorned her offer of steak for his meal that evening. There is no such prude as a whore reformed, she thought to herself. It was too little too late for him now. Too late for him to change her mind.

The only thing he did find it difficult to give up was his illicit smoking. He had smoked for about twenty years, although never at home, and never in Nancy's company. He thought she didn't know he smoked. He never asked her, and she never mentioned it. He smoked seven a day, in an almost slavishly adhered to timetable.

His first was on the way to work, his second over coffee before he started work. Third for elevenses. Fourth and fifth at the start and finish of lunch break. Sixth mid afternoon and seventh on the way home. The only variation on this was if he went out for a drink. That he did go out was due entirely to the company of one man. John Field, or Fieldy as he was known. If there was one person in the world that Tim admired, it was him. He had no worries, lived for the day and was a man so utterly and completely in charge of his own life that it was to the contempt of everyone else. He was an alcoholic, but he had learned to live with his weakness.

Strangely enough, they had met through his brother-in-law, Graham. He had known him on and off for about twelve years, and had grown close over the past seven or eight, following the collapse of the business. Fieldy had been recruited by Graham to do the welding. The man was an artist, a genius, but had no desire to do anything but casual work, and certainly had no skills, need or want to run the wrought iron side of Greyoakes Garden Supplies. Tim had learned as much as the business disintegrated around them. He had learned from Graham that the reason for that side of the business failing was Fieldy's fault. He now knew different.

Fieldy was a true artist. He lived in a one-roomed flat brought by the proceeds of his divorce from Lorraine. Tim had never met her. He had exactly what he needed to live with. He had no desire for a car, besides he drank steadily all day, so would be permanently over the driving limit. He never watched TV, so did not possess such a thing. He had a reasonably healthy bank balance derived from his cartoon work. He was a regular contributor to two men's magazines from his comic strip. If he had any discipline in his life, it was to draw his cartoons about five months in advance. It gave him all the money he needed to live. He had turned down opportunities to syndicate his work, to draw on a weekly basis. He had what he needed, and if he did want anything more, he could turn his hand to a bit of creative welding, sell some original caricatures or whatever. Tim admired him greatly, could talk easily and frankly with him, was his true confidante. He had often had a good drinking session with him down at the social club where he was a regular. Fieldy never got violent or aggressive when drunk, but often giggled incessantly, whilst slipping into a gentle stupor.

"The trouble with being an alcky, Tim. The single thing which makes it tempting to give it all up, never appears at any counselling session, in any text books, or is given in warning by anyone is this.

The poohing. Shit, crap, number twos, excreting, whatever you care to call it. Number two is the number one problem. I go at least three, maybe four times a day. My expenditure on bog paper is second only to my outlay on booze. My bum is so tender and sore, that I am a major shareholder in the Vaseline Company, and produce skid marks to be both proud and ashamed of. Tim, my boy, if you ever join me on this slippery path, just think of the soreness your botty will have to undergo. Strangely enough when I addressed a meeting of AA on this very subject I was asked not to come again."

It was this kind of embarrassing honesty, at his own expense which Tim liked. He knew lots of people, would and could talk to beggars and barons, field marshals and floozies. He always had something interesting to say. Always listened well. Everybody knew his name. Few knew him really well. Tim did.

"The trouble with you Oaksey, old boy," he had once said, "is that you are trying to find something you don't want."

Tim remembered asking him what he meant by it all, and received the withering look and mockery of "physician, heal thyself." In the end he had fathomed that Fieldy was advising him to be true to himself to do what he wanted, and to not listen to anything that anyone else might say or suggest to him. Graham into had seduced him near ruin, because Grahams, not his own, dreams, had caught him.

"Oaksey, I've known Graham from school. He's a cunt. Simple as that."

Tim had riposted with his own witticism, "Ah yes, but cunts are useful."

"Not when they're that big."

He had not seen Fieldy for a month, not in itself unusual, but he felt the need now. Three days before his hospital appointment.

"Evening Fieldy."

"Bloody hell. I thought you were dead. Here."

He poured a glass of white wine and pushed it into Tim's' hand. He always drank white wine. Drank it steadily through the day, from morning through to evening. It had the balance between quaffability and strength in the perfect balance for him. He had two cases a week delivered by the local off license. "Cheers."

"How's the wage slave doing then?"

Fieldy always spoke in a voice which sounded like he was

swallowing something and which danced with minor slurring. It was

always the same. He had developed a kind of twitch, a nervous

slow motion tic which looked like he was loosening his neck from

a tight collar

"Fine. Got promoted."

"Why?"

Straight down the line with him as ever.

"Because I am the best man for the job."

"No one else want it then?"

"You sound like my darling Nancy, such support."

Fieldy shrugged slightly and gave his customary neck movement.

"Just wondering why you've took it. Managing people are you?"

"Yes."

He shrugged again. "That's the entire trouble with work. If you are good at a job, the only way up is to manage other people, even though you may not be a good manager. People who are good managers are rarely good at doing the job, so therefore get no respect from their workforce. Are you a good manager Oaksey?" Tim gave Fieldy an exaggerated smile.

"I doubt it. But I need the money."

"Why? You'd have been better being made bankrupt and starting again."

"We'd have lost the house."

"And?"

"We'd have lost the house."

Fieldy shrugged. "I wonder what is the worst thing. Losing the house, or paying off the debts for the rest of your natural days. Still, this is old ground. How's the wicked?" Fieldy called Nancy the wicked, after the wicked witch of the west. They totally disliked one another. She hated him more than football, which was something in itself. He was too honest for her liking. Honest to the point of rudeness and beyond. They just agreed to differ these days, well at least she did, by ignoring him, and avoiding him where possible. As a result he always tried to go to her and engage her in conversation whenever he could. Just to irritate her. Tim had once nick named him Timex, because he was good at winding her up.

"Nancy is, well Nancy. No change I'm afraid."

Fieldy studiously poured them both more wine.

"Tim, can I ask a question?"

"You don't normally ask permission."

"No, a serious one mate."

"Go on."

"Why do you stay with her? You seem to have separate lives now. You do one thing, she does the other. You rarely go out together."

"We'll be out tonight!"

"Come off it Tim. The Club? You go there with me, she goes with her mother. Together in the same room, that's all. Do you love her?"

Tim looked at his friend. It was a strange line for him to take. He knew that Fieldy and Nancy did not get on, but this was different. He answered his question.

"No, I don't think so, not been in love for a long time. I just, well I owe her. Owe her big time. Because of me, ignoring her about Graham, I've lost everything. I owe her big. I don't know how, but I'll pay her back somehow. Why?"

He shook his head.

"Just curious I guess. Knew I couldn't get by with Lorraine so I ditched her years ago. Just wondered what your motivation was, after such a long time."

Tim looked at his friend. Somehow he felt like he was withholding something from him. Fieldy changed tack. "Is that why you're out jogging? For her?"

"How did you know?"

"Saw you in your get up. Nearly pissed myself laughing."

Tim felt slightly annoyed at the jibe. "No, not for her. For me."

"Suit yourself. Time for the club then?" Tim looked at his watch. Seven thirty. Duty calls. He drained his glass and they left.

The social club, more commonly known as just the Club, was not the most salubrious of settings. It had once been an old school, and had been coarsely converted into a social outlet. The main hall remained for badminton, five a side and the like, as well as the weekly live entertainment and dancing. To the back were three snooker tables, some changing rooms and children's area, whilst at the front, and to the left was a pleasantly furnished lounge, decorated in pale purple and pinks, with comfortable seats. It was there where the bar was, and was the focus of the Clubs activities. There were several small, less well-furnished nooks off.

Tim entered with Fieldy, both being waved in. There was no need for either to show their passes to the doorman. Tim went to the bar and ordered their drinks. Double wine for Fieldy. Pint of bitter for him. Nancy was not yet there, nor was her mother. As he exchanged some words with the barman in walked Nancy's other brother, Simon. He had a new 'friend' with him. Tim liked Simon. He was honest and quite entertaining. He was also gay, much to the annoyance of his mother.

"Hi Simon. Drink?"

"Tim. Nice to see you." He shook hands, then gave him a small hug. They had not seen one another for about a year; he had been working in London.

"Here, Tim, this is Nick. My friend."

Tim reached out his hand and welcomed Nick. He was about five six, wiry, had his hair close-cropped and wore a golden earring on the left. His grip was firm, and his eyes clear and commanding.

"Nice to meet you Nick. Here, let me get both of you a drink."

"Simon, you old toss pot! This your new boy friend then?"

Fieldy was over and giving Simon and bear hug, and did the same

to his friend. When he had emerged from Fieldy's' generous welcome he whispered to Nick in a loud voice,

"Village Alcky, this one."

"I'll drink to that you tart."

The four sat around a table whilst Simon caught up with the news. He was over for a few weeks, since he was changing jobs in the next couple of months, and decided he needed the break. Despite his small diminutive stature, Simon was a very successful engineer, who specialised in trouble shooting, around the world. He had been based in London for seven years, and now was going to work in Aberdeen, working on pipeline installations and maintenance.

"Met Nick here in Turkey about eight months ago. Been together since."

"Turkey eh? What do you do Nick? Similar line to Simon."

"No, couldn't be more different really. I am an accountant."

"Same as Timmy." Fieldy interjected.

Simon laughed.

"Sorry Tim. Nick undersells himself somewhat. He's actually an auditor. International one. Jets all over the world and strikes fear into all who are under his microscope."

"Yeah, yeah yeah. Why is it that we all have to put the handle on our lives by telling one another what we do rather than who, or what we are."

Fieldy slapped Nick on the back.

"Bloody good for you, matey boy. A man after my own heart. Come on, my go. Same again?"

Nancy's mother arrived shortly afterwards. Ostensibly for the bingo. She gave her son a lukewarm welcome and looked disapprovingly at his new boy friend. She definitely did not approve, and she was a little loud in her condemnation once her inhibitions had been loosened by generous helpings of gin. She was with her own friend. A coarse and rough man with a raucous laugh and bawdy humour. When Nancy arrived, it was her turn to display her feathers of disapproval. She hated the Club, didn't in truth really like her mother a great deal, but felt duty bound to see her, and in truth detested Charlie, who sponged off her. Not that her mother minded. She was eighty and enjoyed his company.

Nancy at least welcomed Simon. She did like him, and gave his friend a cordial welcome. He seemed to be somehow familiar to her. She couldn't quite place him.

CHAPTER 6

'Two wrongs make a right.'

"Major."

Curcic saluted his commanding officer in full formality.

"At ease Sergeant. At ease."

The tall straight-backed officer walked to the door and pulled the blind down. His adjutant would understand that he was not to be disturbed. He stroked at his bristling moustache and indicated that the sergeant should sit whilst he rounded the table, sat and flicked a switch marked 'white'. There was a faint hissing as the outward facing speakers created a field of white noise to deter any eavesdroppers.

"Good job the other day Nicolai. Caused quite a stir I can tell you."

"Sir?" The sergeant raised his eyebrows. It was the first time the major had used his first name.

Major Cropwell gave a grin, and lit a cigarette, offering one to his underling, who accepted the offering. "Yes. Apparently, Radagadz has gone mad. He turned up about twenty minutes after you along with the very latest in drugs to get Marcellus to talk. Pity about him. He was a good man."

"Yes, sir."

"Anyway. Our Radagadz chap has decided that revenge is his best ally, and as such has called in on some of our operatives and exacted his bloody vengeance. Moles and Hartley are both dead. It is possible that he has names from them. I do not know. There is another matter too, something which is of great concern to me, but more of that momentarily.

Radagadz."

"Do you want me to act, sir?"

"Yes. Good man. Look, I need your total secrecy on this."

"You always have it, sir."

"Yes, yes. Of course. Sorry to have to mention it to you. Sergeant, you are the best in the business. I don't think anyone else could have got to Marcellus. I am sure no one else could get near to Radagadz. Here."

He passed over a dossier with photograph of the next victim. "He is currently in a small town called Simonovce. Cox is missing from near there. He may have him."

Curcic looked at the photo and nodded.

"I know the place. I will take care of it straight away."

"Good man. Straight back to report to me. Don't use the usual means. Person to person on this one."

"The other matter. You said there was another matter, sir?"

"Yes I did, didn't I? Tell you what sergeant. Remind me when you get back. This matter has top priority just now."

Curcic stood and replaced his beret. Saluted the major and left.

He took the usual route over the border. Changed into a militia uniform and made his way to Simonovce. He had not been there for about sixteen years, but had changed little in that time. A few buildings were new, several were now rubble, but the basic shape of the town remained unchanged. He walked with a swagger and kept his Kalashnikov slung over his shoulder. He entered a cafe and drank coffee in silence, keeping an eye out on the street.

A succession of lorries, trucks and the occasional tank rumbled their way through the pot-holed streets. There seemed to be a lot of activity in the town. His latest information was that there was a push to weed out some pockets of resistance in the hill villages about twenty kilometres from Simonovce. He would have to be careful. But he always was.

He soon located the building where he hoped Radagadz was. It was in a compound, well protected with high fences. He flashed his pass at the guard who eyed him up and down and asked his business.

"I have been posted here, God knows why."

"How did you get here?"

"Convoy. Then foot. I have been travelling for three days. I could do with a good meal."

"Go through."

He walked on through the gates in the direction of the main building and went to the office indicated. A weary looking captain examined his well-worn papers.

"I have no knowledge of your posting here. None at all."

Curcic handed over an envelope to him. It was addressed to Captain Salic, the man in front of him. The network had so far served him well.

"Yes, I see. Why send you here? I do not understand."

"I have been recovering from a wound. My uncle lives in Koren.

He is my only living relative after..."

He trailed into silence. The captain looked up at him and nodded.

Everyone had a tale of woe to relate these days. "OK. There is no organisation these days. Nobody tells me anything. Go to the barracks and Sergeant Berger will give you a billet. You look as though you could do with a meal. Go to the canteen after. You can start your duties tomorrow."

Curcic did as ordered and was soon eating a dish of stringy stew and beans. He sat and talked with some other soldiers, and soon learned that his target was here.

"Be careful near him. He's a bastard."

Curcic nodded his thanks. They had told him exactly where he was, so that he could avoid him. He asked Sergeant Berger for light duties for the rest of the day, explaining that he didn't like to just lounge about.

"Good man. You can take these messages for me. Paperwork to be processed, that sort of thing. Help you find your way around the place."

As he walked the compound delivering the letters he planned his escape route. To the back of the compound was a wall, which had several loose bricks. They would make ideal footholds for climbing. He also formulated his plan carefully. As the civilian staff left for the evening he managed to type an envelope with Radagadz name on, and stuffed in some sheets of paper. At around eight as the majority of the soldiers were settling down for the evening, playing cards, smoking, and chatting he slipped out and walked through the evenings chill air to Captain Salic's office. He walked through it and out towards the main building, having left his top coat behind, so looking like a different soldier to a casual observer. He entered the main doors and took the steps downstairs to where Radagadz was questioning his suspects. He was halted at the bottom by two armed guards. He showed them the letter. He had marked it 'eyes only' and sealed it with wax.

"I am to deliver this personally to Mr Radagadz and await a reply. It is from General Tomasovic."

They nodded and one of them took him down the corridor, past two more guards, and made him wait by a door, whilst permission was gained to go further. A different guard took him to another door.

"He is having a meal, but will see you straight away. Be quick."

He knocked on the door and opened it ushering in the messenger. Radagadz was as he had expected. Painfully thin, slicked back blonde hair, round glasses balanced on a thin nose. Next to him sat another man with the rank of major. His tunic unbuttoned at the neck. Radagadz spoke.

"You have a message for me?"

"Yes sir."

Curcic moved forward with the letter in his outstretched hand. As he moved around the table to the men his left hand flashed the glint of steel and he lunged forward thrusting the blade hard and deep into the majors throat, silencing and killing him in one violent action. He dropped the letter from his right hand and pressed the blade of a second knife against Radagadz throat. The major had now slumped forward clutching his throat and gurgled his dying breath to silence. Radagadz went stiff in his chair knowing not to cry out.

"What do you..?"

He was not allowed to finish his sentence. Curcic allowed him no such luxury. He did not need to gloat, question or tease the man. He was here to do a job. He drew the blade across the other mans' throat, slicing deeply into his neck, killing him with a single motion. Nic pulled his face down into his plate, to stop him falling over and creating a noise, then wiped his blade on the dead mans suit, and re-concealed the weapon. He backed out of the door.

"Thank you sir. No message. I understand." He saluted and closed the door. He raised his eyebrows at the guard outside and exhaled deeply.

"He says to let him finish his meal in peace. Got quite a temper, hasn't he?"

The other man nodded, and indicated the way out. Curcic walked in a casual unhurried manner, away from the room. He went up the stairs and left the building. He had little time left before his act was discovered.

He made his way to the rear wall and quickly climbed over into the narrow streets beyond, running up and away on the cobbles to the top of the street heading for the pine trees which would afford him some cover. He ran quickly and soon had plenty of distance between him and the compound as the siren wailed to lament the discovery of his deed. He took off his tunic and trousers to reveal civvies underneath.

He buried the clothes under pine needles, and pulled on a beret. He felt cold, since the clothes were of necessity thin, but reckoned it a small temporary price to pay. He hurried up and on, anxious to miss the hue and cry which would follow. By dawn he had cleared the mountain over and down the other side and followed the natural valley towards the river. He jumped on the back of a lorry rumbling on the rough road, without being seen by the driver. By late morning he had slipped off the truck on the outskirts of town and approached a garage and bought an old motorbike with cash from his money belt, as well as a warm jacket. He headed west, headed to the border with Austria, twisted the machine along narrow tracks, gunned it down broad highways, and crossed the border using his false passport which gave his occupation as freelance photographer. He explained to the guard that he had had his equipment confiscated by the militia, and was pleased to be out of the country.

Three days after he had executed Radagadz he marched into Major Cropwell's' office for his debrief. The major once more pulled down the blind and switched on the white noise. "I gather you had some success."

"Yes sir. How did you.."

"Oh, well the shit has hit the fan on this one I can tell you. It even made the international papers. Apparently our Mr Radagadz was next in line for the ministers job. Knife eh" Curcic retold the details of his job. Cropwell nodded his satisfaction.

"Knife was the quietest under the circumstances. Couldn't risk anybody searching me and finding a silenced pistol. Had to be knife."

Cropwell nodded "As usual, you have performed your task admirably. Sergeant, I can honestly say that you are the best I have ever worked with."

"Thank you sir."

"It is not praise given lightly, I can assure you. Anyway. The other matter I mentioned last week. Like I said- shit has hit the fan over Radagadz. Hit it before actually. Bottom line is that our minister has pulled up stumps on us. Doesn't think that the British government should be associated with having a team of assassins on its books. Didn't like it much when we took our own out- you know Marcellus- didn't like it at all. I have totally denied any knowledge on the Radagadz thing, said it was definitely not us. Don't actually think he believes me, but so what? They are making a big mistake I can tell you. They don't realise the power, which we can exert by taking out certain individuals. Take out a leader here, remove an opponent there, and the whole thing collapses, like a deck of cards. Impetus can be lost if the driving force is missing. We can foment uprisings, divert attention here and do it in a totally covert manner. I tell you sergeant, with just three more as good as you, we could keep Europe at peace for years. Save thousands of lives by taking out just a few key people. They are making a huge mistake."

Curcic took an offered cigarette.

"Anyway sergeant, now for the official bit. As of now, the department is officially disbanded."

"What happens to me now, sir?"

"Well, officially, like the others I am to offer you a transfer to regulars, or you can take redundancy."

"Redundancy? Not many jobs for hit-men in the wanted ads, sir."

The major walked to his cabinet and pulled out a bottle of scotch and two glasses. He poured them both one. He had never done such a thing before.

"Cheerio." He clinked glasses and drained his.

"Unofficially, I have a proposition to put to you."

"Sir?"

He leaned forward conspiratorially. "This is for you only, sergeant. I have made no such offer to the others."

Curcic nodded his agreement, and the major continued.

"I can use your talents. The country can use your talents."

"But I thought you said that the department was disbanding?"

"I did."

"Sir?"

"Look. There is a certain market for what you do. People, organisations, governments are prepared to pay for a discreet, professional service. I am not talking about the thugs on motorbikes shooting down judges at traffic lights, nor am I talking about terrorists bombing generals. No, what there is, is a market where people need to be eliminated, where the deaths appear natural, or accidental. Are you interested?"

Curcic looked at his mentor. He had worked with the major for ten years. Trusted him totally. He had no doubt that he was offering him a sound proposition. He cast his mind briefly over the ethics of the matter, but discarded them. Two years ago he had been told that he had a progressive, incurable disease. He would be dead in about ten years. He had not asked for the disease, had been singled out for a slow, agonising death, by the Almighty. No he had no qualms about killing anyone. He had done it often enough before. It was what he was best at.

"Before you agree, sergeant, just consider this. Those you have taken out before this have all deserved it. Have been a threat to peace, stability, lives etc. This could be different. The victims will be selected because they are in the way. You may be asked to kill a grandmother for her inheritance, a young mother so that her cheating husband can remarry. You will be paid to do deeds which may trouble your conscience."

"Sir, do not worry about that. I have no conscience. I have no other talent than to get in and out of places unseen and kill efficiently and without compunction as necessary. I will do it. I want to do it."

The major nodded. "I knew you would. OK. I will give you some personal training on how to use and administer certain drugs to simulate heart attacks, strokes and the like. Drugs and methods which will escape the most thorough post mortem. Then we must arrange your cover, install untraceable lines of contact. You will become a very rich man sergeant, or should I say mister Curcic."

CHAPTER 7

'Catch me if you can.'

The trail to delivering messages to Nick was, by necessity and design, a tortuous one. Major Cropwell had always urged the requirement for utmost secrecy. Nick had made it an art form. All his years spent undercover had honed survival skills to a fine point. Now was no exception.

He had gained the habit of constant surveillance, incessant glancing around him, checking and rechecking people close by him, looking for signs of furtive movements, hidden weapons and the like. Now was no exception. He unlocked his private mailbox in the store, which offered such a desirable facility. The contents had been re-routed through similar such mailboxes up and down the country. Hired hands had keys and routinely re-located the letters and packages to the next one. Le Carre would have been proud of the convoluted precautions taken to ensure secrecy. Inside the mailbox, Nick retrieved three large envelopes, one of which was padded. He looked at the typesetting. The two thinner ones were familiar, the third not. He looked around again, all seemed normal. The third package caused a slight furrow to his brow, brought about a stirring concern. He gingerly felt along the contents, paying particular heed to the sealed flap. The polystyrene padding made his sensory examination difficult but he was fairly sure he could feel something there. Something thin, hard. A wire? He could not be sure.

Nick looked around again and stuffed the three letters into the copious inside pocket of his greatcoat. He relocked the mailbox and emerged into the cold daylight which that November day offered him and checked around in his familiar manner. Behind him, to the left he caught sight of a man in jeans, brown short leather jacket and dark sunglasses. It was too dark to make such appendages necessary, but perhaps the man was a fashion junkie. His close cropped hair suggested that this was not the case. Nick pulled his coat to him, protecting him from both cold and from prying eyes.

The jiffy bag still concerned him, but he had thought quickly. Over from the shopping mall lay the crown court. He knew that they had had recently installed X-ray equipment to screen visitors into the building. He hurried over the busy street, dodging quickly between cars and buses, noting a red Rover and metallic green Renault more acutely than the rest of the traffic. Behind him he glimpsed the sunglasses again. He would work quickly.

Outside the court building he saw the short queue forming to gain access to the afternoon session. The black woman in front of him had an open shopping bag so he quickly placed the padded parcel into it whilst pretending to stumble and hold onto her. "Sorry. Are you OK?"

She nodded her assent and Nick stood back allowing several to join the queue ahead of him whilst ostensibly tying his shoelace. He stood back, looked around him as he noticed sunglasses across the road, four lanes of traffic away. The dark lady handed her bag to the security guard, whilst she was scanned with a hand held probe by another. Her bag passed under a machine and the guard behind the screen signalled the policeman opposite. Before she knew what was happening, two burly men apprehended her, and Nick could see the word 'bomb' being mouthed by the screen operative. Nick slipped from the building and noted sunglasses to his left.

The red Rover was slowly crawling along in the heavy traffic to his right. The Renault was nowhere to be seen. Nick, expertly dodged the traffic, skipping lightly over to the pavement opposite. Sunglasses was trying to manoeuvre through the cars, vans and buses, but stopped and jumped in the red Rover as Nick ran quickly up the side of the bus station. Traffic pressing against him was via a one way street. The Rover could not follow him up there. He was light on his feet, expert in melting unseen into the crowd and slipped into the side door of the multi-storey. His car was on the fifth floor. He ran to the wall opposite to have a quick look at the entering traffic. Red Rover was entering, and sunglasses jumped out, running quickly into the car park. Nick acted quickly, he ran up the stairs to where his car was parked. Once on the fifth floor he looked down to the entrance. The green Renault pulled in across the exit, and two more men jumped out. He could hear the squeal of tyres as the Rover was rapidly ascending the ramps. Nick dashed to his car, prostrated himself on the floor and heard the heavy pant of his breath as he scrutinised the underside of the mini. There, running from the sump and along the underneath was two wires. Both red. He knew what they were. His car was no use to him now.

He rolled away, and saw sunglasses tip toeing along the side of the adjacent cars, his hand holding a silenced Beretta. Nick pulled out his knife from the rear of his belt, felt the comfort of its weight. He assessed the situation. In about thirty seconds red Rover plus occupants would be there, right here. Now, there were only sunglasses to deal with. He had few choices. Sunglasses were next to him as he lay under the blue Ford, three away from his mini. He was walking away from Nick, and in a silent series of rapid movements, he rolled from the floor, sprang to his feet and quickly, but fiercely pulled back sunglasses head whilst cutting his throat, the man slumping silently before him. Nick dragged him to the rear of the blue Ford, and relieved him rapidly of his gun and wallet, and then sprinted to the stairs to run and jump down to the ground floor before the red Rover reached the fifth floor. He squashed himself flat against the wall whilst he peered through the small window in the door which lead to the alley at the buildings side. In the shadows of the doorway opposite he saw another man dressed in jeans, this time wearing a camel coloured jacket. He wore no sunglasses. Nick cursed under his breath. "Elliot!"

He knew him from some seven years ago. They had done some training together under the watchful eyes of Cropwell. He had last heard that he had been killed on active service in South America. He was evidently misinformed. Time was his enemy, in moments sunglasses would be discovered and the place would be swarming with secret service operatives. He drew breath, checked the weapon, and walked from the car park with the gun held by both hands pointing directly at Elliot's' head. The man stopped, and began to raise his hands but it was too late. Nick squeezed two bullets from the weapon, throwing Elliot back into the gloom of the doorways shadows. Nick looked left and right, but luck was with him. He had not been spotted. He walked rapidly away slightly downhill to the main thoroughfare. It was fortunately very busy, and with the gun pushed down the inside pocket of his coat, he quickly and happily blended with the crowd.

He took the bus and changed direction five times until he was confident he was not being followed. He had to formulate his plan quickly.

The parcel in his mailbox- a bomb. His car- a bomb. He was being targeted quite firmly. Two cars, five, maybe six men sent to get him. They clearly didn't want to talk. He thought about Elliot. Missing presumed dead, now just dead. Nick reasoned that his reported death was to hide him away, to give him the anonymity, which he needed to be a hired assassin. But then, he was no different to Nick. No different at all. His flat was out of the question. If they could trace his car, they could trace his home. Even though he had been sure he could not be traced by way of his thoroughness, it was a chance he could not take. He slipped from the bus and into a cafe. A hot drink and snack would serve him well for now. The situation before him was clear. He was being pursued- to the death by agents sent from some high office. Anyone who could track him through his elaborate mail box system, trace his car, and possibly his home must have vast resources. At the moment he saw the hand of Cropwell on the tiller, but he would have to rationalise the whys later. He had to get well clear of Nottingham, that much was clear. He took the money from sunglasses wallet-seventy pounds. He counted his own, some in cash from his wallet and his 'spare' which he kept secreted in a money belt. Another five hundred and forty. It was enough. It would have to be. He had considerably more, including three excellent guns in his flat, but they were all gone now. He let them mentally slip away.

He had always had contingency plans for danger and flight. They would have to work now. In three separate safety deposit boxes in Plymouth, Edinburgh and Norwich, he had enough cash and gold coins to start over again if necessary. It now seemed necessary. He rolled a cigarette and picked up the evening paper from the table opposite, quickly locating the classified ads. He needed transport, and had a budget of about four hundred and fifty pounds. Not exactly fast car class, but maybe a motorbike. There were several in the price range. He picked the one nearest to him, and made the call to see if it was still for sale and could he view it immediately.

It was a twelve year old Honda 500. Paint was faded, seat tatty, and the engine blew some smoke. There was no tax, but he needed it for a one way journey only, maybe four hundred miles, probably less.

"How much for cash?"

"It's advertised at five fifty."

"I know. How much for cash? Now."

"Five hundred?"

"I'll give you four eighty, and you can throw in the helmet." "You're joking mate. I need the helmet for my new kwak" Nick made as if to move away, indicating no deal with a slight shrug of the shoulder.

"Here, hang on. Is this OK?"

The lanky short haired man pulled an old helmet from the garden shed. It was peakless, was scratched black, and had the word 'demolition' hand painted in red at the back. It smelled musty, but it would do.

"OK. Here."

Nick counted the money into the mans hand and wrote a false name and address on the registration document. They shook hands and he kicked the beast into spluttering life and drove away to fill up at the nearest petrol station. It was fast approaching night now, and he fastened his coat tightly to him. He had decided on Edinburgh. The oldest of his 'stashes' so probably the safest. It would be a trek north on the bike, about three hundred miles. Six hours or so. He would be there sometime after midnight. He would stop over tonight, get to the bank in the morning and off. He stopped and disposed of Sunglasses wallet down a drain. He would keep the gun a little while longer, since he may need it before he could reach Edinburgh.

The journey north was cold. Very cold. The wind bit through the weave of his greatcoat and made his neck sore where it was exposed to the frost and light snow. He wore no gloves, and by the time he reached Scotch Corner some two and a half hours later he had something approaching frostbite. He could not face much more travelling and at ten o'clock had cleared Newcastle and stopped in Alnwick, finding a nice room for the night at a local hotel.

"By, pet you look frozen?"

"I am that. Lost my gloves. Sorry about the signature. I can hardly feel my fingers."

"There's plenty of hot water, pet. I should have a good soak if I were you. Do you want any supper? The kitchens just about to shut?"

"Please. Anything will do."

"I'll make sure it's something hot. Here's your key."

He ate a mix of steak and kidney pie, peas and chips, washed down with tea, and took the landlady's advice and soaked in the bath. He could gradually feel the numbness leaving his fingers, and felt the pain of the rawness of the chafed knuckles now glowing red before him. As he lay there, soaking and aching he tried to focus on the events of the day. He was always ultra careful, had been well schooled and practised in it for more years than he could number. It was a good job he was. They were certainly determined to get him. First the letter bomb, he recalled the date as being only the week previously. The twenty first. The strange thing about it was that it had been a single envelope. The others were several envelopes thick, from successive postings. He still had them, and could chart their progress from the date stamps. The jiffy bag was posted from Kettering. He had made sure he had gleaned the necessary information, at least. So someone had tracked one of his mailbox forwarding from there. They obviously had to be sure that the letter would be opened directly by him, not smothered by subsequent layers of postings. The net had tracked him well. As for the pursuers, well, he had his suspicions, but could not be sure. The Beretta he had taken from sunglasses had no serial number- standard practise, which made it untraceable. He would dispose of that later. He dried himself and sat with a drink of tea- he would leave the blur which alcohol gave him for the moment, and checked the dates on the other two letters. They were older than the last date of the twenty first . One was last dated November the seventh, the other October thirtieth. He would muse the significance of those dates over the next few hours.

So far, it had the mark of Cropwell about it, but why? He had not offended him, in fact he did some jobs for him. About half of his work was via Cropwell. He had always delivered. Always gave good, efficient service. He would review his cases over the past few weeks, examine what was, and what was not significant. He fell into a deep sleep.

Next morning he felt the soreness in his knuckles. One thing was sure, he must get some gloves before taking the rest of the road north to Scotland. He ate a full breakfast and the kindly landlady gave him some cream for his hands, and pointed him the right direction for gloves. After he had bought some thick plastic gauntlets for thirty pounds he paid his hotel bill and had only a few pounds left after he had filled up with fuel. As he headed north the germ of an explanation of his pursuit took root.

He took possession of his box through the bank where it was deposited. In a private room he pocketed ten thousand pounds in cash and a similar amount in gold coin. He also had a Smith and Wesson plus silencer. It would replace the Beretta, which was currently concealed in a bag in the bushes in the park. He did not wish to risk detection by the banks' security. He replaced the box and left the bank carefully scrutinising all about him. He was sure he was not being followed.

With some of his cash he bought a second hand mini. He liked minis, small and nippy, innocuous, easily overlooked. Just like Nick really. He left the bike parked in a side street after removing all identifying marks. It would no doubt soon succumb to night time crime. With a new set of clothes he drove to the coast and threw the Beretta over the cliffs and to the ravages of the North Sea. He was away and this time at least had the comfort of the car to keep late Novembers chill away. He stopped and ate a meal at a roadside cafe and contemplated his next move. He would not leave the country. That was probably expected of him. He would go to ground for a couple of months, away from the limelight, somewhere common. He was used to living on his own, but desperately wanted some company. He thought back to the dates. He was probably being watched, tailed, supervised or whatever over the past few weeks. He decided to eschew all contacts he had made over that period. Trouble was, he had visited most of his friends over that time. There were few options left.

Then it came to him. Four months ago he had enjoyed a very pleasant couple of weeks with Simons family. He had got on particularly well with his brother-in-law Tim who had invited him back. Now was the time to take up the invite. He didn't have his number, but remembered the house well. It was about three hours drive, he would be there about seven. Tim would be surprised.

CHAPTER 8

'Queer goings on.'

Simon was embroiled in conversation with his sister, at a separate table, whilst Fieldy had wandered off and was chatting to the barman. Tim found himself alone with Nick. He noticed how he looked constantly around him and yet managed to look relaxed at the same time. Perhaps it was a habit. "Where are you staying?"

Nick smiled, allowed white teeth to counterpoint his slightly dark skin.

"Actually, perhaps I shouldn't say, but I believe old Simon is negotiating with his sister."

"Oh. Sorry Nick, didn't mean it to sound like that. No I would be delighted if you stayed with us. We have plenty of room. No problem."

Nick nodded his appreciation.

"It's not quite what it seems you know. Simon and I. We've not 'been together' for eight months like he said. Sure, we've known each other that long, in Turkey like he said. I was working, he was on holiday. Just got on well. Arranged to meet back in London, which we did about two months later. We've met up casually since then on several occasions. Sim makes it seem like we are a couple. We are, as they say, just friends."

"You don't have to explain it to me, Nick. Not my concern really.."

"No, please, I'd rather. He said he was coming up here for a couple of weeks since he was changing jobs, and asked if I'd accompany him. Only too pleased to. I've been working flat out for months, my next job is two weeks away, so the break will do me good. Quite frankly, my job is by necessity a lonely one, so I love plenty of company when I'm off. Simon is good fun. Hope you don't mind me tacking on like this."

"No. Any friend of Simons, as they say."

Nick smiled again, and glanced over to Fieldy.

"Quite a character eh?"

"Yes. He is. A good laugh, and a good friend. Look out, he's coming."

Fieldy performed his neck movement on the way over. "You two talking about me? Like old Oscar said.. mind you'd know that Nick eh? One of your lot eh?"

"Yes indeed. You know, women are all right, but there's nothing like the real thing."

"Good man. You can take a joke. Just like me. Mind you, I am a joke. I drink you know."

"We all drink."

"No. I mean, I'm what they call an alcoholic. People keep trying to tell me that I must stop, that it's bad for me. Well, I don't actually care what other people tell me. In my experience, every one has their own private cross to bear their own particular weakness. They'd be better off doing something about it, rather than trying to reform me. I know my weakness. It's the amber nectar, you know? Well, the wine in my case. I live my life how I like it, and drink only to excess. What's your weakness, Nick? Buggery?"

Tim winced a little. Fieldy had the knack of being, what he called honest, whilst others might have suggested rudeness. He knew that some people could be easily offended by it. It appeared that Nick was not one of them.

Nick shrugged at the suggestion.

"John, really! I don't think.."

Nick smiled and interrupted. "It's OK, Tim. If you are serious with the question, then I will give it an honest answer. Well?" Fieldy smiled back. "Yeah why not? I like honesty. Homosexuality? Never tried it myself. Perhaps I shouldn't condem what I don't know about. You never know..? Go on Nick, educate me."

"Well, you like masturbating don't you?"

"Sure thing. Who doesn't? "

"Well so do I. I bet you like a blow job too?"

"Yeah. Like the old joke about lobster and blowjob, eh? You know, you get neither at home. That's right isn't it Tim?" Fieldy nudged his friend.

Tim was feeling a little embarrassed by the revelation of intimate homosexual acts. He didn't answer Fieldy but allowed Nick to continue.

"Well, I like both. It's just that I choose to do it with a mate. Good night out, plenty of booze, Chinese on the way home, then end up with your cock in someone's mouth. Lovely."

"Blimey. Why not a woman then?"

"I can manage that too. No problem. It's just that a lot of women want some kind of commitment before they do the things you want from them. Not all mind, some enjoy just the sex, but then they usually drift off to try it somewhere else. There are some gay blokes who go for the commitment thing too, but by and large, most men just like a bit of casual, then off. You know us blokes, naturally promiscuous. "

Fieldy nodded his head. "See what you mean. I'd never thought of it like that before. Always hated the thought of a didgery up the old fudge tunnel."

"I remember having a girlfriend at uni who actually preferred it.

Mind you she was a bit weird."

Fieldy and Nick looked at Tim, slightly surprised at his revelation.

"You know. Deep down, we all just respond to our natural, sexual urges. Often, we're governed by the wants of our partners, rather than our own needs. Tim here, did the deed, because some tart wanted to have it that way. Most of us get ensnared in a 'relationship' with the opposite sex and sacrifice our freedom, and individuality into the bargain, when really, a good wank would do. Now you, Nick my boy, have it how you want it. Just respond to the call when it takes you, that's it. Good for you.

You'll do."

"Thanks. Actually, we all make trades in our lives. Sexuality is one. Jobs, relationships, they are some of the others. I regard a job, as a means to an end. I earn quite a lot of money, but once I have reached my savings target, that will be it. I'll use the rest of my allotted time in paying people back."

Tim looked puzzled. "What do you mean? Paying them back?

Revenge?"

Nick laughed and stood up.

"Same again? No paying back comes in three ways. You can repay kindness, repay a debt, or you can exact revenge. I look forward to the day when I can do all three."

He walked over to the bar for refills. Fieldy looked at Tim.

"I like him. Straight-for a queer. No embarrassment, just honesty.

He's OK."

Nancy walked over with her brother. She could not disguise her scowl when she tried to avoid looking at Fieldy. He stood up, at her approach.

"Nancy! Lovely to see you. We've just been talking about you."

She refused the bait, ignored him and spoke directly to Tim.

"Hope you don't mind, but Simon has nowhere to stay so.."

Tim nodded. "Fine. They can have the spare room."

"Oh, well, good. I thought I'd slip off now and get the room ready. Would you like some supper when you get in Simon? I can.."

"Sis, no. Look, thanks a lot. We can call at the chippie if needs be. Don't worry about the room, we can just doss.."

"You will not. I'll see you later."

She breezed off, grateful for a genuine excuse to leave early. Fieldy watched her leave, and shook his head. Tim was going to ask him what he meant by that but was interrupted by Nick returning with a tray of drinks. He took two more over to Simons mother and friend before returning.

"Nice chap that Charlie. Next time I get him a drink, remind me to piss in his beer."

"No point, chap. Enough of the landlords in it already. Why do you think I stick to wine?"

"Ah yes French bottled piss."

"Thanks Tim."

"My pleasure Mr Field. My pleasure."

"Tell me about your work, Nick. Sounds exotic."

Nick looked at Tim. Cocked his head to one side and considered the question.

"Well, it sounds exotic, but isn't. I audit books of international concerns. Jet off somewhere, spend one or two weeks in a hotel somewhere, and add up numbers. Trouble is, a hotel is a hotel whether it's in Spain, Amsterdam or Tokyo. Apart from the staff, you sometimes wake up wondering which country you are in. The work is fairly routine. I have to do it, I don't worry if I upset someone, that isn't my brief. All I do is go in, do it get out."

"Do you enjoy it?"

"The job? Curious question really. I have a theory that only ten per cent of people actually enjoy their work. Often these people just live the life. Another ten per cent are so ensnared by it, that they know no difference. Life, work. Work, life, they just melt into one another.

The other eighty per cent hate it. Do it because they have to live, have to perform the task so that they can get by in life."

"And which are you, Nick?"

"Oh I'm with the majority. Definitely. I don't particularly enjoy the work, but, I do it. It is all I know. The trade is the pay. It gives me something to aim for. How about you Tim?"

Fieldy answered for him.

"Eighty per cent. Definitely." Tim nodded.

"How about you Fieldy? What do you do for a living?"

"Me, well I live. I don't fit quite into your theory. I have become very philosophical about work. I am a welder by training, albeit a long time ago, and can turn my hand to making some pretty objects. Quite therapeutic it is too. I also draw cartoons. I enjoy that too, but my philosophy is each to his own needs. So I do just enough to get me by. I have sufficient for what I want, and when I do work, draw or weld, then I actually enjoy it when I actually do it. My theory is, that if I aspired to earn a bundle, I would have to work hard at what I now enjoy, so much so, that it would then become a chore. I would create a monster which would either kill me, or have to be killed."

"Nice, philosophy. I'll amend my theory. How about you Simon?"

Simon lit a cigarette, and offered them round. Now Nancy had gone, Tim took one. He allowed Simon to exhale the smoke before speaking.

"Actually, I think I'm in the first ten per cent. I actually enjoy my job. Enjoy the challenge that my type of engineering. It makes me think. I must admit, that I often don't like the people I work with. Set of tossers, mostly. Praying to some corporate God, playing silly power games, doing things which are petty and stupid. On the whole, the work is great, but people get in the way."

Nick gave a little chuckle, and raised his glass. "Looks like I'll have to totally revise my thinking in this company. Cheers."

The next couple of weeks went along in the same vein. The four became almost inseparable. They laughed more than they had for ages, they shared similar philosophies, with sufficient differences of opinions to make discussions lively. Tim continued his fitness routine, although he lapsed slightly on the alcohol ban. He continued to lose weight, so he was quite pleased with himself. Pleasure and pain mingled nicely in his life.

The day of his hospital appointment dawned, and he felt quite nervous. He took a barium meal, an unpleasant experience which was a little like swallowing concrete. He was X-rayed, prodded, poked, had blood syringed from him and finally sent away with a dismissive 'we will send the results to your GP. He'll tell you what the next step is.'

And that was that. He would have to wait about ten days. He had taken the day off work, and only Nick was there when he got home.

"Hi Tim? Cuppa? Kettles just boiled."

"Sure. Thanks. No Simon?"

"He's gone to get a new set of wellies or something. Special weatherproof gear for bonnie Scotland. I decided it wasn't my scene. Day off?"

Tim accepted the drink.

"Yes. Actually I've been to hospital for some tests."

"Tests? Nothing wrong I hope?"

Tim shook his head. "I don't know, yet. Got persistent indigestion, heartburn, bit of pain in the side. I don't know. Everyone assures me it will all be OK, but you can't stop worrying can you?"

"No you can't. It's only natural. Have you talked about it with anyone."

"How do you mean?"

"You know, a trouble shared, and all that."

Tim shook his head. "No. Nancy and I, well we don't talk any more. Not real talk. Just swap snippets of information necessary for existence. You know the kind of thing, need more bog rolls. Gas bill came today. That sort of thing."

"What about Fieldy? I know that you two are close."

"No, actually. Not this time. I'll tell him when I have the results. I've told no one. Don't know why I'm telling you now."

"Talk about it if it helps. I have, well, let's just say I have certain experiences which can be shared."

It was only later that Tim understood the significance of that innocuous remark

CHAPTER 9

'Some solutions cost dear.'

Nancy and Nick were alone for the first time, since Tim and Simon had gone to the gym to work out. Nick did not feel the need, he would retain his natural fitness by taking a few days out on the moors, facing privation and nature in all her glory. She gave him a drink.

"Thanks, Nancy for all the hospitality. I, we both appreciate it."

"No problem. It's nice to see Simon settled with someone. Not that I am a rampant liberal mind, but I'm no prude either."

Nick did not dispel her illusion. He and Simon were no 'couple', but he did not gainsay her, being unaware of exactly what Simon had told her.

"I still can't get over the feeling that I've seen you somewhere before. You look so familiar. It's been driving me crazy."

Nick sipped some tea and placed his mug on the coffee table. He was in a position of strength, but would not have mentioned it had Nancy not been close to remembering.

"Actually, I can remember exactly when and where it was. It was the two weeks commencing July 10th, in Magaluf. We were in the same hotel."

Nancy paled at the recollection but remained outwardly calm.

"Yes, of course. That was it."

He smiled at her, and lounged back in the chair.

"You weren't with Tim."

"No, we take our holidays separately. I like the sun, Tim prefers the countryside. It suits us both that way. We've done it for years now."

"Yes, of course you do. Funnily enough I can remember exactly who you were with."

"Oh, yes, Sally. Girls together."

"Funny name for a bloke. Sally. I wouldn't have known his name, had I not met him at your tennis club bash last Friday. It definitely wasn't Sally."

She put her cup down, tossed back her hair and jutted out her chin. "What do you want?"

"Want? What do you mean?"

"Oh, come on Nick, don't play games. You know I was with Ricky. I suppose you'll tell Tim?"

"I don't honestly know. After all it is not my business is it?"

"No, it isn't."

"But then again, I like Tim a lot. I wouldn't like to see him get hurt."

"Fancy your chances eh?"

He gave a small laugh. "Now then, Nancy, no need to recourse to pettiness. No, the thing that made me wonder, made me mention it at all, was why you haven't told Tim yourself? After all, from what I can see- and correct me if I'm wrong- but there doesn't seem to be much love between you. I just wondered why you both don't just call it a day. Find your own happiness in your own ways. Or is it just a sexual thing?"

Nancy felt uncomfortable. She hated that direct kind of questioning, it made her feel inferior, made her feel inadequate. "No, it's not just a sexual thing, although well that..." She tailed off, embarrassed by her own apparent willingness to confess sexual pleasure to a total stranger, and a homosexual at that. " Not, that it concerns you, but it is serious. I will tell Tim when the time is right."

"Why not now?"

"I have my reasons."

"And they are?"

"Why should I tell you?"

"I like to understand people. Like to know what makes them tick. I could always tell Tim myself."

"Is that a threat?"

He stood up, and smiled at her. He decided that this audience was at an end.

"Nancy, do not worry. I'll not tell him. Just be true to yourself. My belief is that life is too short to live a lie. I should tell him, if I were you. But I'm not going to. Anyway I'm off for a pint. Tell the boys I've gone to pick up Fieldy, and we'll be off to the Red Cow. See you later."

She watched him leave. Watched him and felt threatened by him. She just knew she had met him before, just knew it. She recalled the holiday, it had been glorious, save for the accident. Whilst at the hotel someone had fallen, jumped, or had been pushed from the top floor and had made quite a mess on the patio. The rumour at the time was that he was cheating on his wife, and so had got what he deserved. As far as she could recall, the verdict had been accidental death. It was a pity Tim couldn't have such an accident.

Sally arrived for a drink as the boys came in after their exertions and then left in pursuit of Nick and Fieldy. Sally stroked her blonde hair and sipped some wine as they left.

"My, I see that your Tim is getting quite trim now. It suits him. You'll be wanting him back no doubt."

"Hmmph. He's like a kid at school with a new set of friends. You know when he started all this, when he got that new job, I initially thought, ' here we go again. He'll be back to his slothful ways within a week.' Well, I was wrong. He's been at this for about two months now, he's found the happy compromise between exercise and going out for a beer, so that it doesn't seem to put back the weight. Despite that, I still shudder at the thought of him. As he gets fitter, I feel insulted by it all, insulted as to why he couldn't have done it before-for me- when I wanted him to. As usual he's done it for himself. Well it's too bloody late."

"Still wanting to run off with your Ricky then?"

Nancy looked at Sally closely. They shared all their secrets, Sally covered up for Nancy when she went on holidays, didn't mind digging into her own pocket to help her out. After all Sally had two successful divorces behind her. Unlike Nancy, her previous husbands had been rich, and she took considerable sums of money from them when their marriages failed. It was a situation which Nancy would have loved to be in.

"Are you going to run away then?"

"He owes me. Owes me big. I wish..well I wish he would get run over or something. It's more pressing than ever now. You know Nick?"

"Simons boyfriend?"

"Yes. Well, I knew I had seen him before. It appears that he was in Magaluf last year, staying in the same hotel as me and Ricky."

"Oh my God! Did he recognise you?"

Nancy nodded.

"'Fraid so. He also recognised that I wasn't with Tim either. Not that he knew us then."

"Oh, Nancy, will he tell Tim?"

"Well, strangely enough, he says not. But I don't know. It is just more pressing than ever that I do something about Tim. I wish he could drop down dead, then I'd get all the insurance money- the house, everything. Good old Tim's worth quite a lot dead."

"Are you serious?"

"Serious? About what?"

"You know, about Tim dropping down dead?"

"Damn right I am."

Nancy looked across to her friend. She was biting a little nervously at her lip, and had furrowed her brow slightly, emphasising the lines on her forehead, betraying her true age.

"Come on Sally, what are you getting at?"

Sally patted her friend on the knee.

"Just bear with me a couple of days. Just something Richard once said. Look I must dash. See you on Saturday. Lets have lunch at Houdini's."

Sally tossed her car keys on the mantle, and leaned forward and kissed Richard, her third husband.

"Thanks darling. Here, there some ice in the bucket, pour me another G&T will you old girl?"

She did as he asked and poured herself one. Sally looked at him, he was tall, muscular and still had the bearing of his military service. He had been a captain in the marines, and was ferociously fit. It was probably his love for order and fitness which Tim could never get on with. She liked it, liked his virility. She sat on the arm of their soft cream leather seat and sipped at her drink.

"Richard?"

"Yes darling?"

"Do you remember a couple of weeks ago, we had a blazing row."

He blushed slightly and nodded.

"Yes, sorry about that. Got a bit pissed after the regimental reunion."

"No, it's alright, I'm not having a go at you, it's just. Well just something you said."

"Said? Such as?"

"Well, you said that, for a price, you could get me bumped off. Done away with so that to the world it would seem like an accident."

He shuffled uncomfortably in his seat. "It was just the drink talking, that's all."

"Actually, Richard, I don't believe you. You have a way of always telling the bloody, brutal truth."

"What are you getting at Sally?"

"So it is true then? You could arrange for someone to get knocked off?"

"There is a point to this, I assume?"

Sally smiled. He had not denied it. "Yes there is. It is a friend of mine. She needs someone disposing of. Disposing of in such a way that it looks entirely natural or accidental, so that the insurance companies will pay out."

He nodded slowly. "I see. Who?"

"Richard. Could you arrange this."

He put down his glass and looked around.

"What I said that night should not have been repeated. I trust you haven't blabbed?"

She held up her hands, and shook her head.

"I'm just testing the water."

Richard stood and poured another drink for them both, and paced up and down on the rugs, hands clasped behind his back, lips pursed, head down considering the exact response he would make to his wife's question.

"First you must promise never, and I mean never, to repeat this to anyone."

She nodded. He continued. She was no casual gossiper.

"Well, at the reunion, I met all my old pals. We talked about what we were doing, how we had got on and so on, and I had a good chat with my old CO, Butler. He set himself up supplying mercenaries, most of who were armed security men for tyrants and dictators, people who would buy loyalty. It also seems that he has access to professional hit men, and I mean professional. I'm not talking about the guns for hire from the drugs barons, the type who for a couple of grand will walk into a pub and shoot someone then tear away on a motorbike. I'm talking about real pros. Every army has them, undercover specialists who did the job expertly. Anyway it appears that these units have all been disbanded in the army due to political pressures, so there are redundant assassins out there with only one skill to hire out. Anyway, Butler has these people on his books. They are specifically trained to take people out so that it looks like an accident, natural cause, or even some previously unknown disease. But, they cost money. Lots of it. Who wants to know?"

Sally considered his words. She knew he was genuine, knew he could be trusted completely. If the army had instilled just one thing into Richard, it had instilled total loyalty.

"Nancy." She said simply.

He looked across to her, and cocked his head to one side then nodded slowly.

"Makes sense. Tim is a prick. She'd be well rid. Another man I assume?"

She nodded.

"Look, Sally are you- is she serious? - it will cost her more than she has, and she will have it on her conscience."

"Don't worry Richard. Beneath her jolly exterior, our Nancy is quite, quite bitter towards Tim. She has found someone who will give her the happiness she not only needs, but has earned. Tim is in the way."

There was a moment's silence, before Sally continued.

"How much?"

He smiled. "Well, a proper, undetectable, untraceable hit, with all the due considerations of.."

"Richard, cut out the sales crap. How much?"

"Fifteen grand."

"Bloody hell."

"Cheap for a life actually. A big hit, you know president, head of state that kind would cost ten times that, and more. I don't think Nancy has that kind of cash, does she Sally?"

"It can be arranged. Cash on delivery?"

"No. Up front. Gets rid of the wasters that way."

"I'll let you know."

That Saturday Nancy and Sally had lunch at Houdini's. Sally didn't mention her idea until they were alone walking by the river. October was bright and warm that year.

"Nancy, I have found a solution to your problem."

"Oh yes. Which particular problem have you found a solution to?"

"Tim."

"Tim?" She looked closely at her friend. "How do you mean..?"

Sally told her briefly what Richard had told her, she emphasised the need for caution, but knew there was little need. Nancy nodded slowly as the solution sank in.

"Oh Sally. I don't know. I know I've often said it, but when it comes down to it, to actually do it. I don't know."

"It's the perfect solution. Tim wouldn't feel a thing. It would be out of the blue, the kind of thing that could happen to anyone anytime. It's your key through the door of happiness." Nancy walked to the waters edge and kicked a few small pebbles into the blue-grey waters, watching the ripples overlap, fade and die away. She turned to her friend.

"How much?"

"Fifteen thousand."

Nancy laughed. "Well why bother even mentioning it. I haven't got fifteen hundred, let alone..."

"Nancy. I'll put the money up. You can repay me from the insurance if you like. Money isn't an obstacle."

"I don't know. My heart says yes, but my head..., well I'll have to think about it."

"You do that. There is a solution."

That night Nancy and Tim went out with Simon, Nick, Richard and Sally to 'Mothers', the latest nightspot in town. It was plush, well mirrored and the drinks were at a ridiculously cheap price, and everyone got well oiled. They had a private booth and ate a splendid meal. It was the first time Nick and Richard had met.

"Ex army eh Richard."

"Proud of it. Captain.. anyway how did you know."

"I can always tell."

"How?"

"Takes one to know one."

"Cheeky buggar- oh I see. You ex forces?"

Nick nodded. "Yes. Pay corps, then auditor. Not much active service."

"Oh, pen pusher eh? Never mind, you'll get better one day. But tell me, you and Simon here, a couple of bum boys eh? Which ones mum, which is dad? Ever fancied any children of your own?" Richard could get quite boorish when drunk. Nick smiled at his attempts at goading him.

"How about you Richard? You got any kids. Save for your squaddies. I suppose you liked ordering them about. Wiping their pretty little botties for them."

Richard sneered down his nose at him. Tim interjected. He was quite wobbly by now, and saw the opportunity to have a dig at Richard.

"Can't hack the real responsibility of life can you, you army blokes. Don't have, won't have kids of your own because they are real people, not conditioned to blindly follow orders eh? Real children answer back. What would you do Dickie? Put them on a charge? Put them on jankers, or whatever you call it?"

"Look here you arsehole. I didn't choose to have children, nothing to do with the army.."

"Balls Richard. Couldn't have more like. Didn't have the C-I-C behind you giving you the necessary orders. By the left shag shag, by the right pant pant. Thrust two three, come two three. At ease soldier!"

Simon and Nick laughed. Richard was incandescent with rage, Sally tried to calm him, and Nancy decided to try and defuse the situation.

"Tim, not everybody wants children.."

He glared at his wife. "Yes and some of us wanted more children, but others thought more of playing bloody tennis instead. Don't talk to me about wants Nancy!"

Nancy's' face fell, badly hurt by his remarks. Richard was ready to let his fists put a more convincing argument, and Nick acted quickly, pushing Tim to one side and bundling him out of the booth and into the throng toward the bar. Sally put her hands on Richard to make him sit down.

Simon asked if his sister was OK then went after the other two. Richard poured himself another drink and muttered 'fucking pooves' under his breath, whilst Nancy and Sally went together to the toilet. Nancy wiped a tear away from her eye and looked at her friend.

"Tell Richard to make the necessary arrangements. He's gone too far this time

CHAPTER 10

'Blood brothers.'

"Nick! Great to see you. Come in."

Tim gave Nick a firm handshake. When he and Simon had left he had told him to drop in any time, and he meant it. He had made a new friend, and was comfortable with his sexuality. Nancy was less pleased to see him. She felt guilty since he shared her secret. She had subsequently wondered whether or not he had ever told Tim, but doubted it. He would have beat her with the weight of its implications.

"Nick. How nice."

"Nice to see you Nancy. Still swimming, playing tennis etc."

"Yes."

"How about you Tim? Still jogging? " He heard a slight hmmph from Nancy.

"Only occasionally. Once a week. Keeps me going. Mind you I don't take the car down to the park any more. Run it there and back. And what have you been up to? Have you seen Simon lately?"

Nancy got up to make them all a drink. She was pleased to leave the men on their own. Nick nodded in her direction.

"No change there then?"

Tim shook his head.

"Worse than ever. Ever since that night out at Mothers, she seems to be more down then ever. Still that's life. I don't lose any sleep over it. Sometimes wish she'd find herself a toy boy and piss off somewhere. Leave me on my own. Mind you, I mustn't grumble. I've not been the best husband or provider in the world. Many wouldn't have stuck with me through everything she's had to."

"What do you mean Tim?"

"You know, that business venture with Graham."

"Of course, yes, Simons brother. Never met him."

"Best not. Totally unlike Simon. He's a bit like Nancy, only nasty and devious. How is Simon?"

"Not heard for several weeks. He's got a couple of weeks off at Christmas. We arranged to have a drink together. Like I said just a casual thing. Good company though."

Tim nodded, and thought back to their time spent together those few weeks' back. It had been a happy time, one the most pleasant times he had ever had. Took him back to his carefree college days.

"Could I ask a favour Tim?"

"Sure. Ask away."

"I just wondered if you could put me up for a couple of days."

"Sure thing. Stay in the spare room."

"What about Nancy?"

"Balls to her. Stay here, mate. It'll be nice to talk to someone."

Nancy entered with a tray of drinks, and some biscuits. Tim stood up.

"We're off to the pub. Nick's staying a few nights. He can have the spare room. Come on, Nick, let's catch up with Fieldy, he should still be just conscious."

Nick raised his eyebrows to Nancy, making feeble apology for Tim's rude behaviour. She sat down and fumed at him, mentally pulling the trigger.

They caught up with Fieldy at the club. He greeted Nick warmly, and insisted of getting the drinks in. They spent a pleasant evening, and John did his customary trick of wandering off and engaging someone else in conversation.

"Had your test results yet Tim?"

Tim had half hoped that Nick had forgotten what he had shared with no one else. He nodded but remained silent, before making some comment about the dragon woman as Nancy's mother came in. After Tim had bought her a drink he returned to Nick.

"You didn't answer my question."

"What question?"

"About the test results. Look Tim, if I'm prying, just tell me to piss off."

"No, sorry Nick, it's just that, you're the only one I've told, that's all. I'll tell you later."

When they got home, Nancy was already in bed. She had made up a bed for Nick and he had put his holdall in the room with all his worldly goods in. He secreted the gun by taping it to the underside of his bed. He returned downstairs to Tim. It was a Friday night, and so no work for him the next day. He extracted a half bottle of scotch and had poured them both drinks. "Cheers, Nick. Nice to see you again."

"Cheers."

"Do you know, I've never seen you drunk, Nick. You had gallons of the stuff, like we all did, when you were over last time, but as we all fell down, you never did. How do you handle it?"

Nick shrugged. "Just a gift. I like to be in control. Like to be prepared."

"Yes, I've noticed how you always seem to be watching everything that's going on. Old habit is it?"

He shrugged again. "Guess so."

There was a brief silence, before Nick spoke again.

"Can I tell you something about me Tim?"

"Go ahead."

"If you remember, last time, we spoke of philosophy, of what motivated us, and the rest, and I said that I worked for a goal, to pay people back?"

"Yes, I remember."

"Well, I was surprised that you never really closed in on the real reasons. Why I wanted to repay people, who I wanted to repay."

Tim nodded and sipped his whiskey, indicating for Nick to continue.

"What I want to repay, and why is simple. I'm telling you this, because I think you will understand. I think it will help you as well. Look, I work hard, and have got a fair bit of money, not enough, but quite a bit. I have only a few years left, three at best. What I have and have had for about ten years is the knowledge that I will waste away to a slow death. I have an incurable, hereditary disease. Basically, there is a genetic defect which means that my nerves will gradually die off, meaning that I will have symptoms close to like having leprosy, only by the time they appear. It will be far too late. Already, there are early signs that my nerve endings are failing. Look."

He showed Tim his hands. Where the cold had recently got to them on the long motorbike ride north two of his fingers were suppurating badly. They weren't bandaged, but infected.

"They could well become gangrenous. But I will survive a bit longer yet."

"I'm sorry to hear about that Nick. Does Simon?"

He shook his head. "Only my ex army doctor knows. He found it, diagnosed it. In a way it got me out of the army, but that wasn't the direct reason. No Tim, I am dying. Piece by piece, day by day, I am dying. I have told no one else. The reason I am telling you is two fold.

Firstly, I mentioned paying people back. My disease is progressive, and I must soon commence that payback. There are people from school, who either helped me, or hurt me, they will be repaid. There is a wonderful man who helped my family flee from war torn Bosnia- yes you didn't know my real name isn't Nick Church, it's actually Nicolai Curcic. I anglicised it for convenience. Anyway, I digress. The biggest thing I have to repay is the debt to myself. I have done a lot of, well let's just say things I am not particularly proud of, but I owe it to me, to pay a debt. I deliberately chose a life of getting my sexual gratification from men, because I didn't want to pass on the genetic disorder I have down to any children, that is why I choose homosexuality rather than heterosexuality. No my debt to myself will ensure that I don't suffer unnecessarily. Whilst still in control of my life I will end it. I will be in control to the end.

The second reason I am telling you this, is that I believe you have a similar experience to share. You have not yet admitted it. Perhaps not even to yourself yet. Am I right?"

Tim poured them both another drink. He listened to Nick carefully. Heard him explain what drove him. Saw a man admitting the beginning of his own personal demise. He leaned back in his chair and thought briefly before speaking. He glanced to the door to make sure he wasn't overheard.

"The tests. The tests. Well, I had all the tests, got the results. I've got a nasty growth on my liver, around the bottom of the lungs, pancreas. Just about as big and awkward as could be. It's inoperable. They say they could try me on some chemotherapy, but there are no guarantees of success. In fact, there is worse than fifty-fifty chance which could actually make it worse, the pain, that is. I have about a year, that's all.

A bloody year to get my life in order, to give it some meaning. I don't know Nick. I just don't bloody understand it."

He had a tear in his eye, and he wiped it away as Nick gently touched him, indicating the suffering of a kindred spirit..

"What I don't get is this. I know I'm going to die. We all die. It's the only thing in life that we can guarantee. In a way, I'm glad, because I'm worth more dead than alive. At least Nancy, and Anthony will get back the value I have taken away from them in death. That's the one good thing about it. The other thing is the pain and suffering. I just won't be able to stand that. I'm a coward at heart, you know. I would like to do what you are going to do, end it myself. Trouble is, it would make all the insurance policies worthless."

"Why is that so important to you?"

"Because of what I said. Nancy- sure there is no love left, there's approaching hatred- but I owe her. I know I do. It's what you said about debts, and repaying them. This is one which I have to repay. It offshoots to Anthony, the cash, but apart from leaving him behind, I have no regrets where he is concerned. We are friends, he is well balanced and mature. I've given him the best advice I can, shown him how not to fall into the same bear pits of failure into which I stumbled. No, my friend, I can understand what you say, but I don't have the same option that you have."

Nick nodded his head slowly.

"A real pair we are eh. We have the knowledge, which few others possess. We know how, and roughly when we will die, and yet it still isn't enough."

They drank in silence for a few minutes. Tim was glad to have unburdened himself, was pleased to have finally told someone else, and yet he was sad. Sad not for himself, but for Nick. He too had a death warrant, but unlike Tim, he knew exactly what he was going to do. He had it all planned. He lapsed into an off the cuff remark.

"At least there is one good thing about cancer, it makes the weight fall off without having to exercise."

That night in his room, Nick thought about Tim. He had had a raw deal, especially from Graham, but still felt puzzled as to why he still felt so indebted to one half of such a loveless marriage. It was an alien feeling to him. He had never really got close to anyone before, he did not try to comprehend Tim's feelings toward Nancy. He knew it would be a fruitless venture. He thought more about Tim. He had shown him kindness and friendship but offered nothing in return. He could use his skills to put Tim to his death. He could do it, thus relieving him of his anxiety towards his suffering. Yes he would do that. At some point in the next week he would broach the subject.

In the meantime, talk of payback brought up the subject of who was trying to track him down. He drew up the dates again on a notebook. Something happened between the seventh and twentieth, or as near as dammit to put the hunters at his back. He thought back. In between those dates, he had performed two contracts.

Good ones they were as well. On the surface they seemed unrelated, they could still be, but at least one of them could hold the key. Whatever he had done, it was evidently clear that his silence was also part of the contract or contracts. The trouble was, he did not know the source of the maker of the contract. He would have to examine the facts. Meanwhile he still had the two unopened envelopes which were work in hand. He couldn't be sure how safe they were, but suspected they probably were confirmation details. He would examine them later, at least eliminate them from his search for his hunter

CHAPTER 11

'Tarrant and Taylor.'

Nick opened the envelope carefully. It was an envelope within an envelope within two more, all testimony to having been routed and re-routed to avoid detection. Inside was as usual a copy of a newspaper. Inside he searched for a picture, a small article, anything which would be circled, highlighted. He found it. This time an advert for male incontinence. He smiled to himself. Whoever sent this had a dry sense of humour. But there was a point to it. The point was the page number, in this case thirty seven. He looked at the separate sheet of numbers, which came with it and started the decryption process. It was a careful and devious method which Nick had devised himself. Initially he had showed it only to Major Cropwell, but had subsequently allowed to be used by others in the web of the dark world of undercover and intrigue. He hoped it was exclusive to him, but doubted it. It came from one of six people. He only knew Cropwell, the others were ostensibly his contacts, or contacts of their contacts. He did not ask, he did not need to know. The lack of anyone's curiosity kept the whole network secret. He himself only accepted this particular form of contact. All he had to do on decryption was telephone a number, say the password, and five grand would be in a Swiss bank account. Untraceable. Upon completion, the balance was unerringly paid. The system relied upon trust. Just like in his army days, their lives depended on the total trust and professionalism of each knowing exactly what to do.

He began the task. Page 37 was the start point of the apparently random set of numbers on the page. The one directly under was the key. This time it was 10. He found page 10 in the newspaper, and looked at the next number. 18. 1st column, eighth word. Get this one wrong and the whole thing became meaningless. He followed the sequence of numbers. From this opening word the sequence ran 25, 6, 18, 44, 22, 8, 3, 22, 6 etc. From the opening word he counted 26 words and noted down the first letter. He moved on 6 words and noted the second letter, 18 words and noted the third letter. This time the word was a three-letter word and this told him to move back 44 words and start at the first word again, and so it went on. Depending on the devious mind of the message sender he could ride the lines up and down like a dizzying switch back. Eventually he got the information he required. Name, address, age, brief description, type of job required. Time limit. Fee, password.

He read the job back to himself.

Lord James Arthur Tarrant. Thaxted Manor, 77. Five foot eleven, 17 stone. Thick grey hair, walks with a stick. Accidental death, by November 12th. Twenty five (thousand). Password charabanc. He could do this one quite easily. He was vaguely aware of the address, a minor kind of stately home. Normally he did a brief reconnoitre before accepting, assessing the risk. He dialled the number and simply said the word 'charabanc'. The deal was struck. He always checked his account before starting to make sure the deposit was paid. He had never been let down before, and was not on this occasion. He started work immediately. It was after all, October and he had a time limit. He decided his plan of action and drove down to Northamptonshire to seek out his victim.

He was not difficult to trace. The house was an imposing twenty bedroomed manor in acres of rolling countryside. Apart from a burglar alarm there was no security. At the local village he bought a paper and found his lordship staring back at him from page four, giving out prizes at the local schools literary competition.

He had flashy eyebrows, and he smiled at him. He wondered what he had done to earn the right to have his life taken, but he didn't pry. He did not wish to take sides. He had a job to do, and that was that. Over the next few days he made a hide close to the manor and watched the comings and goings through high-powered binoculars.

He saw the Lord often. He always walked the dogs first thing. Took them down the drive, over the bridge on the lake to a small island where his wife was buried, and spent a few minutes making sure it was neat and tidy. Nick wondered about the dogs. Two large retrievers. They seemed docile enough. But he couldn't be sure. The walk took about half an hour, and the old man seemed to do it with some ease, despite the use of a stick. "Be careful old man. Don't go falling into that lake. A chap might drown."

Three days later, Nick made his way to the island before dawn. As the lord and his dogs approached, Nick fired two lightly drugged darts at the dogs from two high-powered air pistols. Lord Tarrant thought he heard a couple of faint 'pops' but noticed nothing unusual. He stood before the grave.

"Well, dear. Here I am again. Like I promised you. Every day. Rain or snow, I'd be with you every day. We'd not spend one day apart."

He heard a groan and saw one of his dogs lay down and apparently fall asleep.

" Bella? Are you all right girl?" The other dog staggered around and slumped down more heavily than the other.

"Donna? What on earth?"

Nick slipped from the bushes at the rear of the island. He had been careful not to leave a scented trail. He wore galoshes. He was sure the only people who wore galoshes those days were spies and assassins. The police could round them all up by simply watching the few outlets which still supplied them. He pointed a gun at the old man as he examined the dogs, and noticed the red -flighted dart sticking from one of the animal's neck.

"What the hell..?"

"They will be fine your lordship."

The man eased up on his stick and stared at the younger man before him. In a couple of strides Nick was upon him. With his left hand he squirted a fine mist in the old mans face. Within seconds he slumped back, in a light sleep. Nick acted quickly. He removed one of the Lords shoes and deliberately made a skid mark on the damp morning grass. At five feet eleven inches behind the mark he rested the mans head on a rock and with one violent action crashed his head onto it. A steady stream of thick dark blood started to trickle out. He felt his carotid pulse through thin rubber gloves. He felt the pulse fade and die, along with his life. He quickly moved to the dogs, removed the darts. They would be awake in about three minutes. Have headaches but would be otherwise fine. Nick surveyed the scene. Placed the walking stick at an erratic angle in the mans hand, and backed into the bushes, slipped into the water at the rear of the lake and took the short swim to the tree lined shore. That way he was out of direct line of sight from the manor. Once ashore he donned wellington boots to hide a damp trail and steadily walked through the woods to his car and he stripped off, put on dry clothes whilst standing on a large plastic bag, and carefully packed them all away. He hid his guns in a secret compartment in the cars' petrol tank, and drove on whistling. He was staying at a boarding house ten miles away and had filled his car with fishing gear. It gave him the perfect excuse to be out in the early hours, and back for breakfast.

"Catch anything?" The landlady asked.

"Only an old trout. Well past its best. Chucked it back. Mind you I'm starving."

He tucked into a full breakfast, and stayed on for another night. In the local pub that night he got the confirmation he required.

"Heard about his lordship. At the manor"

"No, what?"

"Took his dogs out this morning, as usual, and must have slipped on the wet grass and cracked his skull open. His butler found him, with the dogs sniffing round him."

"I heard they were drinking his blood."

"Don't be daft! How could you know that?"

Nick faded into the background, and finished his drink. He went back to his lodgings.

"I'll be off in the morning Mrs Drew. I'll stay for one of your excellent breakfasts, couldn't set off without one of them, could I?"

He had another commission when he got home. Different this time. Gordon Richard Taylor. 55. Address in London. Tall, balding, gold capped front tooth. Married to wife Thelma. This one was trickier. It had to look like suicide, and he had to leave something at the scene, something incriminating. Fee was forty grand, by November 18th. He whistled.

"Someone doesn't like you Mr Taylor."

Before he telephoned the password 'Highlife' he spent a couple of days in London. He could see why it was a tough commission. Taylor seemed to be an important man at a merchant bank. He worked late often and his movements were unpredictable. Nonetheless he made the call.

Taylor lived in a house in Hampstead, but kept a small flat in the city, for when he stayed back. To Nick, that was the best bet. The family house was busy, lots of people coming and going. His flat was easier, although access was difficult through a security-guarded entrance. He did a thorough reconnoitre, and discovered that his apartment was overlooked by another taller building. Taylor's flat was the top floor and his roof skylight represented the way in for Nick.

The overlooking building was an office block, some ten stories taller than Taylor's building. Disguised as a workman, he hid in the roof space overnight until, at around ten thirty silence finally descended on the building. It was tricky this one, but over the next two nights he managed to set up a rope from the office roof and managed to climb down onto the roof above Taylors flat. It would be difficult to gain access, but he could make an entrance via the glass, and down into the flat. Entry was relatively simple. It was making an effective escape, which was more difficult.

He thought and planned it over the next week. Firstly he broke a top floor window in the office block whilst working for the telephone company. He apologised to the manager, and said he would repair it the next day. That evening he had glass delivered to the top floor so that he could start first thing in the morning. At eleven he lowered down the fresh panes of glass to Taylor's roof, carefully and excruciatingly slowly, so as not to make any noise, or attract any attention. One thing was for sure, it would be safe from prying eyes until he needed it. Nick had to wait another night, since Taylor was working late and at last over the weekend of the ninth and tenth of November. Over the next two nights he carefully and expertly removed one of the windows, and replaced it with one, which he soft puttied in. Its own downwards weight would keep it in place. He removed all evidence both inside and out of Taylor's flat. When he needed to act he could not be distracted by having to cover his tracks. By Monday the eleventh all trace was clear, and each night thereafter he made entrance to the flat and waited patiently in the bathroom for Taylor to stay over.

Thursday was the day. The fourteenth. At around eleven fifteen, Nick heard the key turn the lock and saw the light flood the room. He heard the door shut, and heard footsteps across the room, heard a heavy sigh took in the sound of a coat gently thud to the floor and then caught the sound of a glass being filled with spirit. Nick looked through the crack in the door. Taylor was alone. He acted quickly, silenced gun in one hand, spray in the other. He wore his galoshes and thin rubber gloves. "Freeze!"

He held the gun directly at Taylor's head.

"What the..!"

"Quiet. Put down the glass."

"What do you want?"

"I said quiet." He took a step and squirted the spray into his face. Despite being such a tall man, he soon fell forward in a faint, caught by the efficacy of the spray. Nick nodded at the small aerosol.

"My narcotic friend. What would I do without you."

It was a useful tool. It acted in seconds, and lasted about five minutes. In such a low dose, the natural narcotic would evaporate leaving no trace unless a post mortem was carried out within two hours. He had been introduced to it by Cropwell. Nick acted quickly. He attached the mans belt to the crossbeam over the skylight. He pulled Taylor onto a chair, and hoisted him onto and across his back. He was heavy, but Nick was strong for his size. He lifted him, and with a free hand, fastened the rope around Taylor's neck. He kept him upright, and balanced on the chair, then kicked it away and watched the mans weight pull against his neck making a 'crack' as it did. Nick stood away as Taylor kicked his way to a violent death, and as he stopped, he noticed the warm damp patch spread across the mans charcoal grey trousers.

Nick checked around, locked and bolted the door, casually tossed a cuff-link with the letters J.K.K. under the bed, and using a chair climbed back to the skylight and pushed away the loose pane, dropping down a rope to make good his escape. He replaced the chair. A note carefully typed and supplied to Nick for the job. He read it.

'I can't begin to tell you, Thelma, the desperation you have driven me to. I have found out about you and Jeremy. I cannot live without you.

Gordon.'

It was signed. He had no doubts it would pass close scrutiny. He left the lights on and climbed the rope, pulling it up behind him, and using some carefully aged putty, sealed in the window, and pushed in small tacks into pre-formed holes. He walked carefully back along his set route, and laid a short roll of roof felting, already splattered with pigeon droppings. No one would notice scuffed roofing should they examine the roof from above.

He made his way to the office roof, stuffed all tools and ropes into his large holdall before gently lowering it over the side into a skip on the other side. He waited until around ten o'clock

the next day, and casually walked out of the building, smiled as workmen tipped some rubbish into the skip, covering his evidence, and strolled off into the streets and into anonymity

Taylor's body was discovered on November the seventeenth, it was a minor scandal, once the suicide note had been discovered.

CHAPTER 12

'Romance.'

"Well Tim, Helen. You have both performed a difficult task well.

How did you find it?"

Tim squinted against the sunlight streaming low through Joanne's office window, and smiled weakly to himself. He knew what she was getting at, knew that she was adopting a counselling 'hat' towards them. He had seen such an approach before by different bosses at different times. In fact he had seen just about every approach conceivable, from carrot and stick, bullying, coaching, friendly buddy-buddy, touchy-feebly type approaches through to indecision and failure. He had seen them all. Joanne was good, she tried to encompass all the tricks of the management trade in one persona. If he had been younger, much younger, she could have been him, or vice versa. It didn't matter really.

"Something funny Tim?"

She blew out smoke from red lips. Her arms were crossed and her head on one side in faint inquisition.

"No, sorry Joanne. It's the sun, making me blink that's all."

She pulled down the blinds slightly, shutting out November's low dazzle.

"No, I must admit I didn't particularly enjoy it- firing people. People I have known and worked with for years, but, well I always knew it had to be done."

"Yes, I was the same. I hated it if they started to break down and cry. I preferred the ones who got angry- at least I could deal with them better. The ones who cried, well I felt like I wanted to give them a hug."

"Tim?"

"No. No hugs from me, Joanne. It was just a sad occasion. I am trying to put it behind me, after all the new computer goes on-line next week. I shall bury my feelings by jumping into that."

Helen turned and looked at Tim. She glanced at Joanne first.

"I don't know if I'm being soft or what, Tim, but I don't think burying problems is a solution. It only puts off the inevitable."

"Helen's right Tim. Keep these feelings out in the open. If they are kept hidden, they just fester and.."

"Yes, yes, yes. I've heard it all before. Can we just get on?"

Joanne looked at him, surprised at his sudden shortening of temper. He had always seemed so calm, totally unruffled. Lately, he had been getting a shorter fuse. She wondered if the pressure of the job was too much.

"OK, that will do for now, thanks. Oh, Tim, can I have a quick word?"

Helen knew that that meant privacy. She too, recognised Tim's new shorter temper, she suspected Joanne would tell him about it, and quietly left. Joanne looked through the strips of the venetian blind. Looked out onto the cool world outside, and tried to formulate her words the best she could. She too, found it difficult sometimes to do unpleasant things, or ask unpleasant questions. She did what she advised against, buried her feelings deep and put on a false exterior. It was one thing practising, totally another preaching. She was good at preaching. "Tim?"

"Yes, I know," he said heaving out a sigh," I shouldn't snap, unburden my feelings toward you, or Helen. It's just that sometimes we spend too much time looking back, rather than looking forward. I know I have spent a lifetime doing it. Sorry. Just, when we take decisions, we alter people's lives. We shouldn't forget that. Sorry."

She nodded and lit another cigarette, and paced the room. Tim lit one of his own. He knew she had something to say. "It wasn't that I wanted to talk to you about Tim."

"Oh?"

"No. I have had the results of your medical."

"Oh."

Tim decided not to speak. He knew what was coming.

"I had er, well I hoped you might have told me before I got official notification."

He smiled.

"You know me Joanne. Hide things deep, rather than confront them."

She picked up the letter on her desk and scanned it quickly.

"Normally, Tim, we don't get details of any illness. Patient confidentiality and all that, and of course this is no exception."

"What does it say?"

"Oh. Just that there is a serious complication to your health and that we may wish to reconsider our offer to you in view of this development. That is all."

"A bit vague isn't it?"

"Like I said.."

"Yes, patient confidentiality. What you want to know is what is wrong with me, don't you?"

She bit her lip and nodded. She was about to say that it was entirely voluntary, but he cut her short. He stood up and walked to her by the window, and cleared his throat. He felt his tie tighten around his neck, and they stood side by side watching the outside world as he spoke.

"Well, my dear. It seems that over the past few years I have had a nice little cancer growing inside me. It appears that since I am quite a large framed person that it grew and grew in the ample space inside me. The thing is so big now that it covers my liver, spleen, pancreas, lungs heart- just about everywhere really. Bottom line is that this time next year I'll be pushing up daisies. "

"Is there nothing?"

He shook his head.

"Just too fucking big- sorry. No, they said they could gamble on some chemo, but chances were, that it would make me worse. They have prescribed me some hefty painkillers for when the pain gets too much. Now, well I can cope without them. Trouble with me, Joanne, is I'm a coward. I really can't stand the thought of all that pain."

"Oh, Tim, I'm really sorry."

She put her hand on his shoulder. She now knew what Helen had meant about wanting hug those she had broken bad news to.

Tim forced a smile, and took her hand from his shoulder, felt the softness, the frailness of it against his large paw like mitt. He patted it slowly, gently, then released her.

"Look, Joanne, I'll make it easier for you. I'll resign from the team leaders job. Get someone else in. Pete Marsh, let him have a shot."

Joanne looked closely at him. She had the seed of a tear in her eye, and felt it difficult not to actually cry. Here was a man before her, whom she genuinely liked, had felt to be a kindred spirit in many ways, and she had fought a tough battle with her boss for her to get Tim the job, to give him the chance which had been denied to him for so long, and she was truly delighted with the response he had made. She knew they could work well together. Now, he was expecting her to turn the knife in him, at this, his lowest point.

She managed to keep the tears back.

"That's not what I want Tim.

Not at all."

"But I thought..."

She shook her head slowly. "No. What do you want to do?"

"Me? Why, well I haven't given it any thought really."

"You said earlier that you only wanted to look forward, that you had spent your whole life looking back. What is there for you to look forward to?"

"Not much, that's for sure."

He sat back down, and felt a tear trickle from his eye. He let it go. There was little point in pretending not to be upset. He had plenty to be upset about. She sat next to him and took his hand. It felt right that she should offer some comfort to what was a dying man.

"All I'm saying Tim, is, well that as far as I'm concerned, this changes nothing. If you want to continue doing the job, installing the new systems and the like, then I am happy to let you do so. If you want to resign, leave even, I'm sure we can grant you sick leave in the circumstances. It won't affect..."

"My pension? Yes, thanks Joanne. I know what you're trying to say. Let's face facts. I have about a year, but the nature of the beast is that it starts to get bad, very quickly. All this weight I've lost recently? Well it ain't the exercise, sister. No I think I've can probably work for about another six months. Fact is I need to work. I need the money, and more importantly I need the distraction it gives me. In fact the installation will be a fitting epitaph to my years of mediocrity at Fenners.

" Tears made a definite path down Joanne's face. She could no longer control them. She didn't want to. She kept a firm grip on his hand. Trudy looked in from the outside about to say goodnight but noticed them huddled together, holding hands, and chose discretion.

"What does your wife have to say about this?"

He smiled, then laughed gently, making a kind of faint snorting through his nose.

"My dear Joanne. You have never had the pleasure have you? Well neither have I, not for a few years, anyway, sorry. No my beloved Nancy does not know, nor will I tell her. As I said, I am a coward at heart. I don't believe she will care anyway."

Joanne shook her head and stood up, wiping away her tears with a tissue, and poured two slightly stale cups of coffee. "I didn't realise things were not well, as they should be at home."

"And how should they be?"

"Well. Loving, caring. Open. I don't know Tim. I am thirty, and I don't know. I've never been married, had a couple of disastrous relationships, but always assumed the problem was mine. I never really thought that other people could struggle as well."

She lit another cigarette and offered him one. "How long have you..?"

"At least ten years. We struggled for a while before then, but I would say the last ten years have been a complete waste of time."

"Actually I meant, how long have you been married?"

He laughed.

"Twenty four years. It was good at first. We shared dreams together, you know? Wanted the same things. She always wanted a big family. Four she said. I agreed. I am an only child and was a bit of a loner as I grew up- still am I suppose- and always wanted the house to be filled with noise, she was the same. I got the job here, a few years after university, and it had plenty of prospects you know? So we bought a big house, and planned to settle down and breed forever. We had Anthony a grand little lad, and everything was wonderful. I was in for a chance of promotion, and they sent me to night school for six months to get computing skills up to scratch with a view to setting up one of the first computer dependent office systems around. Nobody had those skills then, and they chose me to get them. We developed a good circle of friends, and since Nancy was at home more she wanted more than just washing and cleaning, and rightly so. So I encouraged her to join these clubs, tennis, swimming, local committees and the like and she loved it all. I tried to take up tennis as well, but have never been particularly athletic, and besides I had night school and looked after the baby when Nancy was out. Then she became pregnant, we were both happy, but she slipped whilst playing tennis- well actually in the shower- and well, the bottom line was that she lost the baby, and could have no more. My world just seemed to cave in at that point. I took it all badly, hit the bottle, and at the same time found out that the finance for the new computer systems was not forthcoming, and fell out with Morris about it, along with a couple of other things as well, and managed not to finish the course. Well, you know the rest of my career here. I lost a bit of interest in work, turned up, did it went home, to find a wife who despite the tragedy we had suffered seemed more intent to go out than ever. She didn't really want to talk about it, but then in truth, neither did I, and so as the years rolled over us, we just lived separate lives, in the same house. Then, well I had a disastrous business venture with her stupid brother who ripped me off so much that I'm still paying off the debts. If my life weren't so short I'd be still paying them off after I'd retired. But, that's another story. Well since then, it's been almost total warfare between us. Well, total cold warfare.

I've got to the point where I can't stand her, and yet, well I still owe her."

"Why? You've put years into your marriage. Why don't you just walk away?"

"Why? Where to? Look, believe me, it's more complicated than that. I just owe her that's all. What I'll do about my last months well, that's another matter entirely. I don't feel inclined to tell her, Joanne. I just can't. It will be my pathetic revenge on her."

Joanne looked at him, saw the sadness within him, felt compassion for him, and more. Slowly, deliberately she leaned forward and looked into his eyes. She kissed the tears from his face and pressed her warm soft lips against his. He moved back slightly, slowly, but enjoyed that soft fragrance, which he had forgotten, had existed for so long now. He kissed her back, mixing his feelings of sadness with confusion and desire. He knew she was not kissing him out of pity.

She pulled away and held his face, glancing for the first time through the windows into the office. It was six o'clock, there was no one there. She hadn't thought of any complications her actions might have brought about. She had acted by instinct. She looked back into his eyes.

"You need to be loved. You need me. Dammit Tim, I need you."

They went to Joanne's town flat, it was small and modern in design, and surprisingly, to Tim, untidy. She always had seemed such an organised person to him, but his mind was on different things now. Before they were properly through the door she wrapped herself around him, squeezing closely her lips to his, touching him tenderly, and more enticingly with her tongue. He felt the old fire burn again, felt it race and engage him as he lifted her up and ran his hands underneath the softness of her blouse onto the even more tenderness of her skin. They sank onto the sofa, feverishly unbuttoning her blouse and sinking his mouth around the softness of her breasts. He felt her gentle moan of delight as her nipples hardened to the persuasive probing of his tongue. He heard her gasp as his hand slipped beneath her skirt, and she pulled down tights and lacy pants in one swift movement. There was a musky moistness about her, a scent of mystery, of passion and he tasted it, licking his lips, and devouring the fruit with eagerness. He had a hunger which now he feasted on. Joanne leaned over as he kissed her, tasted her, sent shivers of pleasure through her, and unfastened his trousers before he burst them open from the pressure within. She pulled him up, kissed his lips, tasted her own sex and pulled him into her, gasping at the joy his penetration gave her. He sweated at the task, teased nipples and thrust his way to an almighty, burning crescendo, flaming across the sky like some bright comet. She cried out as she felt the warmth of him flood her, not the cry of pain, the cry of a million excited emotions rushing at her and taking her by surprise. She had not felt like that before. Ever.

They slipped across to her bed, and slid under the covers for warmth, and the delight of more intimacy. This time, it was gentler; more measured, more delicate, and rewarding in a different way. They hadn't spoke since they had entered her flat, and as they lay back, she lit two cigarettes and switched on the kettle by her bedside for a drink.

"Joanne. Wow! I didn't expect..I mean I hope you don't think I've taken adv.."

She pressed her finger to his lips. Touched him to silence.

"Tim. Strangely enough, I think I fancied you from the moment I met you. If I analyse my own feelings, I think it is probably why I fought so hard to get you. When you told me about your illness, I wanted to kiss you, to hug you, but when you told me of your loveless marriage, of the starkness of your few remaining months I knew I had to seize the moment, not just for you, but for me. I see some of me in what you told me. Saw me looking for something, saw me ending my time alone and sad. I want us to spend the time you have left with me. I will love you when you're fit, care for you as you fail, weep for you when you're gone. God Tim, I need you."

He looked at her. She was pretty. He had always thought so. He had had a brief fantasy about her, but that was not unusual. He had probably fantasised about every woman he had met. Now, well it was different. She wanted him, and she had revived feelings within him which were dormant. And yet those same feelings confused him. He enjoyed the passion- that was fantastic- and he enjoyed holding her soft small body to him, and yet, mixed in among the pleasure was the pain. The pain of his guilt toward Nancy- not that he felt guilty about cheating on her, he felt pretty sure she had cheated on him enough times- but guilty of his debt to her. If you added his melancholy over his illness, if only served to confuse him. He was enjoying the moment, but as to what she had just said about taking care of him to the end, he would need to consider that. He considered what Nick had said to him the previous weekend, maybe he was right. Live life for yourself not for others. If Tim would be happy spending his last moments of life with Joanne, then why not? He might chat with Nick later. He turned to Jo, who was pouring them both coffee and kissed her on the shoulder. She smiled and turned and pecked hi on the lips.

"I do believe I would like to do this again some time."

"Me too. Why don't you move in with me?

CHAPTER 13

'Home truths from a field.'

"Oh it's you."

"Charming as ever, Nancy. Is Nick in?"

"You'd better come in, John. He's just nipped out. Said he be back soon."

Fieldy gave his customary exaggerated stretch to his neck and sauntered into the house. She led him into the living room. Strangely, despite being so close to Tim, he rarely came to the house. But then he was so un-close to Nancy. She indicated for him to sit and he sat in the middle of the sofa, his arms stretched along the back.

"I've just made a drink of tea. I don't.."

"Tea would be lovely, Nancy. Thank you."

She returned with the drinks and sat opposite him. He broke the icy chill, which was hanging in the air.

"Bet you didn't know I drank tea did you?"

She shook her head, and gave a weak smile.

"You don't like me do you Nancy?"

She sipped her tea and said nothing.

"It's alright you know. I can understand it. We can't all get on.

It's just that I often wonder why. But then I know that really.

So do you."

"I don't know what you mean John."

"Yes you do. Do I need to remind you?"

She put her cup down, and raised her eyebrows "So we once went out together. That was a lifetime ago."

"Ah, yes. I was so much wiser then. You must admit Nancy it was good whilst it lasted."

"Like you said. While it lasted."

"Tim never found out did he?"

She sipped at her tea.

"Why should he. We weren't married or anything at the time."

"No, but you were together. Well at least he was at university and you waited dutifully at home for him. Don't you feel guilty about that?"

"Don't you?"

Fieldy smiled and shook his head. "No, dear girl. The sex was good. You always were a good shag."

"Do you have to be so crude?"

"Are you still? Are you still a good shag Nancy?"

"You'll not find out. That's for sure."

"I wonder if I told Tim. I wonder if I'd find out then? Ha!"

He defused the situation. "No, sorry Nancy, couldn't do that to old Tim. Don't know if I could raise the necessary to stand up to you either. Mind you, you have others to sort that side of your life out."

"If you're going to go on like this, you can wait for Nick outside."

"Is Ricky good at it?"

"I don't know what you mean."

"Ah, Nancy, Nancy, Nancy. You were never any good at lying were you? I don't know how you've kept it from Tim for so long. Mind you he never looked very hard did he? Well?"
"Well what?"

"Ricky? Are you going to run away with him?"

"How do you know about him."

Fieldy touched his nose and moved his head from side to side.

"Ah yes. Good old Fieldy. Always pissed. Never does any harm to any one does he? Thick as two shorts. Well, my dear, Fieldy sees a lot of things. A lot of things he keeps close to his chest. He talks to a lot of people. Good old Fieldy knows who's screwing who, I can tell you. What are you looking for Nancy? Why don't you just leave Tim and move in with Rick? You'd both be a lot happier, I can tell you."

"Why the hell should I?"

"Don't you want to?"

"That's not the point."

"Then, Nancy dear. What is the point? Is it just sexual gratification?"

She shook her head. He continued.

"You, you forget that thick old Fieldy, drunken old Fieldy knows you better than you know yourself. That's the real reason we never made it together isn't it?"

She said nothing. The truth of his words were peeling back her defences, and she could only huddle into an emotional ball for cover.

"You see, I know what's wrong with you. I know what's wrong with you and Tim. I know why your marriage died."

"Come on then. Enlighten me."

"I will. You see you were always the homemaker- sure you liked your fun, liked to tease a bit, liked the extra seconds snog with a stranger under the mistletoe, you're no different to anyone else for that. When you first met Tim, he was something different. Something out of your league. He went to university for Gods sake. You never knew anyone so bright as him before. No, Nancy you were used to the likes of me. A bit of rough. A good shag after a night out, and scant prospects. Tim was different. He was witty and charming and clever. Still is mind you. He offered you something different. A way out of your personal gutter. Don't forget I knew your family.

Went to school with Graham. Worked with him later. I knew you didn't have an easy life. You saw Tim, aye, probably loved him, for a while and saw your escape ladder. You see Nancy, I know you. I know you wanted a nice family, lots of nice things, a nice house, caring husband and father, you know, all the things I couldn't give, nor wanted. You took to Tim, and it all went well, all until you lost the baby."

She glared at him. Why was he saying all this?

"What happened took your womanhood from you. You couldn't have any more children. It was the essence of you, which was now denied you. I'm right aren't I?"

"Look here John. If you've come here to reopen old wounds then piss off now. I don't need reminding how upset I was when I lost Lucy. I don't need it, certainly not from you."

"Hear me out, my dear. Hear me out. It was your search for your lost femininity, which led you to keeping fit, getting a tan, and keeping yourself desirable. I think for a while it was all aimed at Tim, but, well, old Tim sank into his own well of pity didn't he? He couldn't sort himself out, let alone you. Was it then that you started your affaires?"

"John!"

"No need to hide it from me, Nancy. Like I said. Old Fieldy knows most things. I suppose most of them were just for the excitement eh? To make you feel desirable again, to make you feel like a complete woman. But you're not are you? Not complete. Why this affaire you have with Ricky is just the last rush of hormones stirring in your pants. That's why you can't leave Tim isn't it? It's because you know, deep down, deep where it really matters, that once the thrill of the sex has passed over there is nothing left. No conversation, no love, no children. He can't give you what you really want, but then nobody can, can they? Can they Nancy?"

She had a tear at the corner of her eye. She felt anger surge through her.

"John, you were always the total bastard weren't you? Always hurt people, always looked after yourself. Like Lorraine. Look what you did to her.."

He shrugged his shoulders.

"It's what I am saying about you and this Ricky. Me and Lorraine, well I was young, so was she and we followed the path of drink and hormones into bed. It was great whilst it lasted. We had good times, enjoyed the sex, but when that lacked its old sparkle underneath there was nothing. I wanted to do certain things, and yes I was selfish, and she wanted to do others. In the end, we did the right thing by calling it a day and by leaving it alone, splitting up and going our own ways. That's exactly what I'm saying about you and Ricky. Once the thrill of the rush is over. Once the hormones have done their job, what's left? Nothing. Sure you can play a bit of tennis together, go for a swim, but what is really left? You and Tim reached that point years ago. For your own sakes, you should have split up and gone your own ways. You might have found something more worthwhile and less shallow than little Ricky."

She breathed in deeply. "How dare you, you bastard. How dare you preach to me about morality?"

"Morality? Shit, Nancy I'm no good at that. Why for the sake of a good screw I'd do it with you now. I have no morals, but then I admit it. All I'm saying is be true to yourself. Why don't you just leave Tim and make both of you happy?"

"Because he owes me. Simple as that. He screwed everything up by blowing all our money on that venture with Graham. Despite everything I told him, warned him about Graham."

"That's funny. I told him the same things about Graham too. Mind you I didn't know him that well then, did I? My advice came after the business folded. But then again, so is this advice to you."

"What too late? I'll say. You've got a bloody nerve John Field. A bloody nerve. Tim owes me. If it wasn't for me then he'd have left Fenners and gone down with the business. It was only my intervention that made him carry on working, otherwise we'd be bankrupt."

Fieldy raised his eyebrows.

"Funny that. Tim says, if you hadn't insisted on him working at Fenners he could have been better employed full time, and spotted Grahams little tricks and saved the business. But then I guess you've never voiced that to one another have you? Sad this. Anyway, Nancy I've enjoyed our little chat. Just like old times eh? Mind you, you couldn't take the truth then could you? Never listened to yourself, and you're not doing it now. Thanks for the tea.

Pubs are open now. Tell young Nick I've gone for a wander down to the Gate if he fancies a bevy. You can come too."

"Piss off."

"Charming, absolutely charming."

She watched him walk in his casual rolling motion down the path and into the street and away. She hated the brutality of his truth. Why couldn't he just let things lie. But then he was right, and she knew it. She knew he was right about her and Tim, that was no secret. That relationship had died years ago, for whatever the reason. And deep down, she knew he was right about Ricky. He was there at the moment, and she knew that it probably wouldn't last, but for as long as it did she would enjoy it. She smiled to herself, and wondered about the contract she had made. Soon Tim would be gone, and she would have her inheritance from Tim. She felt no regret now, she had rationalised it all to herself. She would have the house, the insurance money, everything and be rid of Tim. She would not miss him. Who knew?

In the fullness of time, once free from him, she might meet someone who would care for her and love her properly. In the meantime Ricky would do

CHAPTER 14

'Departures.'

Nick had gone out to open an account in a false name to arrange the sale of his gold coins. It wasn't particularly practical to carry them about. It was a difficult transaction, and the manager was suspicious of him, despite all his papers being in order. He had another deposit account in the same name in Cardiff, and had to produce pay slips.

It was only later that Nick realised how careless he had been. It was what confirmed Cropwell as his adversary. On leaving the army they had set Nick up as a bogus employee of an international firm of auditors. He had four different names, partly to keep the Inland Revenue away from his large payments, and partly to open accounts, get accommodation and the like. He used the name of Trevor Hughes, one of the four. He had not used it for about four years.

It was the following day when he first became suspicious. He looked out the bedroom window and saw a car at the bottom of the street. BMW. He wondered about it. Usually surveillance cars were anonymous, understated things. In this case he was right, but to the rear of it was a telephone operative climbing the pole. What made him suspicious was the fact that he had a walkie-talkie, or mobile phone whilst up the wire. Now he knew enough about regulations to know that perhaps, the mobile should have been left in the van with the other man. To most it seemed a small piece of trivia. Noting such things had kept Nick alive for a long time now. He decided to test them, since he was still up the pole some two hours later, and taking his gun, told Nancy he was going out for a while. Nick jumped into his car and kept an eye on them as he drove past only to notice a silver Ford pull out behind him and another van indicate in front of him. The van turned across the road, blocking the way, Nick quickly spun the car round in the opposite direction. He heard the crack of his rear window breaking, and managed to avoid the Ford slewing sideways toward him, attempting to hem him in. More bullets were fired, and he squeezed his mini through a pedestrian walkway, scraping the sides as he did, before making good his escape. His heart was racing as he saw his pursuers get smaller in his rear view mirror. They reigned in their weapons, not wishing to start a full-scale drama. One thing was sure. he was no longer safe at Tim's'.

He had only gone a mile or two when smoke started to belch from his engine. The gunmen's bullets, having damaged his car after all. He took it to wasteland, to the rear of an old slagheap, through undergrowth and down rough paths before finally abandoning it. He removed everything he needed, ammunition, spare cash and torched the car. He needed to hide away somewhere else. He ought to flee, but they would expect it, so he tried a different approach. Two hours later, in the saloon bar of the Gate he tracked down his quarry.

"Nick old man! Drink?"

He nodded, and sat by him.

"Fieldy, can I ask a favour?"

"Sure thing. Anything."

"Would you mind if I moved in with you for a few days? I'll doss on the sofa."

John looked surprised.

"Not making a move on me are you?"

Nick smiled. "Do you want me to? No. Just need to lie low for a few days that's all."

"Escaping from wicked eh?"

"Sorry?"

"Nancy. Wicked witch of the West."

"Something like that."

"Course you can. Mind you, it's not that big really, but you're welcome. Here."

He peeled a spare key from his key ring.

"Before I forget. I wander in and out at all hours. Don't worry about me. Go when you want."

"Do me another favour?"

"Phone Tim later, say I've gone away unexpectedly for a few days.

Don't tell him where I am."

"Why?"

"He'll find me soon enough."

"You've got the old curiosity stoked up now my boy. Just tell me in your own good time."

Fieldy phoned at about six thirty. It was Nancy who answered.

"Sorry John, he's not home yet. Probably working late. No I don't know when he'll be home. I'll be out in an hour myself. OK, I'll tell him Nicks gone away. Bye."

When Tim arrived home it was nine thirty. He had a lot on his mind. The sudden outburst of passion with Joanne was unexpected, but welcome. It confused him as well. He was pleased Nancy was out, not that she would ask awkward questions, nor that he would care if she did. What confused him was himself. He had determined not to be saddened by his own impending doom. Such things happened in life. They were fairly typical of his luck. He had wondered how he would pass his last few months, and had decided to take time out with Anthony, to spend more time with his few friends, and not to be at all morbid. He had thoughts about writing, but no that was too late for him to start. He didn't know what to put to paper. In short he had decided to go out in a brief blaze of glory. He heard what Nick had said about repaying debts, he would try to do something approaching the same himself, but apart from Nancy, and Graham, had few debts he really needed to settle.

Now, well, Joanne had arrived on the scene. He liked her in the few short months he had known her, and now, well, there was more. He wondered if it were pity, rather than love, but he knew what he felt. It didn't seem like lust, although there was real sexual power in their first embrace. He tried to remember his first feelings towards Nancy, or to the others he had dated all those years ago. The memory is a poor judge of emotions. He knew he had felt something for Nancy, but he didn't recall it being like this. No, at least he could live the remains of his life in some pleasure, and not a little regret. One thing was sure, it would be with Jo rather than Nancy. She could still get the pay-off; his debt would be paid.

He chose Jo. He would tell her the next day, at work. He prayed she would still feel the same in the morning. Why was he so consumed with doubt all the time?

He looked down at the post- it note by the phone.

'Nicks gone away for a few days.'

He looked around the house. It didn't quite seem right. He felt ill at ease, perhaps it was guilt at his own licentiousness, after all, he had been faithful all his married life, not necessarily by design, he admitted, but had never been a lothario. Tim entered the kitchen and switched on the kettle. The cat was at the back door, so he opened the door for it to enter, and fed her as she rubbed against his legs.

"Strange. Not like Nancy to leave the door unlocked." He said to himself. He checked through the house just to be sure. Everything was secure, so he took his drink to bed, and had an early night, he felt exhausted, but smiled to himself.

"Better than jogging."

Nancy had come in sometime during the night but he was asleep. They still shared the same bed, but had not made love for quite some time. She never asked, and he never pressed her. She had also taken to changing in the bathroom, out of sight in the past two years. He needed no more signs that their marriage was dead. As he ate breakfast, she joined him.

"Work late last night?"

He gave a non-committal grunt.

"Did you get the message?"

"Message?"

"About Nick."

"Oh, yes. Where's he gone then?"

She shrugged. "I don't know. John called with the message."

"Fieldy? How did..never mind. You didn't fall out with him did you?"

"John? Why?"

"No, not John. Nick."

She shook her head. "No he went out in the morning, came back, then said he was nipping out again. Not seen him since. His stuff's still in his room."

Tim drove to work humming to himself. He must rid himself of the inane grin he had permanently pasted to his face. He just prayed that Joanne felt the same way. He arrived early, he usually did, but instead of coffee and cigarette in the canteen made his way to the office. She was there already, but then she usually was. At that moment she was bending over the desk, looking for something upside down in the drawer.

He gulped, at both her provocative posture and his own embarrassment. He prayed again, as he gave a half-hearted knock and walked straight in. As she turned he blurted out "about last night.."

She gave a wide smile and turned to him and gave him a soft lingering kiss.

"Yes, fantastic wasn't it? I wish you could have stayed the night."

Prayers answered!

He sighed. "Yes it was. I can't stop thinking about you. About us."

"God, Tim, me too. I feel like a star struck schoolgirl. Here."

She offered him a tissue. He looked puzzled.

"Lipstick? "

"Oh, yes. Not my colour. People might talk."

She giggled. "We ought to 'work late' again tonight don't you think?"

"Of course Jo, but, well you know time is of the essence and all that, well I wondered- if it wasn't too presumptuous- wondered, what you felt about, well.."

"Tim! Get to the point. Trudy will be here in a minute."

"Yes, sorry. What do you think to us living together?"

She put down the files she had been glancing at.

"Do you mean it?"

He nodded, and felt suddenly foolish, felt suddenly afraid of rejection. He heard Trudy open the outer office door.

"Yes please." was all she said.

Trudy knocked on the door and entered with a jug of water for the coffee maker. "Morning. You two been here together all night?"

"Partly."

Tim smiled and suppressed a giggle.

"Look, I'll catch you later, there's a problem with the interface I'd like you to help with."

"Fine, we should be able to bed the thing down between us."

She gave him a broad smile as he left. Trudy looked up as the coffee aroma began to seep its way into the room.

"Am I missing something here?"

"I don't know what you mean."

Tim felt distracted all day. Felt the office eyes burning into him, felt slightly dangerous. He found himself gazing over to Joanne's office, and caught her winking back at him, more than once. He felt happy. After sorting out the details with her, he would deliver the message to Nancy. That would be a pleasant bonus. He wouldn't have to witness her fake sympathy as he deteriorated. He wouldn't tell her. He then thought of Nick. Strange he should vanish like that, but then, perhaps not. Maybe he had a call from work. But why Fieldy? Obvious Dr Watson, he thought aloud. He's staying there.

He giggled aloud, then stopped. "What if he and Nick were together? What a thought!"

Ian was passing. "You OK, Tim? You've been like a dog with two cocks all morning."

"I'm fine, Ian. Never better."

That evening he waited outside for Joanne, she was late and half ran from the office and jumped into the passenger seat of Tim's' car. She pecked him quickly on the cheek. "Sorry about this, lover, but Morris has just dropped me right in it. He has an important client over tonight, and has asked me to join them for dinner, and tomorrow I've got to go with him, with them both to London, to help finalise the deal. He knows how busy I am, and well, he doesn't know anything else, but it screws our social life up doesn't it? Look I'll have to nip home, get changed and out. I'll have to stay overnight in London, so won't be back until Friday afternoon sometime. Sorry."

Tim was annoyed but didn't show it.

"Good old Morris, Put the evil eye on me again. About what I said this morning?"

"Yes. You move in to my place. It's ideal. You can give Nancy the kiss off and she can have the matrimonial home, like she wants can't she? All I want is you. Look, Tim, must dash. Tell you what, follow me home and I'll get you the spare key. You can move your stuff in whilst I'm away. Then we can spend the weekend in bed."

She kissed him, and went to her own car and he followed her home, then left for his own house with the key to her flat, and her heart. On his way home, he decided to call in on Fieldy, just to satisfy his curiosity. He walked up the grey concrete steps to his friends' maisonette and rang the bell. Fieldy answered.

"Hey, Timmy. Come in. Drink?"

He entered the cluttered rooms, and smiled a broad grin when he saw Nick sitting on the settee reading a magazine.

"Well, well, well. What will Simon say to this?"

Fieldy pressed a glass of wine into his hand.

"Don't be a prick Tim. It's not like that at all. I think our Nicks' up to something, but he won't tell me what. You never know your luck do you? He might have been poking your dear Nance. After all he does swing both ways doesn't he?" Nick gave a false grin. "Funny, both of you. I'd appreciate it if you didn't tell anyone I was here Tim."

"Fine by me. I suppose you'll tell us when you're ready?"

He nodded. "Do me a favour Tim?"

"Sure."

"Would you fetch my bag from your house. There's a bit of money in it, a change of clothes, and a couple of large envelopes with old newspapers in them. Put the bag inside another one."

"No problem."

"Make sure nobody follows you here mind."

"Nick, what the hell is going on?"

"Please. Both of you. Just trust me a little while longer.

Somebody is after me. You're in no danger. "

"OK. Look, Fieldy, I just popped by, because I thought you'd be here, and well I'd like a chat. Later. At the club."

Fieldy gave a mild shrug. "Sure thing."

"Look I'll catch you both later. About eight thirty?"

Tim wondered what kind of scrape he had got himself into with Nick. After all, he didn't know much about him, and was always watchful. He had nearly told him something about himself the other evening, but didn't quite. He would trust him to come clean in time.

Tim parked his car at the side of Nancy's and had the feeling he was being watched. He glanced around him. He suspected Jim and Sue Roberts's house and keened his eyes in the darkness but could see nothing. Weren't they away? He shook his head and entered his house. Nancy was there, so was his meal. He popped it in the microwave and went upstairs to change. When he came down, he felt nervous. He knew he had to tell her, and although he had few doubts that she would not be disappointed, thirty years of knowing one another was a big break to make. He sat at the kitchen table and moved the food around the plate. She was looking closely at the evening paper.

"Are Jim and Sue on holiday?"

"I think so. Why?"

Just thought that I saw someone. I'll go and have a look in a bit."

She shrugged her shoulders non-commitally. Tim tried a mouthful of food. He was too nervous to eat. It was now or never. "Nancy?"

"Yes." She didn't look up from her newspaper.

"I'm leaving you."

She was chewing some gum, and stopped her jaw movement. Slowly, carefully, she looked up at him. She had a mocking smile on her face."

"You are doing what?"

"I don't think you mis-heard me, but to get rid of any doubts I will say it again. I am leaving you."

"You! Leaving me. Bloody hell, that's rich. After all these years of me grovelling and scraping, after all these years of mental torture from you, you are dropping me in it? You've got a bloody nerve mister."

"Oh shut up Nancy. I know you've been screwing around behind my back for years. I never said anything, because, quite frankly, I didn't care. Neither did you. What's more, I know that you'll be pleased to see the back of me. Why if it weren't for the huge yoke of debt, you'd have been gone years ago. Shut up and listen. I'm moving out, and I know, that in a perverse way, I owe you. A divorce will mean we share fuck all between us. We can sort out details later, but for now suffice it to say, that as far as I'm concerned the house is yours. It'll stay that way until the day I die, when you will inherit the lot. That's no different to how things are now. Difference is, that you'll be able to have your affaires in the comfort of your own bed."

"You've got a nerve Timothy bloody Oakes. After all this time. You should have done it years ago."

He leaned over and hissed slightly at her.

"Nancy, we should have both done it years ago. We can either do it by screaming and shouting at one another or we can just agree to part. You will get everything in time. I have no desire to stand in your way over anything."

"Sure. You say that now, but wait till your new little tart starts to get her way, she'll want her share. Who is she anyway? "

She stopped, and gave a wicked smile.

"Assuming it is a she?"

"Very funny Nancy. I have met someone else. Don't worry, I'll not embarrass you, it is a she. She has her own place, and has no desire for anything of yours. I'll move my stuff out tomorrow. I only want my clothes, and a few books and records."

"And how am I supposed to live?"

"That my dear is over to you. I'll continue to pay the bills, for a while, and of course, all the debts. I'll work out what I can afford for you for an allowance, but I think you will have to find gainful employment, otherwise...well we can sell up and share the debts."

"Bastard."

He laughed.

"It's the money isn't it that upsets you? You'll not go short. Besides, I'm sure you'll find somebody quickly, that is if you haven't found somebody already. Good luck to you,

Nancy. I hope you can find the happiness we never had together. I know I've found it. I'll be gone in twenty four hours."

She looked at him, felt a surge of intense relief, anger and frustration. She looked at him again, and shook her head. So Fieldy hadn't told him, if he had, Tim would have used the barbs against her. She nodded, and smiled to herself. Let him have her, he would be gone soon, and she would have everything anyway. His pleasure would be short-lived. It would serve him right.

"Who is she? Anyone I know?"

He shook his head. "Not just yet. I'll tell you in due course.

Let's get this over with. Do you agree?"

She nodded. "There are the old cases in the loft. You can take them."

"I'm not going to take that much, but I'll start tomorrow. I have to go out tonight, but I'll be back to sleep. I'll use the spare room."

She nodded. "OK. Yes. Let's be jolly bloody civilised about all this shall we. Going to see her are you?"

"No not tonight. See you later."

Before he went out he looked around the Robinson's house. He saw nothing, and yet still felt uncomfortable He drove away with Nick's belongings in a rucksack in the boot. As he climbed back into the car, he noticed something on the passenger sides floor. It was Joanne's mobile phone. She must have dropped it when she jumped in his car after work. He stuffed it in his coat pocket. It was switched off, so it wouldn't disturb him. At eight thirty he met Fieldy at the club.

"I gather Nick is still in hiding?"

Fieldy nodded. "Strange one that. I wonder what it's all about. Wronged lover or something like"

"Don't know. He'll tell us, when he's ready. But enough of him, I've some news."

"Oh yes?"

"I'm leaving Nancy. Told her tonight."

"About bloody time too."

He said nothing more, but got more drinks from the bar. Tim didn't have another. He had brought the car.

"Don't you want to know why?"

"Not really. But I suppose you're going to tell me anyway."

"Fieldy! You can be most infuriating at times. I've got another woman."

He put his glass down and stared, open-mouthed at his friend.

"Well, fuck me- that is a bit of news. You old dog! So you don't tell me everything after all."

"Actually, it all happened a bit quickly."

"Anybody I know?"

"Joanne from work."

"What your boss! Nice one."

"I'll bring her over to meet you at the weekend."

"Want my approval do you?"

"No, not particularly. I just want it all in the open. You're as good a start as any. Look, here's the bag with Nick's things in. Will you take them to him? You won't lose it will you? Don't let me down."

"Have I ever?"

"Yes, actually. All the bloody time."

CHAPTER 15

'Action in Priory Close.'

Tim went home early from the club. It was around ten when he turned into the estate where he lived. He hoped Fieldy would remember to take Nick's bag back with him. As he started the turn just before his driveway he felt a bump at the front end of the car.

"Shit!"

He got out and looked for a torch. He had no such thing. Nancy would have one in her car, she was well organised like that. He didn't really need one, even in the cold winters air he could tell it was flat. Some louts thinking it entertainment to smash bottles in the road no doubt. He rolled up his sleeve and unfastened the boot. Inside the jungle of discarded papers, old boots, a spade, just in case of snow. Mind you it was from last winter. He hadn't moved it since then. He heaved a sigh and lifted the carpet, unfastened the two plastic lugs and lifted the hardboard wheel cover, then pulled out the spare. As it hit the ground, it did not bounce, but made a dead 'thud'. He kicked it. "Shit, shit and shit again!"

It was flat. He never checked it; he lifted back into the car. He would have to get the foot pump, it would be in Nancy's car. As he did so he scraped his knuckles on the boot lid, drawing blood. He examined them in the boots courtesy light, and somehow managed to refrain from swearing once more. Pulling a none too clean handkerchief around his knuckles, he pulled his coat to him and made his walk back to his house- for one more night at least. He could feel his knuckles ache and it reminded him of Nick. His knuckles were in a terrible state, a by-product of his own terminal illness. They had a lot in common, including bad knuckles. He at last, in his final months had found some happiness. He hoped Nick could do the same. Meanwhile, he was in some kind of trouble.

Tim bit his lip and looked up the street to his house. On his left he passed two men sitting in a silver Ford. The interior light was on, and as he passed he heard the indeterminate garble of a short wave radio crackle. He slowed slightly, but did not know why. In front of him, he saw the curtains twitch in the upstairs room. The spare room. That was strange, he thought. Nick had his stuff. He clearly didn't want to return. He walked on, trying to puzzle it all out and walked up his next door neighbours path as if to go in via the back door. Then he half climbed, half fell over the small fence into his own garden. He sidled up to the French windows, and looked in through the open curtains, they never closed them. He froze momentarily as the cat rubbed up against his legs and meowed at him. She was hungry- again.

Inside the house he could see two men. He was unsure as to whether there was another upstairs. One was at the window, the other man was sitting opposite Nancy obviously talking to her, but he could not hear what he was saying. The man at the window had a walkie-talkie. Tim pulled back. What the hell was going on? He flattened himself against the narrow part of the wall, and thought quickly. In his pocket he still had Joanne's mobile phone. He quickly ran down the bottom of the garden and squeezed behind it. It was a favourite place of his, just big enough for a garden seat, for him to hide from Nancy's' nagging, and have an illicit smoke. He dialled Fieldy's' number. It rang five times. "Come on, come on."

The answer phone clicked in.

"Yeah this is Fieldy. Leave your name etc. I may get back to you if I feel like it."

"Nick! Nick! Pick up the phone. It's Tim. Nick, it's urgent.."

"Hello."

"Nick?"

"Tim?"

"Look, what the hell's going on? There are some men in my house.

They've got Nancy. What is all this about?"

"How many men?"

"Two, maybe three. I think there are another two down the street in a car."

"What sort of car?"

"A silver Ford. Look Nick what.."

"I'll be right over. Where can I meet you?"

"Oh, er you know the footpath which leads to the park?"

Nick did. He had scraped his mini through there earlier. "The path goes past the bottom of our garden. I'll look out for you."

"Fine I'll be about fifteen minutes. Don't move, don't do anything."

The phone went dead, and Tim cursed as he waited. His knuckles hurt and he was cold. About twenty minutes later he heard a low whistle and peered over the fence at the bottom of his garden. He didn't see anything, but seconds later, he heard the bushes rustle to his right. "Nick?"

"Yes. It's me. Anything happened?"

"You were quiet? Nick what the hell is going on?"

"I'll tell you later. In the meanwhile, stay here. I'll sort it."

"Nick?"

Nick pressed his face close to his friends.

"I'm serious, Tim. I'll sort it. Don't move until I call you. If I'm not back in fifteen minutes, call the police."

Without a further word he disappeared up the garden. In the dim light he could make him out crouched against the rear wall, then he lost him, catching him a split second later at the back bedroom window. How had he got up there so quickly? He was like a cat.

In a trice he was through the fanlight in seconds, Tim did not know whether it was already open or not. He waited and strained to hear properly, but could not. Against his friend's advice, he sidled back up to the French windows. He could not believe what he saw.

Nancy was on the floor, her hands over her head, and Nick was kneeling over a mans' body whilst pointing a silenced revolver at the other mans face. He lay down like Nancy and in one cat-like motion Nick sprang over to the now prone man and hit him hard with the handle of his pistol, knocking him senseless. He heard him tell Nancy to stay still, then carefully peered through the window. He raced to the French window and called 'Tim' in a low voice.

Tim gulped.

"Here!"

He found a silencer pointed at his face.

"Pillock!"

Tim went inside.

"Nick what the fuck is..?"

"Tim? Thank goodness. What is going on?"

Nick peered through the curtains again and told them to be quiet.

Tim felt strange comforting his wife. Nick spoke quickly.

"Look I can't talk now. It's obvious these men are after me.."

"But you've killed him!"

Nancy shrieked pointing at the man near the window. "Sorry. No choice. Look shut up and listen. Have you got the rest of my stuff Tim?"

"Fieldy has it. He's bringing it home after the pub shuts."

"Shit. He may be in danger already. Look, give me your car keys.."

"Sorry mate, it's at the bottom of the street with two flats."

"Take mine for Gods' sake. Just who are you?" He smiled. Can't tell you. Look get some rope, I'm going to tie you up. I'll be back in a minute."

He slipped out the back way, after reloading his gun.

"Tim, where is he going now?"

Tim shook his head. "Don't ask. Just get the rope Nancy." He felt his side hurting. Stress, no doubt.

"I'm going to phone the police."

Tim took the receiver from her and half shouted through clenched teeth. "Just get the fucking rope!"

Nick returned about four minutes later. "The rope?"

Tim gave it him.

"Sorry folks, but to protect you, I'll have to tie you up. Nancy just say what you saw, Tim say you got in and saw these two on the floor. Any questions they ask you about me, tell the truth. Don't cover up for me. I can take care of myself."

"I can tell that, but.."

"Tim, the less you know, the less you can tell. Come on, I'll have to tie and gag you, make it look good. Sorry, but there it is. Nancy?"

She looked nervously at him. Her heart was beating quickly. She had already seen him burst through the door and down one man with two gentle 'pops' from his gun. He had shouted her to lie down as the other man yielded his weapon up. He was a lethal weapon. She looked at Tim, and he nodded. Nick tied her firmly but comfortably. He did the same to the man on the floor, then it was Tim's turn.

"Sorry mate." He tied him tightly and whispered into his ear.

"I'll be in touch on Christmas day. Look out for me. Explain everything then."

"But.." Tim didn't have chance to tell Nick he was leaving Nancy when he was enticed to sleep by a swift blow to the back of the head.

When he came to, he had a headache to end all headaches. Blue flashing lights entered and left his sight as he came back to reality. He was untied, and on his back. Nancy was sitting in the armchair with her hands over her face. She was crying. A sheet covered the man by the window, and he could not see the second man. The room was crawling with both uniformed and plain clothed police. He was being tended to by a paramedic.

"He needs to get to hospital."

"In a minute. I need some answers."

A small, dumpy blue suited man with thinning grey hair, and smoking a cigar walked over to him.

"Are you Oakes?"

Tim nodded.

"What happened here? Tell me what you saw."

Tim felt giddy and started to wretch. The paramedic pushed the blue suit away.

"Question him later. He is concussed. I must get him to hospital. Now."

Superintendent Wright surveyed the chart on the wall. He drummed his fingers impatiently waiting for Inspector Sheridan to arrive. He was on his way, but Wright was not a man to be kept waiting.

At last the small, tubby man in the blue suit entered.

"Sorry, sir.."

"What the hell is happening Sheridan? Three dead. A couple held hostage? What is happening? I've already had a call from the Home Office. I need to be able to tell them something. What have you got?"

Sheridan scratched his head. "Very little, at the moment sir. Key man is the householder, but he's unconscious at the moment. Wife only knows assailant as Nick. Friend of her brothers, can't be sure of his surname."

"What about the other man in the house, the one with the gun?"

Sheridan raised his eyebrows.

"Taken the fifth as it were. I think he's waiting for someone to spring him, if you know what I mean, sir."

"Spring him? From custody? Do we have the necessary security?"

Sheridan smiled and shook his head.

"No sir, not like that. I mean he is waiting for a 'connection' to spring him."

"Who is he, Inspector? Who were the other three?"

"That, I don't know for certain. We're checking out their credentials now. My guess is they'll all be fake. I personally think it's an MI5 type thing. Secret service and all that."
"Well, they won't get away with playing their blood-thirsty games on my patch, I can tell you. All three shot?"

Sheridan nodded. "Yes sir. Two in the car, close range, silenced pistol. One in the house twin shots to the forehead. Again silenced. Mrs Oakes- the lady in the house- says she saw the last one. Quite shaken she is. Says two men forced an entry and asked her where her 'guest' was. Seems he was lodging there. Waited about an hour, then husband came home, and so did the suspect. Bound the occupants and fourth man. Left her, but coshed the men. Took her car- a red Micra- I've circulated all points with details. Jenkins is at the hospital waiting for Mr Oakes to come to."

"Is he seriously hurt?"

"No, sir. Just concussion. Jenkins will call me the minute he can talk."

"Do we have a description?"

"Sir. Five six or seven, small frame, close cropped hair, light brown. Unshaven at the time, and was wearing black jeans, black leather shoes, casual pale yellow shirt and brown leather jacket."

"Good. Keep me informed. I want him, and I want him quickly."

Sheridan did not move.

"Is there something else Inspector?"

"Yes sir, there is. I don't know if you recall last week in Nottingham. Two men killed in a multi- storey car park?"

"Yes. Drugs related so I understand."

"I'm not so sure, but the mans' description fits someone seen running away from the scene."

"I thought they'd caught a couple of local yardies for that?"

"Yes sir, but.."

"But what? I don't want you chasing shadows Inspector. Focus on what is needed right now."

There was a knock on the door, a duty sergeant poked his head round. "Sorry to disturb sir. Mr Oakes has come to at the hospital."

The inspector stood, and the supers' telephone went as he left.

"Are you OK, Mr Oakes?"

Tim nodded. His mouth was dry, his head hurt, and so did his stomach and side. "Never felt fitter."

"I need to ask you a few questions, sir. It's very important. I've had a version from your wife, just need to know from you what happened?"

Tim, licked his lips, and remembered Nick's words to him. By telling the truth, as he knew it, he would not become incriminated, not that he was. Nick could evidently take care of himself.

"Well, I got home at about ten, maybe just after. I'd been out with a friend, and got a puncture a couple of hundred yards from home, and found my spare flat too, so I walked home to get the foot pump."

"Notice anything unusual?"

"Two men in a silvery grey car, that's all. Wondered what they were doing out so late."

Jenkins nodded to Sheridan, and Tim continued. "Anyway, walked in the house, and the next thing I knew was me being hit over the head and passing out. That's about it." Sheridan nodded.

"Yes, sir, that fits with what your wife says.

Tell me about your lodger."

"Lodger? Oh Nick. Is he all right?"

"It was him sir. Him who hit you, tied you up."

"You're joking!"

"Tell me what you know of him."

Tim lay back on his pillow and asked for a sip of water, before continuing.

"Nick. I first met him, about two months ago. He came along with Simon- my wife's brother. Anyway seemed nice enough, then turned up last Friday on his own. Asked if he could stay a few days."

"Why?"

"What do you mean why?"

"Why did he want to stay with you. Did he give a reason?"

"No, not really. Look, officer, he was a really nice bloke. We got on really well, and I said for him to drop in next time he was in the area. I guess he was in the area."

"Do you know his surname, his permanent address, his job?

Anything would be helpful?"

Tim sighed. "I can't believe he'd attack me like that."

"You don't know the rest do you sir?"

"The rest? Nancy? Is she.."

"She's fine sir. Untouched, shaken but fine. No he shot someone.

Someone in your house at the time."

"Who?"

"That I don't yet know, sir. The details, about this Nick character?"

Tim managed to pull a veil of puzzlement over his face. It wasn't difficult, he was puzzled. Wondered what Nick had been up to. Wondered who he really was.

"His real name is Nick Church, or rather that was what he told me-actually no. He told me his real name was Nicolai Curcic."

"Foreign, sir?"

Jenkins slipped out to telephone the name through to intensify the search.

"Not that you'd notice. I think he said he came from Bosnia, originally, but I know no more than that. Whether he was born there, and came over as a child, I couldn't say. Anyway, what else is there? He's an international auditor or something like that. Jets off abroad a lot, audits foreign companies. Was based in London, I think, but Simon may be able to tell you better."

"Simon?"

"Yes. Simon Worrall. Nancy's brother."

"Nancy will have his address. He works in Aberdeen."

Sheridan put away his notebook. "Anything else you can remember sir? Any reason why he would want to tie you and your wife up. Any reason why he would shoot someone? Do you think he was being followed, chased or anything?"

Tim shook his head.

"I'm mystified. One thing though. Yesterday- rather the day before- he left our house and moved in with my friend."

The inspector took out his notebook again.

"His name is John Field. 27 Morven Close. His number is 554277. "

"Thank you sir. I shall call on him. Now take your rest, I'll be

over to see you later in the day."

CHAPTER 16

'Hue and cry.'

Nick put his foot down in Nancy's' Micra. He guessed he could drive it for no more than another twenty minutes. He was in a spot, having only a few pounds on him. The rest of his cash was in Fieldy's' possession, and he had left the house at Tim's call without his money belt. The five hundred he kept there would get some distance between him and Burton. He needed cash. It was eleven, and he saw a petrol station ahead. He would have to rob it. It was as simple as that.

He pulled in, and looked around. It was deserted. There was only a youngish looking man in the shop. The sign on the door said that it closed at midnight. At least there should be a full days takings in the till. Nick put ten pounds of petrol in the tank, to avoid suspicion, and walked carefully to the booth. He had already removed the guns silencer and hid it behind his belt. He spoke with an Irish accent and offered the ten pound note to the cashier, as he did he pulled the gun and held it to the terrified young mans face.

"Give me all the fucking money or I'll blow your fucking head off!"

He handed the cash over, shaking in terror as he did. Nick looked at the money he had put on the counter. Two hundred at the most. "All of it!"

"T-that i-is a-all. Everybody pays by credit card these days.."

Nick hit the man on the temple with the guns handle and quickly pulled him to the small room behind the counter. There was a safe there, but he would be wasting valuable time by opening it, or trying to. He pocketed the money, took a pack of rolling tobacco, papers and matches, a bottle of coca-cola and a pack of gum, then walked quickly to the car. A man had pulled up on the forecourt and was unscrewing his petrol cap. Nick smiled and called over, still in his Irish accent.

"He's just gone to the bog. Not be a minute."

He drove of. He would not have much time. The assistant would be discovered in about five minutes, so he drove into a dimly lit pub car park. It was chucking out time, and he put the Micra, behind the main building under an overhanging tree. Nearby stood a nice gleaming gunmetal grey Jaguar. As he locked the Micra a man strolled to the other car. Nick screwed on the silencer as the man turned his back on him to unlock the door. With a quick glance around to make sure he was not being watched he silently skipped over and pushed the silenced muzzle into the nape of the mans neck.

"What.."

"Just stay quiet and everything will be fine. Unlock the car."

"But.."

"Unlock the fucking car!"

He did as he was told.

"Start the engine."

He watched carefully as he selected neutral and turned the key listening as the engine purred into life.

"Out."

He ordered then bent down and pulled the lever to flip the boot open.

"Quickly. In the boot. Don't piss about with me, or you'll get a bullet."

The man nervously climbed in the boot. He was tall, and the boot shallow. As he lay there curled uncomfortably up, he saw the man scrutinise his face and Nick smiled.

"Sorry."

He pulled the trigger and closed the boot after him. He didn't like senseless killing, but right now, he had to get away. With this machine, he could put quite a few miles between him and his pursuers. Besides. They were looking for a red Micra. He tossed the keys away as he steadily drove out of the car park, and headed back in the direction of the garage. It was on the way to the motorway. Already the blue flashing light of a police car was on the forecourt. He did not look.

"Sir, sir!"

"What now Jenkins?"

Sheridan was puzzling his way through the motivation for the crime. Despite what the Superintendent had said, he had a gut feeling that the Nottingham killings were connected to this.

Armed robbery at a garage near Derby."

"Deal with it Jenkins, I've got this as my top priority."

"No sir. Small man, short hair, driving a red Micra. Had an Irish accent mind."

"Is there a video camera?"

Jenkins was beaming, and nodded.

"Then what are we waiting for?"

They reran the CCTV over the monitor. It was jerky, but nevertheless they saw Nick fill up with petrol, hold the gun to the assistants head, take the money, and the tobacco. "Not your usual armed robber eh sir? Just taking one pack"

"Yes, strange that, Jenkins. Evidently just fancied a smoke."

He froze the video on a close up of the mans face.

"So Mr Church, or Curcic. We have a picture of you. No luck on the car?"

"No sir. All cars under instructions to stop any small red car on sight. Nothing yet."

Sheridan sat back in the chair and told his subordinate to get the picture blown up as soon as possible. It was one fifteen. He wondered about the man. If, as he suspected, the three victims were MI5, or some other clandestine outfit, he would have to be quite something to take three out so easily, and expertly. He robbed the garage for one reason.

For some money, to help him get away.

He would know he would be caught on video, and fairly quickly since the alarm had been raised quickly. He only took one pack of tobacco. Why was that? Certainly no ordinary villain this one. He pondered the points, then crashed his fist on the table.

"Of course! Jenkins! Jenkins!"

"Sir?"

"We're not looking for the Micra. He will have dumped it. It's too obvious. Look, get some patrols to check out car parks, quiet lanes, even driveways for it. It won't be far from here. He did this as a decoy. The little shit's jerking us around."

An hour later the call came through.

"You were right sir. About two miles from here, in the Holly Bush car park, around the back. All neatly parked, locked up etc. I've sent for SOCCO to get it printed."

"Well done Jenkins. Mind it doesn't help us does it? Any reports of stolen cars close by?"

"I've checked out two sir. One a TWOC, other a drink driving excuse I think. That's all. Been a quiet night round here."

Sheridan lit a cigar, ignoring the signs which disallowed smoking.

"Trouble is, he could have taken something that won't be noticed until morning. Make sure anything reported round here is dealt with urgently sergeant."

"Could he have gone to ground, sir?"

The inspector scratched his chin. "Possible. But somehow I doubt it. I think our friend may be well away from here by now. I'm off for now. Catch you later."

Nick liked the Jaguar. It ate the miles effortlessly, and it owner had thoughtfully filled the tanks for him. He took the M1 south then cut away cross-country at junction 19. He was heading for Norfolk. He had a 'stash' there. It would be fine. He stopped once to roll out some cigarettes and relieve his bladder, otherwise drove without stopping. He kept to a reasonable speed, not wanting to attract attention. He figured he had the car until daybreak, to be safe. He would be where he intended by then. He reached his first goal around three. Down twisting narrow lanes he headed past Swaffham, and slowed considerably down. There were no houses for miles when he reached the gate to the field. He locked the car and set off over the damp cold grass to the pylon in the field, and winced as his hands touched the freezing metal. He shinned his way up, negotiated the overhang of spikes and started to feel for his goal. With shivering fingers he snapped back two clips and loosed a thin cover of metal. Below that was a wallet containing two hundred pounds- a decoy, but useful just now- and he fished further down with his fingers, locating a piece of plastic wire which he extracted. Fastened to it was a key. He hung it round his neck and quickly descended to the ground and back to the car. He rolled another cigarette and felt the cars heater take the chill away from him, then he carefully drove back down the main roads and towards Heathrow. He parked it in the long stay and walked toward the main terminal building as dawn showed her cold face to the world. He disposed of the car keys and parking permit carefully in a bin, then caught a bus to the city.

He neared his destination, and before he did, carefully, meticulously did a survey of the area to make sure his top floor apartment was not being watched. He smiled as he entered the musty smelling flat. He had had it for about seven years, and in a precaution to being detected, had sold it- to himself -some six months previously. Hidden away under floorboards, behind pipes, and in a hollow joist was his new identity. One which he had never used before. He looked in the mirror. "Welcome home Mr Jemsom."

He shaved, pulled on a short black, but grey streaked wig, and pasted on a thin moustache with painstaking deliberation. With a faded brown suit on, and spectacles. Trevor Jemsom left his apartment, and went to the corner store to purchase some provisions, a newspaper, and solitude.

George Sheridan was tired the next morning. he had been up until about four, and returned to the station for eight thirty. He sent for a bacon sandwich and reviewed the night's events. There had been only one more car reported stolen, and it had been traced half wrecked near Matlock. It didn't have the mans' trademark. As the grease dripped down his chin the super entered.

"Report Inspector. What has happened. Any hot leads?"

He put down his breakfast and wiped his hands and face with his handkerchief, noticing his superiors disdainful looks in the process. Sheridan repeated the scenario at the garage and that they were working on the theory that he had taken another car and was probably well away by now, The Superintendent nodded and looked at his watch.

"I've someone coming to see me at nine, regarding the victims.

I'll brief you afterwards."

He swivelled on his heel and marched out. A very methodical, and upright gentleman, was our Super. Sheridan continued with his breakfast. He refused an interview with the press, for now, and noted the sleek black Rover pull up. It had MOD number plates- that in itself strange, since they were largely discontinued as a preventative terrorist measure. He watched the dark green uniformed man appear. He was about six foot tall, slightly swarthy, with black slicked hair and a pencil thin moustache. He carried a swagger stick, and looked incapable of mirth. He was shown into the Superintendents office and the doors closed. Jenkins interrupted his thoughts.

"Don't know if this is anything sir?"

"What is it?"

"Businessman. Henry Arthur Theobald reported missing by his wife. Apparently he went out last night to the Holly Bush to meet a business acquaintance Not been seen since."
"So? "

"The Holly Bush pub sir. That's where we found Church's Micra."

"Check it out Jenkins. PDQ. By the looks of the chap the supers got with him, we may need some up to date info. Report straight back to me."

The superintendent emerged an hour later, the military man disappearing back into his car and away. He clearly had no need or desire to speak to Sheridan. Wright summoned Sheridan to his office. He was red faced, and for once appeared slightly nervous. As Sheridan sat, he stood, and went to make sure the door was firmly shut. He lit a cigarette. Sheridan had never seen him smoke before. He gave the inspector a broad grin.

"Good news. We've got him."

"Curcic?"

He nodded in an exaggerated manner.

"Yes, yes."

"Where? When?"

"Oh, apparently he was caught trying to steal a boat at Brighton.

Got picked up by the coastguard when he got into difficulties."

"How did he get to Brighton?"

"As you said, Sheridan. He stole a car."

"From where sir? We have no reports..."

"For Gods sake Sheridan, I don't know all the details! It's out of our hands. He's in custody. The special branch have him."

"Special Branch sir? That chap was no spec.."

"Look here inspector, and this is a direct order. Drop the case. He is arrested, locked up, and will be dealt with in due course. Apparently a serial killer -being tailed by undercover special branch officers, who took his bullets last night. Bad show that. Anyway, we've come out of it well. Been praised at division for our promptness, and the rest. All over and done now. You can close down the case. It's sorted. Just get it written up."

"With respect sir, this doesn't add up. A serial killer? We've not been warned to look for some serial killer. Why the military man?"

"Curcic is ex army, gone wrong, that's all. Had a car hidden round here to get away. Army likes to keep this thing quiet."

"I thought you said he was being tailed by special branch?"

"I did.."

"Why the army..?"

"All singing from the same hymn sheet Inspector. I've been told to tell you that you are to be commended for this."

Sheridan shook his head. "No, it doesn't add up. I have done nothing to earn a commendation, and besides, you said earlier he had taken a stolen car to Brighton, and now you say he had a car hidden. I don't get it."

The superintendent stubbed out his cigarette. "Like I said. It's over. Wind it all up Sheridan. It's over. That's an order."

"Yes sir." Sheridan stood. He was about to say something again, but thought better of it. There was certainly more to it than he was being told. The commendation? That seemed to be there to buy his silence. He closed the door behind him and he smiled to himself.

"It'll take more than that."

He walked back to the incident room and called those present to order. He told them the official line, and closed down the operation. He could see the superintendent watching across the corridor. The men dutifully filed away statements, took down critical incident paths, and returned to their other duties. Jenkins returned at about eleven thirty.

"I hear they've got him."

"I hear the same. Only thing is, I don't believe it."

"Sir?"

"Look, Jenkins, this is between you and me. I don't believe the official line, serial killer? Bollocks. Not taking out those three like he did. Did you find anything out?"

"Yes. Theobald left the pub at closing time. The landlord knows him well. He was about the last to leave. Not seen since."

"Run off with another woman?"

Jenkins shook his head.

"Doubtful sir. Not got a full set, if you know what I mean. Accident ten years ago with a shotgun. He no longer has the necessary equipment."

"OK. Look, follow it up. See if you can trace the car. Check airports and the rest. If Wrighty asks, say it's a suspected kidnapping. Seems a bit odd that he disappears the same time as our Mr Curcic dumps his getaway car. Give it top whack Johnny eh?"

"Yes sir"

CHAPTER 17

'The plot thickens.'

"Tim! What on earth has happened?"

Joanne had found out about all the excitement when she had returned back from her business trip with Morris. She had missed the news until she breezed back into Fenners expecting to see her lover. She almost fainted when she had heard the news. He was currently at home, off work by doctors' orders. He was still at Nancy's' when she called round to see him. She was in luck, Nancy was out at that moment, but was expected back at any time. He was pleased to see her, and gave her a quick peck before ushering her through the door.

"Come through, I'll make a drink."

"Tell me everything."

Tim told her the official version, but left her curiosity dangling by telling her he would fill in the rest of the details later.

"So this Nick is some kind of serial killer? It makes you go cold, just thinking about it."

"I still don't believe it myself. Apparently he's been caught now, in Brighton. I'd like to go and see him, if allowed. Anyway, it's complicated it a bit for us hasn't it?"

She slowly shook her dark auburn hair. "I'm not sure, exactly what you mean?"

"Well, it's Nancy. She's petrified at being on her own in the house."

"Does this mean what I think it means?"

He leaned forward and took her hand, kissed it gently, and stroked her hair.

"No, not that. I still want you. Still am going to move in. Just leave it a few days, that's all."
"You're not shirking away from this are you? Having second thoughts?"

"No. Definitely not. In fact in some ways, lying there in hospital, it made me realise what the end could be like, without you. I felt so cold, so alone, so desperate. If it hadn't been for the thoughts of you, well I would probably have ended it all there and then. Just knew I couldn't do it- coward you know."

"So this is her is it?"

They hadn't heard Nancy enter. Joanne was on her knees in front of Tim, holding his hands, gazing into his eyes. She raised to her feet nervously as she confronted his wife. In truth Nancy was not what Joanne had expected. She was slim, attractive, a little too sunbedded to look natural, but her blonde hair was perfectly cut and groomed. The same could be said of Nancy regarding Joanne. She had expected an older woman, a woman looking for some final fling of pathetic excitement with her husband, she was no such thing.

"You're younger than I thought you'd be. Pretty too. Tim, you have managed to surprise me."

She looked at Joanne, looked closely at her pale skin, soft lips, wide brown eyes.

"I suppose I should scratch and kick at you, scream obscenities and demand you unhand my husband. Quite frankly I can't be bothered. All our years of marriage have worn me down. All my fight has gone now. Please, sit down. By the way, what is your name?"

"Er, Joanne. I didn't expect to see you. When I heard about what had happened I just dashed over here, never gave you a thought- sorry."

"Don't worry about me. Am I right in thinking you won't make any claim on the house?"

"Yes." She answered slowly, now unsure whether Tim had told Nancy about his illness.

"Good. All I want from him, is to make sure that the will stays the same, that I get what is due to me. After all he blew it away, not me. Agreed?"

"Fine. Seems a bit odd to me, Mrs Oakes, you may have a long wait to get it, maybe another forty years, who knows?"

"Yes, and he may get knocked down by a bus tomorrow. I can wait. We just need to agree some living expenses. I'll maybe consider a part -time job, for the niceties in life." Joanne was a little confused. Had he told her? She still decided to play cagey.

"I have a good income of my own, but I will not pay a single penny of it to you. You and Tim sort that out, it is nothing to do with me. Now, Tim, you can move your things in today. Right?"

He looked across to Nancy. She shrugged.

"May as well get it over with. Take what you said you'd take.

I'll probably stay over with Sally for a couple of days anyway. Good bye Joanne."

She turned away and went upstairs, for her own packing. She was going to stay with Sally, she had already decided such and Sally was to pick her up around six. She had had news that the police had found her car, and she could have it back early next week. She was beginning to have doubts whether she would move Ricky in, but she would think about it. She smiled to herself.

"Poor cow. Doesn't she know he'll be gone sooner than she thinks.

Serve her right."

An hour later Tim had two cases full of essentials. He did not return his key but agreed to telephone Nancy first, should he require access.

"Oh, by the way, you dropped this. Came in handy the other night."

He said to Joanne as he climbed in the passenger seat. "Thank goodness. I thought I'd lost it. Cancelled it. Mind, they'll send me a new PIN, so I can use it in a couple of days. What do you mean came in handy?" That went better than I could have hoped. I never expected to meet her. Never gave it a thought. She's quite attractive isn't she."

Tim smiled. "Which question would you like me to answer first?"

"Sorry Tim. Let's get home first, you can tell me about the ordeal in full detail back there. I think we'll have a night in tonight. In fact we might even spend the weekend in bed if you're up to it."

"I banged my head, nothing else."

He told her the full story, how he had used her mobile phone to summon Nick, how he had whispered that he would contact him on Christmas day.

"He won't be able to now will he? Being locked up."

Tim shook his head. "Don't be so sure. The only thing that will make it difficult is the fact that I never had chance to tell him about us, that we would be together, here. He doesn't know where you live."

"But if he's locked away..?"

"I saw him work. Saw how quickly he climbed onto our roof, saw him take out one man, disarm the other. I tell you, I have never seen anything like it. Now I know that about him, some of the other things he said make me wonder about what he really does, and who those men really were. I'm sure, if he was a serial killer, like they seem to be saying, that the two men who bundled past Nancy into the house would have given some indication who they were. She said it seemed like they were trying to rob the house as they forced

her in, then all they did was ask her about Nick. That's why I want to go and see him."
Joanne put her finger to his lips, gently rubbed her long fingernail down the side of his face, kissed him softly and pulled him toward the bed.

"We can think of that later. In the meantime you have some work to do."

Tim went to see Fieldy the next night, and took Joanne with him.

"He's a bit blunt sometimes, a complete alcoholic, but I like him."

He said to her as he rang his doorbell. Fieldy opened the door, made his customary neck movement and smiled.

"Ah the hero and his fancy bit. Come in. Drink?"

Tim nodded and squeezed her hand. She was looking round the room, and her eye was drawn to his drawing board. She walked over and looked at what was on it. Fieldy returned with two (crystal) glasses of wine. She smiled and looked up at him.

"Sliding Tackle. I love that. Do you..?"

He handed her the glass and scowled slightly, but turned it into a smile. "You know it?"

"Sure thing. I read it all the time. I have some clippings on my fridge door haven't I Tim?"

He shrugged. He hadn't noticed.

"You'll be telling me next you like football."

"No, I love it. I'm having cable next week for the England match."

"You never told me that!" Tim exclaimed.

"Sorry, darling, wanted to surprise you."

Fieldy nodded and took her hand, kissed it and returned it to her.

"Tim. If you ever get tired of her, let me know will you? Beauty personality, and a lover of the beautiful game?. Joanne. I like you already. I think I shall call you Jo-Jo."

Tim leaned over. "You should be flattered. Only people he likes get their own pet names."

"Do I do that? Bloody hell, you're right. I never noticed it."

"Too sauced up, that's why."

"Sit, sit. We can go out for a drink. Where do you fancy?"

"Just a couple. Thought I'd show Jo the flesh pots of the club."

"Trying your best to put her off aren't you? First me, then the club. Blimey, you'll be introducing her to Nancy next."

"Oh, I met her yesterday."

"Bloody hell. Better have another drink."

He returned with the bottle and topped up their glasses. "Got over your excitement then Tim?"

Tim nodded.

"I knew there was something odd about Nick. Like him mind. But a serial killer? Surely not. I've met killers before, met mad men too, perhaps I'm close enough to one to know one when I see one. There's a core of steel about Nick, a strength you rarely see. But he's not mad, and not dangerous- unless you're his enemy. I'd bet he was on the run. Probably nicked something secret, that sort of thing."

"Did you see him on Wednesday night?"

Fieldy shook his head. "No, he'd gone when I got home. Never had chance to give him his stuff."

"Still got the bag?"

"Yeah. Back there, behind the chair."

Tim got up and fetched it, emptying the contents. He hadn't looked at them before, but there had never been the need. Clothes spilled out, along with a box, and two envelopes. Inside the envelopes were two old newspapers, and two sheets of paper with numbers typed on them. Tim put them to one side. The box was locked, but he decided to force it. Inside was cash. Three thousand pounds in cash. A stiletto type knife, a small aerosol spray, a key, and half a carton of bullets. Joanne touched each thing in turn.

"Well, I never met him, but it strikes me that he was fairly well prepared- for something."
"Have the police been round?"

"Yes. Yesterday morning."

Tim looked surprised at his reply. "Not today?"

"Timmy, old man, I'm not that pissed to miss out a day you know.

It was yesterday morning. Youngish chap, frizzy hair, bad breath. Asked me about Nick, what I knew about him. Well I know fuck all about him. Just said he was a mate of Simons, had been over before and was OK. Asked if he could crash here a couple of days, that was it. I told him that Nick had probably fallen out with Wicked."

"Wicked?" Jo asked.

"Tell you later. The only reason I was curious was that he is supposed to be locked up somewhere. They are supposed to have caught him Thursday morning sometime. Odd that."

Fieldy shrugged. "Come on the club. Our jo-jo's in for a treat

CHAPTER 18

'Cover ups and mystery.'

"I did tell you it was a mistake."

"I hardly think recriminations are in order Major."

Cropwell resisted the urge to shrug his shoulders. Instead he reached for a cigarette, and lit it, standing up from the chair. He didn't like to be sat in one place for too long, it made him feel uncomfortable, made him vulnerable. He exhaled some smoke and looked closely at the man now peering from the window. He was tall, stocky, and had an untidy mane of gingery blond hair, which he constantly swept back from his forehead. His face looked as if it had been chiselled from granite, square set, hard lips, broad nose, pale green eyes deep behind rimless glasses, beneath a forest of brow. He was not a man to be trifled with, but then neither was Cropwell.

"Well, Major what next?"

The Major made a point of hesitating, as if in thought, but there was no need, he had already worked out what he was going to say.

"Forgive my repetition Gordon, but it must be said. He is the best there is, the absolute cream. He's been free almost five years, and he will have accumulated considerable wealth in that time, and knowing him as I do, he will have secreted it well away from even our prying eyes. He will have stashes all around the country. We certainly won't be able to flush him out through desperation. But I have told you that before."

"Yes, yes. Get on with it."

"You shouldn't have tried to take him out. It was a mistake, a big one. The chances were such that he would never have made the connection. The real beauty of a lot of his work was his detachment. He only used what he needed to know, the rest was excess baggage. Travels light does our sergeant. In and out, does the job, forgets it. Onto the next. Now? Well he will start looking."

"Major, you have made your point to me several times. I have told Him, that as well. Like He says, we must now deal with it again. Not make the same mistakes. Potentially it's twice as bad. We have a queue of reporters lining up wanting to know why secret service agents were so easily slaughtered without as much as a hint of resistance. The blackout is so far holding. But only just."

Cropwell nodded.

"I know. This is my proposal. We stick to the serial killer line we've so far used. His name is out, but that is of little importance, he will have a few names he can use. No, we need a scapegoat, and I have one."

"Go on."

"One of my ex operatives, Jack Dorigo, has been recently released from a prison near Lahore. He had a break down, shot several villagers on the wrong side of the border about three years ago. Anyway, apparently he's a broken man. Well doped up, and released into the care of his elderly mother."

"So this Dorigo. How did he manage to get freed in the first place."

"Blood money."

"Explain."

"In that part of the world they operate a system of blood money payments. The authorities accepted that he was deranged, even the most biased could see that. Blood money payments are paid to the families to replace the income they could have expected from the deceased. All the families accepted the pay-offs."

"After three years? And who paid this money? Forget it, I won't ask. Go on."

"Well that's it. Released madman, ex SAS and all that. A bit Rambo-ish I admit, but should work."

"So we hand him to the police, or just release it to the press."

Cropwell shook his head. "We must do it. We cannot risk some snooping reporter find out it's all a fabrication. This is what we do- rather this is my suggestion.

Dorigo flips when his mother passes away- dickie heart, no surprise. Probably the shock of having to cope with a deranged son. Anyway he goes looking for his old CO- the one who gave him his original orders, a man called Oakes. He goes there, goes berserk when he finds it is the wrong man, and kills the security agents trailing him, escapes, catches a boat, gets picked up. Found hanged in his cell a couple of days later."

Gordon was nodding slowly. He sighed gently and frowned.

"I appreciate what you say about no fabrications, but how water tight is all this?"

"Ducks arse."

"How? No, let me play devils advocate a moment. Dorigo and Curcic. Look similar?"

"Dorigo is slightly taller, slightly fatter. Shave his head, they could be mistaken from a distance."

"So don't let those closest to Curcic mustn't see him."

"Already can cover that. Apart from those up in Burton, few people know him. An anonymous man, the sergeant, part of his success."

"OK. Bury him quick eh? Oakes. This CO Oakes. That's a bit thin."

Cropwell smiled. "No sir. there is a Captain Oakes living in the town, wrong address , unlucky for the real Mr and Mrs Oakes, who were involved."

"Is this Captain Oakes Dorigo's old CO?" Cropwell shook his head.

"No. There was a Captain Oakes in Dorigos regiment, but he lives in Australia. Dorigo got it wrong- mental instability you see."

"OK. I'll trust to your network. Thing is, we need to act quickly. How will he get to the south coast."

"Stolen car. I can arrange it easily enough."

The other man looked at his watch.

"You'll have to work quickly. It's ten already."

Cropwell smiled. "Do I assume we are to proceed?"

"Yes. We have little choice. It should head off the problem of Curcic, for a short while. He still remains a problem."

"Yes, but shall I proceed?"

"I said yes, didn't I?"

The major smiled. "He'll be picked out of the sea in about an hour."

The other man looked closely at him.

"His mother?"

"Unfortunately had a sudden heart attack two days ago. As we speak, a Mr Thomas is reporting his blue cavalier stolen. He'd been away a couple of days, found it missing on his return. It's currently abandoned in a car park at Hove. I have a man in the coastguard helicopter as we speak."

"You had all this planned didn't you. In advance. You're a bit of a bastard Cropwell."

"I have heard it so said." He smiled.

"But how did you know?"

"I didn't. How could I? Just knew that, after Nottingham, he'd turn up soon. Actually sprung Dorigo then. His mother did actually die of natural causes, but he doesn't know it. He's so pumped up with drugs that he doesn't know anything. I had someone to nurse him once he was freed. I thought this might crop up sooner, rather than later. When I heard around midnight what had happened I set the ball rolling."

"You assumed I'd agree then?"

"It is for the best."

The other man swept back his hair and fell silent as Cropwell's secretary brought in coffee. Cropwell handed her some papers and she left. The other man sipped his drink.

"What about Curcic? He's still a loose cannon. How will we get him?"

"We won't."

"What?"

"He'll come to us. To me. If he can make the connection, he may come for you, but, well, I know he's bright, but even this may be beyond him. No, the fact that we have acted by getting Dorigo to take the fall for him, will show him that someone out there loves him. I'll send out coded messages to his mail points, but I guess he'll not be using them for a while. This is the best way. We'll have to be patient. He'll find me, don't worry."

"And then what. Take him out then?"

"Take him out? You've been watching too many movies. I haven't decided that yet. Trouble is, he is far too valuable to get rid of. I'll think of something. Besides, he may be of use to us."

The other man put down his cup.

"This is all a bit too, well bloody melodramatic for me. I know the stakes are high, but for me, this Curcic still is too dangerous. He was considered dangerous enough six weeks or so ago when he was commissioned for this mission, and we decided then that he would have to go after it. Now, he's just as dangerous, maybe more so going by what he is capable of. I am nervous about all this, Cropwell. Very nervous."

"No need to be. Like I have said before. If we had stuck to my original plan, it would all be secure now. Insisting on sending teams of bungling men to get a real pro has nearly exposed everything. Fortunately I can recover the situation because I fore guessed all this. I made contingency plans for it. I always do."

"Sir."

Sheridan was trying to light the nub end of his last cigar when Jenkins came in.

"Yes, sergeant, what?"

"Just got a call from a Mr Thomas. Been in hospital the past few days, just reported his car stolen. About five hundred yards from the Holly Bush, and.."

"Let me guess. It's been found in Brighton."

"Hove actually sir. The boys down there said they'd ring me back with the finger print results. I asked them to keep it hush-hush."

Sheridan gave a wry smile. "I wouldn't bet against it being covered in Curcic's prints."

"Sir? What are you getting at?"

"Nothing, Jenks, nothing. Don't chase that any more. Redouble your efforts on Theobald. I should try the airports and ferries."

"Oh." Jenkins face dropped. It was a mammoth job.

"Concentrate on the car. The car."

Jenkins left and a young policewoman came to the door.

"Sir?"

"Yes? Oh hello Maureen. How are you?"

"Fine sir, thank you. It's just that there's a Mr Oakes in reception wanting to have a word."

"Thanks Maureen. I'll be right out."

He followed her out, and shook hands with Tim.

"And what can I do for you this fine Monday morning Mr Oakes?"

"Well Inspector. I have a couple of days off at the moment, and I wondered if it was possible for me to visit Mr Curcic. Nick. Despite everything, he was once my friend."

"Come through."

Sheridan led him into an interview room.

"Yes, strange do this one, and no mistake. He's not here you know."

"Yes, so I understand. He's somewhere on the south coast, I believe."

"Do you know, Mr Oakes, I don't know exactly where he is? Case has been taken over by Special Branch, but.." his eye twinkled. "I will find out. I think it might not be possible for you to speak to him, you're a prime witness, but I could. Still a couple of loose ends for me to tie up."

He stood and offered his hand to Tim, who took it.

"Leave me your number. I will find out exactly where he is. Go and see him tomorrow. You can come with me if you like."

"Really? That's very good of you Inspector. I know it sounds daft, after everything that's happened, but I still cannot believe he is what they say he is. Here, my number. It's different from the one on file, I've moved out. Left my wife."

"Sorry to hear that sir. Anything to do with.."

Tim shook his head.

"Pure coincidence. No, we were parting quite amicably, when all this happened. Thanks Inspector. I'll expect your call."

Sheridan frowned. "Split up from his wife?" He scratched his head.

"This gets more complicated by the minute."

CHAPTER 19

'Jemsom. Sons and lovers.'

Nicks' hair was growing quickly, but then it always did. He combed the lengthening brush on top his cranium. The moustache was complete now, and he carefully dyed both, over streaked with grey. A little more lifelike than the rug. It was time to discard that. He had been hidden away for nearly a fortnight now, and had spent his time catching up on sleep, found time to finally relax. He had made a daily trip to the shop for fresh provisions and newspapers. They lay in front of him unread. He was about ready to catch up with the world. Nick had indulged in alcohol, to gluttonous excess, and rediscovered his taste for Indian cuisine. The combined results were a small belly developing in front of him. For now, it went with his alter ego. Trevor Jemsom should have a belly. He patted it. "You'll have to go soon. I'll need to trim down, once I can work out what the hell is happening."

Besides, he had told Tim that he would see him at Christmas. He would have to consider both if and how he should do it. He poured another brandy, and picked up his sheets of papers, on which he had scribbled, thoughts, notes, ideas, and circled a couple of items. It was clear to Nick that the dogs were set after him sometime immediately after two jobs he had done in November. Lord Tarrant, and Taylor, the suicide.

From what he could find out, from his brief excursion to the library, a few days ago, all he had was that Lord Tarrant had died childless. His heir was Jeremy Arran-Harris, under secretary of state for agriculture. He had inherited vast wealth, a title, and had not long after his uncles death decided to take the Chiltern Hundreds. He must have been the contractor. He had benefited so much. That was a dead end. Taylor was vice president of a merchant bank, but he knew that, from stalking him. The papers majored on the suicide note. Obviously he had taken his own life since his wife was having an affaire with a Jeremy Knighton. It didn't make sense. His wife had got everything in his will, save for the insurance money. Nick gave a wry smile and thought about Tim. That was the reason he couldn't do it. It was his only collateral. Still. Whoever wanted Taylor dead wanted some discredit on the house. It was probably contracted by a business associate or adversary. It wasn't plain to Nick nor was any connection with him. He tossed the notepad aside. He genuinely had no idea who was hunting him. It was obviously someone in the net of assassins. Cropwell had the resources, but not the motive. Nick could think on to some people he did not get on with, people who might have some desire, however flimsy to wish him dead, but not the major. They had always got on well, worked to high professional standards. It was the trench mentality. Each depended unconditionally on the other.

He could not work it out. He glanced at the newspapers. He would read them first, with two weeks worth he could track any coverage his chase was causing. First reference was in the stop press.

'Three dead in suburban shooting horror.'

Next day was better.

'Burton killings.- serial killer being sought. Police and special branch are searching for an as yet unnamed serial killer who murdered surveillance officers. Mr and Mrs Oakes were thought to be extremely lucky to have escaped his attentions.' and so on.

'Police today named the wanted man as Nicolai Curcic' Nick nodded. At least they had spelt his name right. 'Nicolai Curcic was picked up following a dramatic sea chase today.'

He poured himself another.

"Funny. I don't remember that. I'm sure I would have" He read on intently. Tuesday's paper nearly choked him.

'Mass murderer Nick Curcic was today found hanging in his cell in the cells at Guilford..'

"Bloody hell!. I'd definitely have remembered that."

He read on until all information had been gathered, and the papers moved onto other gruesome titbits, more trivia for the masses. He put them down and rolled a cigarette. Unconsciously he rubbed his slight mane. What did all that mean? He worked through a logical train of notions. He could draw only one conclusion, but would not wager his life's savings on it. Someone had decided to do away with him- that was blindingly clear- he reasoned that someone else had equally decided that he was to be set free. The shootings had attracted media coverage, and so his identity of Nicolai Curcic had been sacrificed to satiate the demons of Fleet Street. Whatever, it seemed a clear message that he was no longer being hunted. Or was it a ruse to flush him out, and who was the dead Nick Curcic? He sat down and looked at the bottle, then at his watch. He would need another to see him through the night to find a convincing solution.

"Anthony? What a surprise. I thought you were staying in Southampton?"

He shook his sons' hand firmly. He was a handsome young man. Tall, square set jaw, he had the look of his mother, but he was unmistakably his son. He looked a little grim, and eyed his fathers' new home with some suspicion. Tim was not yet back at work, but Joanne was.

"Sit, please. Coffee? Or shall we nip out for a quick drink?"

Anthony shook his head.

"No, thanks Dad, I'm only up for the day. Driving, I don't like to, well you know."

"Yes." Tim felt slightly awkward and embarrassed for once with his son. They had always managed to blend the difficult liaison of father and friend seamlessly. Tim knew why he was here, knew who had told him where he now lived. He had been meaning to telephone him and tell him first hand, but it was the most difficult thing he had ever had to do, and as usual had put it off. 'Never do today what you can put off until tomorrow' was his favourite anti-cliché.

"I don't need to ask why you're here."

"No. It would have been nice to hear it from you. What happened?

Mid-life crisis?"

Tim walked to the kitchen and brought back the coffee. His mind raced, trying to legitimise his thoughts toward his recent actions. He had no need, not to Anthony. He decided to speak honestly.

"Well, son. No doubt you know that our marriage hasn't exactly been idyllic?"

Anthony gave the faintest of shrugs.

"Well, it's no mid-life crisis, I can tell you, no last surge of testosterone wanting me to prove my manhood. No, it is no mid life crisis. Just the opposite."

"Opposite? What's the opposite to a mid-life crisis?"

Tim shrugged his shoulders. "End-life crisis."

Anthony gave a hollow laugh.

"What at forty seven?"

"Yes. At exactly forty seven, or eight."

Anthony looked closely at his father, had his brow furrowed. He had lost quite a bit of weight. It suited him. He looked more closely at him. Noticed the faint orange hue to his skin, a slight tightening around the eyes. He felt the disconcerting tug of disquiet pull at his stomach. His mother had said nothing to him other than they had split up and he had run off with a 'tarty little trollope'.

"Er, Dad. Are you trying to tell me something?"

Tim felt a blush of relief. They always connected on the same wavelength. He would have normally countered with a 'what do you think I mean?' He needn't now, not with Anthony. "Well, let me put it like this. Bluntly? I'll be dead within a year. I have a huge cancerous growth, been growing for years. Doctor guesses seven or eight years, but it is only a guess. Anyway, to cut a long story short, the weight loss you see isn't entirely due to a new lifestyle. It's starting to eat away at me. In six or seven months I can expect to be in considerable pain, then down to a miserable end."

"Dad? I'm so sorry. Mum didn't say.." He was choking on tears.

"Mum doesn't know."

"What?"

"You heard. I don't want you to tell her either."

"Dad? Why?"

"Look, Anthony, I want you to promise me you won't tell her."

"But Dad.."

"Please. Promise."

"OK. I'll promise, but I'd like an explanation. And, well the other?"

"Ah yes. My bit of the 'other'.

OK, first things first. Mum and I have lived separate lives now for well seven or eight years, it's difficult to be precise. About the time the cancer started. Who knows, perhaps the two are related? Anyway, I know that I have not always done the best for her, never been the best provider. Just the opposite, in fact. I took away the things we had aspired to, the things we worked for all those years. We have nothing in the bank, and the house is mortgaged up to the hilt."

"Is this due to that business with Uncle Graham?"

Tim nodded. "Yes. I have decided that the least I can do is to leave her a good legacy. I have bumped up my life insurance and well, when I die she'll be a wealthy woman. As much as we don't get on now, I will be happy that she will get some benefit from our life together."

Anthony stood gently nodding his head. He was looking down at his feet, trying to take it all in. He was bursting with questions and tears in equal measure, but didn't know what they were.

Tim continued." I fell in love again, only recently. With my boss actually- and before you make any comment, my boss is a woman. When I got that feeling again, after so long, well it made me feel alive. Made me want to live, but any lasting pleasure is denied to me. I just have to accept it. I hate it, but I have to accept it. What I considered, was that if I told your mother, she might take pity on me, feel some twisted sense of duty toward me to see me through my final days. I couldn't stand the volte-force you know. It would have felt so false. Then, well there is Joanne. I want to spend my last with her."

"Does she know?"

"Joanne? Yes. She wants us to cram as much living into the last months as possible. As long as I am able, we'll be together, do things together. In the New Year we're off to Jamaica for a week. She's a wonderful woman you know. I want you to meet her. How long are you here for?"

"I said I'd go back tonight to see Kerry."

"Kerry?"

Anthony laughed.

"Seems you're not the only one with a surprise, of the romantic nature. Yes Kerry. We've been living together for about six months now. I think it's fairly serious. We've known one another for nearly two years. Why do you think I've not been particularly keen on coming home that often? Sorry, but, well I know what a fuss Mum would make. Grandchildren and all that. Well, I can tell you that that is way off yet.

We must get together."

Tim nodded his agreement.

Despite his obvious upset, Anthony managed a smile. "You mentioned a drink? I think I will."

"What about your drive?"

"If I could use the 'phone, I'll tell Kerry I'm staying over tonight after all. I'd like to meet this Joanne woman."

Joanne arrived home shortly after six that evening. Tim had decided to surprise her, and hadn't warned her about Anthony. He was in the bathroom as she arrived, and Anthony was in the armchair with his back to her. As she took her keys from the door she called out."

"Hello darling. I'm home!"

"Anthony grinned to himself, he had his fathers humour.

"Hello darling." He replied, and stood to face her. Her pretty face went paler than usual, and her jaw dropped, then she reddened.

"Who?"

Anthony smiled and offered his hand.

"Anthony Oakes, at your service."

"Anthony..you must be.."

Tim appeared from the bathroom.

"...my son. Anthony, Joanne. Joanne, Anthony."

She awkwardly shook hands. It was indeed a surprise. She looked quickly at him and flashed a smile. He was his fathers son, but different. He looked at her. Another time, other circumstances, he would have found her desperately attractive. She was a beautiful woman. He could see why Tim had been attracted to her. He had, half expected someone nearer his fathers age. It was a strangely pleasant surprise.

Joanne wasn't sure whether to kiss Tim on greeting, as she normally did, Tim saved her embarrassment and pecked her on the cheek as he took her coat from her. He did not indulge in any passionate embrace; after all she was not a trophy to be paraded, particularly in front of his son.

"I thought we might eat out tonight. Anthony's staying at his mothers overnight, he has to be back in the morning. I thought we'd eat early, rather than later, since it will give Anthony chance to spend a couple of hours with Nancy before he dashes off tomorrow.

She smiled and nodded. He was full of surprises.

The evening went well. It could have been awkward. Father, son and mistress, but it was a pleasant evening. Joanne had noticed how much alike they were, in their mannerisms, sense of humour and taste. They spoke almost casually about Tim's disease, and that too was a relief for Joanne. She knew that it was important to Tim that Anthony should know. It had just happened sooner, rather than later. They parted amidst laughter and tears, and arranged for Tim and Joanne to go to Southampton to meet Kerry one weekend after their holiday. As they parted, Tim made Anthony repeat his promise not to tell Nancy.

That night Anthony broke his word to his father. He hated doing it, but felt duty bound to tell his mother. It was not a decision he took lightly. To say she was shocked was to understate the case. He was surprised to the depth her feelings ran. All she could say was 'no, oh no.'

"Mum, please, don't tell Dad will you? I did promise him, and I hate to break that promise, but I feel you should know. Are you alright Mum?"

Nancy bit her lip. Her mind was racing. "Yes, Anthony. I'm fine, honestly. I won't tell anyone. I wish he had told me earlier- himself. Oh God."

Anthony allowed himself a grim smile. It was a proper response.

That night Joanne awoke and felt the bed to be empty by her side. She lifted herself up and squinted at the faint red glow from the clock. It was three twenty two. Where was Tim? She could hear a faint sound from the bathroom, and slipped out of bed to see what it was. Through the half closed door she saw Tim, sitting on the toilet seat, dressing gown on, his face in his hands and gently weeping.

"Tim? Whatever is the matter?"

He gave a wry smile. His was no sobbing, wracking weep of lament. It was the soft waves of remorse ebbing and flowing through reality, hope and regret.

"OH, Joanne. I'm fine really. Just sad. Sad about seeing Anthony. Sad that I will only meet his 'Kerry', probably never get to know her properly. Sad that I'll never have the experience of being a grandfather. Isn't that odd. I have never regarded myself as being old enough to have grandchildren- never gave it any thought really- but now, well it isn't an option is it? I am crying over my life Joanne. Crying at the waste. You know when I first learned about this cancer, well it didn't really matter. I was to die. So what? Speed the bloody day.

I was in a loveless marriage, and hadn't seen Anthony for a while. After tonight, with both of you, it highlighted what I will miss. There's you. You Joanne. I haven't felt this way for years, decades. I wonder if I ever have. If I did, it was never like this. I feel I love you so much, feel cheated that it will soon be gone, taken away and consigned to history's' scrap heap. Unread and unlamented. I wonder if I ought to run away and spare you the future agonies.."

She bit her lip, felt a tear find its way to the corner of her mouth, tasted the saltiness of the pain. She shook her head.

"Darling, I feel the same about you. Feel the intense flame of love for you. I don't want you to die, God knows that. But if it's a fact then let's make the most of it. We have a lifetimes living to cram into twelve months. We have a lifetimes loving too. I'll not regret it, not one bit. After you have gone, I will need memories to carry me through the rest of my life."

She kissed him, stood by him and pulled his head gently to rest on her thigh. He exhaled slowly, and continued his grief.

"I will miss you. Miss your softness, your tenderness, the passion of our love making, the fire of your concern. You know? In a way, I'll miss Nancy. Miss the nagging, the bitterness and the resentment. I'll miss Fieldy, and his brutal, simple philosophy- hey, do you realise? I've not told him about me. My God, that must be a first! He is, was always the first I told about anything. The only people who know are you, Anthony and Nick."

He stopped. His tears had dried now. He was encapsulating his thoughts into words, brief sentences of summary, but could not where Nick was concerned. He looked up at her. "You never knew him did you?"

She shook her head.

"I liked him. Like Fieldy, he seemed so straight- Yes I know he was gay- I mean a straightforward person. Not got Fieldy's' attitude, but he knew what he wanted, but then we are kindred spirits you know? He is a dying man too. Known about his degenerative hereditary illness for a long time. He had longer than me to prepare, had distilled his thoughts into the purity of his ideal. He wants to pay people back for the good and the bad they have done for him."

Joanne looked forward. "Is that why he killed those men? Revenge?"

He shook his head vigorously.

"No. Definitely not. That was an act of pure survival. He was being chased, hunted, and did what he had to escape. No, there is even more to him than I first thought. I must get to see him again.

You know, I will see him again. Maybe I can learn from him, some ideas on how to cope. He will tell me, he has a natural honesty. If I am good at one thing, then my instinct toward people is good. It has never failed me."

She looked down at him and bent down to kiss him. He slipped his hand beneath the softness of her negligee, felt the firmness of her breasts, and heard the gentle gasp at his caress. Like she said, there was a lot of loving to catch up on.

CHAPTER 20

'Death and suicide.'

Sheridan called around to see Tim the next morning as arranged. He hadn't told the police at Guilford, where Curcic was being kept in custody. He wanted the element of surprise. Somehow, none of this made sense to him.

They set off at around ten, Sheridan driving. It would give him chance to find about him from Tim, to know the man better.

"Tell me Mr Oakes.."

"Please, inspector, we have a long journey, call me Tim."

"Thanks. Well, Tim, this is a funny job and no mistake. Tell me, did he have any other aliases?"

Tim frowned. "No. I only knew him as Nick Church. I told you I believe that he revealed his real name to be Curcic, didn't I? No, Nick it was, nothing else. Why?"

Sheridan fished in the glove compartment for some mints, but found none. He lit a cigar, first asking Tim's permission. He didn't mind, it gave him the opportunity to light a cigarette. The officer continued.

"My oppo, sergeant Jenkins found out some other things about him.

Does the name Dorigo mean anything to you?"

Tim shook his head.

"Well, seems that your friend also goes by the name of Dorigo. Ex army, SAS in fact. That explains why he could shoot so well. Any thing familiar there?"

"Well, again. I think he said something about once being in the army. I'm sure he said he was an accountant or something, can't be sure."

"I don't know about being an accountant Tim. Anyway, his history seems that he went a bit haywire. Should have been on a secret mission in Iraq, but cracked under fire. Shot up a Pakistani village, got locked up, and freed a couple of months ago due to some diplomatic initiative. Stayed with his mother, but she died a week or so ago. The story is that that tipped him over the edge, got him mad, shot somebody in Nottingham, hence the undercover men. Does that make sense?"

Tim laughed and watched the grey countryside hurtle by as they drove south.

"Not the slightest, inspector. Look, I know that I didn't know him for a long time, but well, I get gut feelings about people you know?"

"And what did your gut feeling tell you about him?"

"A decent man. Straight to the point, honest, that sort of thing."

"Could he kill?"

"That I can't answer. I sometimes wonder if anyone can answer that. Who knows, given the right situation, stimulus, motivation- who can really tell? But there is also one thing that worries me a bit."

"And what's that?"

"You said he was released to stay with his mother?"

"Yes. Does that fit in with your timescale?"

"Timescale?"

"Yes, you know, when you first met him?"

"I suppose so, just about. But then.."

Tim stopped and mulled over his thoughts. He wasn't sure whether to share them with Sheridan or not. After all Nick had whispered his promise to see him at Christmas hadn't he? He hadn't told anyone else that. He looked across to the inspector and lit another cigarette. Sheridan had certain suspicions about the case, that much was obvious. Like Tim, he didn't believe he was the serial killer he was portrayed to be. He decided to share his doubts.

"A couple of things really puzzle me inspector."

"Go on."

"Where was he staying with his mother?" Sheridan shrugged slightly.

"Can't be 100 % sure, Cheshire somewhere."

"Are you sure?"

"I can find out for definite. Somewhere around there. Why?"

"Something he once said. Said his mother, being Bosnian was still there."

"Bosnia?"

"Yes. I'm sure he said that."

"Could it have been a lie. A cover, you know the whole Bosnian thing?"

"I don't know. I don't think so, but I have no proof either way."

There was a silence as the car slowed to manoeuvre through road works. Tim opened the window slightly, disposing of the cigarette end, felt the icy breath of December and closed the window. The inspector spoke next.

"You said two things? "

"Yes. First his mother, then, well you said he was released from some Pakistani gaol a couple of months ago?" Sheridan nodded.

"How come Simon had met him six months ago then. In Turkey."

"Simon? Who would that be?"

"My brother-in-law. Nancy's brother."

"Ah yes the poofter- sorry."

"Don't be sorry inspector. He isn't. Nice bloke."

Sheridan didn't answer. He made a mental note to get Jenkins to

get in touch with him and find out. His thoughts were interrupted

by his telephone going off.

He grumbled as he pressed the button to connect him. He was still driving through the road works. It was Jenkins.

"Look, Jenks, I can't talk now, in roadwork's, and the heavens have just opened up. Look we're about two miles from the service area. I'll pull in and call you back OK?"

The rain was driving and icy cold and both men were pleased to off the motorway for the moment. They had made good headway and were about an hour from their goal. A break and a coffee would be welcome. Tim went to order the drinks whilst Sheridan called back on his mobile phone.

"Yes, Jenks? What is it?"

"It's Curcic sir. Just got word. Found hanged in his cell this morning."

"You're fucking joking man."

"No, sir. Thought I'd better call, save you a journey."

"Anything else on that?"

"No sir."

He walked into the cafeteria with his face looking at his boots.

He broke the news to Tim.

"Never!"

"'Fraid so. Just got the word through. Seems that our journey has been wasted."

Tim shook his head.

"Never.

Look, inspector, something else about Nick was that he had an incurable disease. He had four or five years left, he told me. He said he wanted those four or five years to do good. To repay the kindness of others. The very last thing he would do was to take his own life. Not now. I just don't believe it."

"I have known it before, Tim. People like him- if his profile is to be true- if they get cornered, it's the only way out. Mind you I'm surprised that it could happen knowing these cases. I'd like to think it couldn't happen in my nick. Still. May as well turn round now. Not much point, unless you want to view the body?" Tim shook his head.

"Not really. A bit macabre that for me."

He was interrupted by Sheridan's mobile again. He answered it at the table.

"Yes, Sheridan here."

"Sir. Jenkins. More news."

"Get on with it."

"Well, we've been circulating all the secure car parks first- you know the ones which register car numbers parked there?"

"With a view to what?"

"Theobald sir."

"Yes. You've dropped lucky?"

"Yes sir. Seems his car is in Heathrow car park. I've contacted the nearest nick, said you might want to be there to inspect it."

"Yes. Yes I would. Well done Jenkins. Got the number?"

He took down the number of the police station and contact- a sergeant Dawkes. He rang the number.

"Sergeant Dawkes?"

" Yes."

"That wouldn't be Jack Dawkes would it?"

"Yes. Who's calling?"

"George Sheridan."

"Blimey! I thought you'd be retired by now. Long time no see."

Sheridan knew he could catch up on old times later. "Look, Jack. My man Jenkins has phoned you about a possible abduction hasn't he? A bloke called Theobald, and his car has been located on your patch. I am about an hour or so away, and I wondered if it would be OK for me to check the car over with your boys?"

"Of course. It will be nice to see you again. Look, I'll do it personally. Call in at Hounslow Nick and we'll go together. I'll give you directions.."

Sheridan apologised to Tim but explained about the diversion.

He didn't mind. Might prove to be interesting.

They drove eastwards in silence, Tim thinking deeply about Nick. He could not believe he would take his own life. Perhaps he, like the inspector had said, realised he had nowhere to go and...

They arrived at Hounslow police station at just before one, and Sheridan and Dawkes greeted one another warmly. They had been on the beat together for nearly three years in Durham where they were both born. They had lost touch a few years ago, but pleased to see one another again. Tim was introduced as a friend, so as not to complicate matters, and was invited along for the ride. Dawkes drove them over with another constable in the back of the car. They spoke to the gate men who indicated that the car was on the fourth floor, and so Dawkes drove slowly up until they located the grey Jaguar, and checked out the number plate. It was Theobald's all right. Sheridan walked around it, looked closely at the outside and in searching for visual clues. It was mud splattered underneath from driving into a field, and inside he could see nub ends of rolled up cigarettes in the opened ashtray. An empty bottle of drink was in the passenger foot well.

He smiled slightly. Curcic had taken rolling tobacco and such a drink from the garage robbery. It was locked.

"Any chance of getting in it Dawkesy?"

"George! You know me better than that. Weller!" He called to his constable.

"Give Jimmy in the AA a ring will you, and SOCCO. Give it a dusting. Is it what you've been looking for George?"

He nodded. Tim stood back, not really interested. He couldn't stop thinking about Nick. Twenty minutes later the familiar yellow van of the AA turned up. Sergeant Dawkes and the patrolman knew each other well.

"Open it up from the passenger side Jimmy. Save any prints for forensics on the drivers side. "

Jimmy was quick. Very quick. In less than ten seconds he was inside, but set off the alarm, which was piercing. He opened the bonnet and disconnected it, knowing exactly where to cut the wires. The shrieking left an echo in their ears until it subsided. Dawkes stepped over.

"Thanks Jimmy. Let's have a look."

Inside they could see the cigarette ends more closely. The interior still smelled slightly musty with stale tobacco. There would be good prints on the steering wheel. Dawkes popped open the boot from the internal release lever, and as Sheridan carefully looked in the back seat for further clues, the sergeant went to the back of the car and lifted the lid. "Jesus!"

Sheridan banged his head on the roof as he looked up, and Tim walked casually over to see what the buzz was. In the boot, curled up and with a congealed pool of blood soaked into the pale grey carpet of the interior lay the cold body of Theobald. All four men looked aghast at the sight before them. Tim had to turn away, and even two hardened officers such as Dawkes and Sheridan still managed to be shocked by such things. Dawkes looked at his colleague.

"Now are you going to tell me what really brought you all the way down here?"

It was late when Tim got back home. Late and he was tired. His side ached badly, probably the stress of both the journey and the revelations he had encountered. Having neglected to take his painkillers with him, he was now suffering. Joanne was concerned by his state, of both body and mind. She gently massaged his shoulders and sent him to bed for plenty of rest. What with the pain, visions of the body in the car, thoughts of Nick hanging from his belt in a police cell, he gained little sleep that night.

The next morning Sheridan was summoned to the superintendents' office. He was not in a good humour.

"Tell me inspector. Are you aware of what a direct order is?"

"Of course, sir, why..."

"Then hear this. So you are under no illusions whatsoever, this is a direct order. Drop all your dealings with both the Curcic and Theobald case. Special Branch has them both. There is a probable terrorist link with Theobald's murder. Is that clear?"

"Absolutely sir."

"If I discover anything to the contrary, I shall have you on a disciplinary charge before you can say 'traffic.' Is that plain enough?"

"Yes sir."

He walked from the superintendents' office to his desk. He dialled a number.

"Jack? Is that you? Great. This is George Sheridan. Exciting day yesterday eh? Just like old times. Look, do us a favour. Send me a copy of the dabs from the car, to close the file this end, yes, special branch have it. OK. See you again. Next time we must get a drink together, Bye" He put down the receiver then dialled again, this time to Guilford to request a copy of the prints for Curcic and his death photo. All routine stuff. It would not raise an eyebrow.

"Jenkins!" He called.

"Sir?"

"Ah good man. Orders first. All enquiries regarding Curcic and Theobald are to halt immediately OK?"

Jenkins nodded.

"Typical. Just when we get something interesting to investigate. Oh well."

"Oh, Jenks, just get me a copy of the dabs from the car in Brighton will you? Then I can close the Curcic file."

"Actually, sir, they came this morning. Here."

Sheridan placed them in the file after copying them, and retrieved Simons phone number in Aberdeen, before sealing the folder, and stamping 'Case Closed' on it. By Friday he had all the information he needed. Simon had verified his story that he had first met Nick on holiday in Turkey, and then several times in London in the preceding months. It was certainly at odds with him being locked up in some stinking Pakistani gaol during that period. The photograph proved to be inconclusive. The video footage from the garage was indistinct, and he couldn't say one way or the other if the photograph from Guilford and the man at the garage were one and the same.

The fingerprints were interesting. The ones from Heathrow were different to the ones from Guilford, but the ones from Brighton matched those from Guilford. He had an idea. It was a one off, but he would follow it up anyway. He inserted the pictures of Curcic into a mugshot book and called in on Tim.

"Just for routine Mr Oakes, Tim. It's just that I have some doubts about one of the men who was supposedly one of the undercover agents shot by Mr Curcic. I know it's a long shot, but just have a quick look in this book, see if you can identify him will you?"

Tim looked through the book. Carefully scrutinised each one several times, but by the time he had spent a good hour perusing it he admitted defeat.

"Sorry inspector. I don't know any of these men."

Sheridan smiled.

"Never mind sir. Like I said, just a long shot. Anyway, I have to say, that officially the case is closed now.

Take care now."

He took the photographs out of the book before driving off.

Interesting that, him not recognising his own friend

CHAPTER 21

'Contracts and cancellations.'

Nick was confused, but had decided that action was necessary to prevent his senses from becoming dead. He had given serious consideration in going to Switzerland and clearing his accounts enabling him to set up fresh somewhere new. Such a course of action was not in his nature. One thing about his 'job' that he enjoyed was the planning, the skill and excitement it gave him. Besides he had other things on his mind of late. He had always put thoughts of his own illness on the back burner, knew it was there, it was his motivation, but an unconscious driving power not meriting serious consideration. Since he had met Tim, it all seemed different. It was the first time he had met someone similarly challenged, allied to the fact that he felt genuine friendship toward him, suddenly his neatly packaged box of psychological spurs and motivations seemed inadequate. He had made a promise to him to visit him at Christmas. He would keep that promise, and now that was but a week away. He would do some work, to keep him mentally fresh, but did not relish the idea of picking up his jobs from his usual drop off points. Now was different, there was still the chance that a letter bomb might be waiting for him, or that the points were being watched. He would confront that situation later, but not now. There was still the work, which he had picked up from Nottingham. Trouble was time might be against him, they all had an expiry date. They would still be at Fieldy's flat, or at least that was where he had left them, in his rucksack.

He decided.

Off his backside, and up to retrieve the bag, check the work, see if it was still valid and do it. It would keep him sharp, and besides, he needed to go back to see Tim. He had promised him.

He caught the train north, deciding to preserve some of his money by not buying a car. Besides his fingers were getting a little more numb than usual of late. His tendency to grip the steering wheel tight probably made the situation worse. Trevor Jemsom booked into town centre commercial hotel. He was lucky, he could stay right over Christmas and beyond, although the manager warned him that he would have to fend for himself on Christmas day, all the staff were off. Nick said it was no problem, he would be seeing family that day.

That evening, around nine he slipped up the single flight of stairs to Fieldy's flat. It was Thursday, he knew his friend would be out at the club. It would have been nice to join him. He listened carefully at the door, and could hear nothing, so he quickly and efficiently slipped the lock and entered, closing the door quickly and silently behind him. No one was there, as he expected, and he allowed himself the luxury of the light. He was wearing his disposable gloves, no trace of his visit would be evident. Quickly looking around the flat he soon located his bag, behind the sofa, resting against the wall. It was how he had left it, everything still there. He wanted to leave a note for Fieldy but decided against it. He locked the door behind him and returned to his hotel.

The money inside was welcome, as were the two envelopes with the newspapers intact. He would scrutinise them immediately, to see if he could still get the work he needed to occupy him. Nick spread the newspaper wide on the bed, at the correct page. In front of him he had his note pad, and the typed sheet with the cipher on. He placed a piece of card under the paper and wrote in fountain pen, just a precaution against being detected by pressing through the paper with a pencil or biro. He worked quickly, noting down each letter as it came up. The first one read.

Lanoline, Bertrand. 30 Rue des Ananas, Perpignan... He shrugged. As appealing as the south of France was, it was not really practicable for the next couple of months. He would sit tight in England for now. He drew out the next assignment and started to decipher the code. Again he worked quickly, just noting down the letters. When the name first appeared he smiled, then shook his head, rechecking his work. It remained the same. He finished the decryption.

When he had completed it he looked at it and laughed. Stood up, stretched and retrieved a half-bottle of scotch from his case, and poured some in a glass. He laughed again and shook his head,. then looked at the target again.

'Timothy Oakes. 18, Priory Close. Burton. Age 47, six feet, fifteen stones. Sandy hair, small scar right cheek. Accident. 15 thousand. January 14. Byzantine.'

He shook his head again then put his jacket back on and went into the street to make the call from a coin box. He spoke only the password and replaced the receiver having had the acceptance confirmed. He bought some more tobacco and returned to his room once more.

"Tim? Bloody marvellous. This must be Nancy's doing."

Nancy poured Sally a glass of wine and bit her lip as she handed it to her friend and confidante.

"So what's it like to be free and single then Nancy? Has Rick moved in yet?"

She shook her head.

"No, and he's not going to either. Made a big move the other night, brought his case with him, cheeky sod, told him I wasn't ready for that yet, needed time to myself for a bit. A lot actually. Anyway, he took the hump a bit, suits himself. I think we may be approaching our best before date, but that's another matter."

"Sorry to hear it. I thought that you and him....?"

"Just the sex, Sally. He's as shallow as Tim beneath the sex. Men eh? Anyway, there is a bit of a problem."

"Oh?"

"Yes, about Tim."

"Tim? How can he be a problem now? Is it the money? If so..."

"No, it's not the money. No, It was something Anthony told me in confidence a few days ago. It's been driving me crazy ever since."

Sally put down her glass and lounged back in the chair.

"Well, come on Nancy, out with it."

"Tim. He's dying. He's got cancer."

"Oh. Sorry, I didn't realise... Nancy, did you not know?"

She shook her head.

"He's still not told me even now. He told Anthony in confidence, he thought I had a right to know, despite everything."

"I know he's been a bit of a pain in the arse and everything, but I wouldn't have wished that on him."

Nancy cut her short.

"Seems he only has about six months to live, then he will be dead. Incurable, apparently."
"How awful."

"Yes, and what's more he has told Anthony that he will still be leaving everything to me, despite him moving in with that bitch."

"Bitch? I thought you would be pleased? Anyway, in a way it solves your problem doesn't it? Sorry to be brutal about it all darling, but face facts. You wanted him dead, now he's going to die? Horrible as his end will be, it is what you deep down, wanted isn't it?"

Nancy lit a cigarette. Sally was surprised, she had never seen her friend smoke before.

"Trouble is, my dear friend, is that I have put this, this contract out for him."

"Oh yes. I suppose..oh!"

Reality dawned on her friend at last. She could see why she had suddenly taken up smoking.

"You are worried that he will be killed before he dies? Is that it? Well, there's irony for you."

"No. If he only has a few months left, then it would be wrong to take away the scant time he has left."

"Nancy. I don't see the difference? You were happy to take all his time away before, now, well, well you might be doing him a favour."

"Look, it's difficult to explain, but deep down, somewhere, there is still the merest shred of humanity toward him. Probably Anthony has something to do with it, I can't rationalise it. Thing is, I want to stop the contract."

"But the money? You are committed to.."

"I don't give a damn about the money. Once he's gone it will get paid, don't worry about that, no I want him to end his days naturally, in peace. I can wait another six months. After all I've waited long enough."

There was a long silence, unusual for the two. Sally poured herself more wine and walked about the room. Nancy looked at her, raised eyebrows demanding an answer.

"Well I don't know do I? I'll have to talk to Richard."

"Richard?"

"Yes my love?"

"This er contract that Nancy has taken out on.."

He stood up from his desk and furtively looked around, as if expecting to be overheard. "Not a topic for open discussion Sally. What is it?"

"She wants it cancelling."

"What! You must be fucking joking. Like I said, it's not a fucking joke this you know. Not something to be taken on lightly, I told her that at the time. This is serious. Bloody serious. I told her. I told you. What the hell does she think she's doing?"

"Look, Richard. She's found out that he's only got a short time to live, due to an incurable illness."

"And she wants to save some money eh?"

She shook her head.

"No. She realises her commitment. That is not the point. She wants him to live his last few months in peace."

"Good old twinge of conscience eh?"

"Look, can she cancel it?"

"I doubt it."

"Try will you? She is quite insistent."

He looked at his watch.

"Trouble with this sort of thing is that there are safeguards, everything secure to protect the identity of the assassin. There is no way to contact him, still I'll phone Butler and see what he says."

Sally left him whilst he dialled through to his associate. She knew he was not best pleased, but then neither was she. This was a very serious matter indeed, it was not a game of second chances. After an hour or so he emerged from his room. He rubbed the stubble on his chin and looked angry. She raised her eyebrows at him.

"Fat bloody chance. I knew this would happen. Butler is absolutely livid. These things are not like buying a new lipstick you know. Everything is carefully, professionally and totally secretly arranged. The only fall back is the confirmation. If it is not confirmed, then the contract is off, or can be rearranged. I told bloody Nancy to be totally sure. You remember don't you?"

She nodded. "The confirmation?"

"Made yesterday. The hit is on. No way back now."

"Shit."

"Yes my dear, shit indeed."

He walked over to the cabinet and poured himself a large scotch. Sally joined him. For a moment they stood side by side and in total silence. He swirled the drink in his glass, downed it, poured himself another and looked at his wife.

"Nancy. What will she do?"

"Do? I don't know. Why?"

"Butler."

He stopped, drank some more and continued.

"Butler is concerned. If any of this gets out, we are all in the brown and smelly."

Sally gave a nervous laugh.

"Gets out? Why should it?" He put his drink down and took her by the shoulders, staring into her eyes.

"Look here. When I said serious, I meant serious. Deadly-fucking-serious."

"Richard. Let go! You're hurting me."

He kept his grip.

"This is not just a matter of getting a fine if we're discovered you know? If word gets out there will be no hiding place. I don't mean the police either."

He released his grip. Sally's brown eyes were wide with fear. She understood what he meant.

"You mean?"

"Of course. These men are totally bloody ruthless. The thing that worries me, is if it's not too late."

"Too late?"

"You're good at repeating everything I say aren't you? Yes too late. They may have already decided that the risk is too great and be sending out a few special orders themselves."

She sat down and started sobbing.

"Pull yourself together woman. Here."

He handed her another drink.

"I'd better have a word with our Nancy. Tell her to keep it shut, or else. In the meantime, I think a last minute Christmas break might be nice eh?"

She nodded slowly, her tears still flooding but the sobbing subsiding.

"Where?"

"Who gives a fuck? Anywhere.. Look, see what you can do, I'm off to see Nancy."

"Richard? On your own?"

"Yes. I need a word."

"Come in."

She led him through to the lounge. It was late for him to call by, after all it was ten thirty. She had already changed for bed, and was recently showered and in her dressing gown. She was finishing off watching a video.

"Sit down. What word would you like?"

"Tim. The er contract you put out on him."

"Oh. Nancy has asked you then?"

He nodded.

"Can't be done Nancy. Can't be done. Look, I told you at the time, how totally serious this was, didn't I?"

She stood up and poured herself a vodka, and offered him one. He chose scotch. She sipped it as she stood by the fire. She had a stern look of defiance about her.

"Just cancel it. Tim deserves his last few months in peace.

What's the problem?"

He stood and closed to her, staring into her eyes, emphasising his point.

"The problem is, is that the contract has been accepted. There is absolutely no way out."

"Why?"

He shook her by the shoulders.

"Because it is? This isn't fucking Tesco's you know. Tim will be killed. The money has been paid. There is no way to contact whoever it is doing it. No way out sister."

"Let go Richard. There must be."

"There isn't!" He did not relax his grip.

"Richard. You're hurting."

His eyes were wide and staring.

"No way out. No fucking way out."

She ducked and wriggled out of grip, panting slightly at the exertions. He was still wild eyed.

"You must not tell any one. Just let it take its course or.."

"Or what Richard? Or what?"

"Or, you may not live long enough to regret it."

"What? I'll go and get police protection if necessary?"

He took two steps toward her, but she backed away. She was frightened by him. Saw the fear within him. He stopped as he saw her backing away, and shook his head. His eyes narrowed slightly and he exhaled deeply.

"Nancy. Just promise me, you'll forget all about this. You must just let it take its course. The police, press, anything like that will bring a deadly vengeance down. These guys are totally ruthless. Do as I say, just let it happen. I feel sorry for Tim, disease and all, but well, we will live on long after he is dead, come what may. Do you promise?"

She looked back at him. He was a big man. Strong and virile, and yet he feared what these others could do. What could she do to save Tim?

It appeared nothing.

She nodded slowly, and walked back to the fireplace and picked up her drink. She could smell the muskiness of his perspiration.

He put his hand gently on her shoulder this time.

"Promise?"

His voice was softer, kinder, asking her to comply. Men, underneath they were all the same, ruled by fear, dominated by inertia. She glanced at him again and nodded, touching his hand with hers, looking into his eyes. He nodded back and patted the back of her hand before letting go.

"Good. Look I must dash. See you later. Any problems, then talk to me OK?"

She nodded. Men could be so stupid at times.

Tim felt the pain crawling over him much more of late. He was, despite his original ambitions, becoming more and more dependent on painkillers. He was to return to work on Monday for the last two days before the break for Christmas. It would be a nice, gentle reintroduction to work. He considered Joanne. If anything they were becoming closer than ever. He more than ever regretted his imminent demise, but now he was waiting to see Bob, his doctor and friend.

The receptionist called his name and he went down the short passage to Bob's surgery.

"Hello Tim." The doctor smiled when he saw him, then stretched a bit of a false grin across his lips.

"How are you coping?"

Tim shrugged. "Just coping Bob. Pain's getting a bit stronger this last week."

"Been overdoing it at all? You know stress, that sort of thing.

How is your wife coping?"

Tim smiled. "I've left her. Got another woman, whom I love dearly, I've decided to spend my last with her. No, before you ask, it isn't stressful at all. I've never felt happier, or sadder."

"What do you mean?"

"Well? for a long time now I have been in a loveless marriage.

Now, well, at last I've found happiness, but my time is so short.

Bob, it isn't fair."

"No, I'm afraid you're right Tim. It isn't fair. Look, I'll give you a prescription for some stronger painkillers, to help you through. After Christmas, we'll probably try some steroids, to build you up."

"Ah, yes, the kiss of death."

"What do you mean by that?"

"Oh, I've seen it before. Pump up the body, then that's it.

Slippery slope from then on in."

Bob smiled.

"Yes. But you know I've never kept anything from you don't you Tim. You are right. The steroids will restore some bulk, you'll feel fitter than ever for a while, then.."

"You may as well give it to me straight Bob. What will it be like? Painful?"

"Probably, but we'll give you drugs. Depending on which way the cancer goes will determine how you finally go. Probably will be liver failure that gets you. You'll feel feverish, tired, restless and then go yellowish and then, well..." Tim nodded.

"Before the end, before it gets too bad, whilst I'm still conscious, I'd like to take the decision into my own hands. but not suicide. Do you understand what I'm saying Bob?"

He nodded equally slowly.

"You mean, you'd like to die early, but not by your own hand is that it?"

"I suppose so. Can you help?"

Bob shook his head. "I couldn't do that Tim. But what I can do is promise that you'll feel no pain."

"Not good enough."

Bob looked at his long time friend and nodded.

"I'll see to it."

There was a moment's silence. The doctor wrote out his prescription.

"Do you want a sick note? There's no need to work you know?"

He shook his head.

"No. I need a bit of distraction. Besides, I'd like to spend as much time with Jo as possible."

"Jo? Your new lady friend?"

Tim nodded and watched the doctor write.

"Anyone I know?..not Joanne Woodward?"

"Why not?"

"Bloody hell Tim, I would never have guessed. Well, good for you.

Enjoy it while you can.."

Tim stood and held out his hand and shook the doctors' hand. He had a tear in his eye, and took the prescription and left the surgery without a further word. This got harder by the minute.

CHAPTER 22

'Chasing shadows.'

Sheridan took the file home in secrecy. This was troubling him deeply. All word on the Theobald and Curcic case was totally silent. All files were inaccessible, he had never known the like before, but then he reasoned to himself, he had never had to recourse to checking on a case after it was taken from him. It had happened before, and would no doubt happen again. In previous such cases, the logic had always been sound, and usually he had received a call after the case was finally finished, just out of courtesy. He didn't honestly know whether files would have been inaccessible before, he had never checked.

This case was different, painfully different, and he felt as though something was deeply wrong about it. He had decided not to talk to anyone else about it, not even Jenkins. He had made a few extra discreet enquiries, and pooled all the information before him at home. He had three days off before Christmas, which meant he would be on duty over the festive season. He didn't mind, let the men with families enjoy their brief moment with them, he had none, but a spoiled marriage behind him. His mistress, duty, had stolen Helen from him twelve years ago. He spread all the papers before him, and wrote his connections on a blank sheet before him.

So far, the fingerprints from Brighton and the Cavalier matched the ones from Curcic (?) at Guilford. They also matched the ones taken from the Oakes house. He marked that fact with a query. The prints from the Theobald killing were different, so not the same man. The next thing he found curious was the file itself. The final version, just before he closed it under the superintendents direction also matched the prints from Mrs Oakes red Micra with the Guilford Curcic. However, he had originally received them on the morning he was summoned to see Wright and had temporarily slipped them into his drawer, and they had in turn been shoved to the back of his papers. They were crumpled a bit, but he now carefully compared them using a hand held magnifying glass with those of the Guilford Curcic. Even he could see they did not match. He then took those from the Theobald case and matched them. They were the same. He scratched his head and lit a cigar, the smoke hanging over his table like some disembodied spirit studying the evidence with him. He walked around the table and spoke out loud to himself.

"Simon the queer first met Church nine months ago in Turkey on holiday, and at odd times since. According to the official line, Curcic was in some Paki gaol. Right then Sherry my boy, add that to two different sets of prints and add the fact that Tim Oakes didn't recognise Guilford man as Curcic, and you don't have to be Sherlock bloody Holmes to work out that there are two men involved. Now.."

He shuffled some papers and drew heavily on the cigar.

"..now it seems to me that Church- Simons boyfriend, and the one who Tim Oakes knows is definitely the one who killed the men in Priory Close and shot Theobald. He was probably unlucky, just because he happened to be in the way when Church had to escape the net which was quickly closing in on him. Now then Sherry, that means that he has killed at least four, and probably the two from Nottingham, making six. Obviously not a man to be pissing around with. So at the moment, he is free, maybe even abroad? Who knows? But.."

He looked at the photographs from Guilford.

"..but who are you? You've taken the fall for the shootings in Priory Close haven't you?, and then fallen on your own sword. Or were you pushed?"

He stubbed out his cigar and opened a can of beer, swigging eagerly at it, gulping down the contents in one smooth sucking action. He fetched another from his fridge, put his hands down the front of his trousers and scratched away for a moment before lighting another cigar and sitting on the chair with his feet resting on one another.

"Why? I can't believe that the super, and every other buggar but me has made a mistake on this, but it must be that the real Church- the live one- is quite important.

Important enough to have a cover for him to get away with killing these undercover whoever's. Big name this one, and that's a fact. The trouble is Sherry my lad is what do we do now? The Chief? "

He shook his head. Maybe he should forget the whole thing and get on with it, but he couldn't. It rankled with him, particularly where Theobald was concerned. As far as he could tell, he was an innocent victim being denied any hint of justice. Sure the legal system was far from perfect but this? It was wrong. In some ways, he could let the undercovers go. They probably knew the score, front line troops as it were, but Theobald? No. He remembered telling his widow, a nice lady, smart, living in a nice house, in a nice neighbourhood. He had already suffered a nasty accident some years earlier, and had overcome the obstacles it had placed in his path, and now he was gone. She had been heartbroken, and so had their two children. At the moment, their grandson was too young to understand where his grandpa had gone. Sheridan shook his head. They deserved better.

He thought on long and hard. He thought of possible scenarios, but generally disliked conjecture. He thought about press coverage, but dismissed it. If the cover up was telling him one story, it would tell the press the same. He could draw only one conclusion, could follow only one path. He thought of Tim Oakes, knew what he felt about it, and had a good feeling about him. He knew he was concerned about his friend and confused by his death. He would chance his arm with Tim.

It was two days before Christmas, and the inspector had called to ask if he could speak to Tim after work that night. Tim was happy to oblige. He arrived around seven, and Tim introduced him to Joanne. Sheridan sat and spoke to him.

"Tim, do you remember a few days ago, when I asked you to identify some mug shots?"

"Yes?"

"Well I was lying to you."

"Lying? Why? "

"Look, I'll be honest with you. I think that this whole thing with your friend Nick Church stinks. The photos I wanted you to identify were the ones taken at Guilford."

"Of Nick? I don't remember seeing a picture of him."

"Here."

Sheridan showed him the photos of the Guilford Curcic.

Tim shook his head.

"This isn't Nick."

"Are you sure?"

"100% certain. It's nothing like him."

He showed them to Jo, but she shrugged, having never met him.

"I thought so. Look, Tim, and this is unofficial, I believe that your friend could still be alive."

"But how? What is happening?"

"I don't know. Is there anything about him you can tell me which might help. This case is officially closed, and if my boss finds out I'm even thinking about it, then I'm history."

Tim shook his head.

"Like I said, just a nice.. hang on, there is something. A couple of days before the shootings he suddenly left us. He had been staying with us you know?"

"Yes, I remember you telling me."

"Well, I got word that he was staying with Fieldy."

"Fieldy?"

"Yes, John Field."

Sheridan nodded.

"Well he sent a message for me to take his belongings to him at Fieldy's. I took them over on the night of the shootings."

He stopped. He realised that he was about to perjure himself.

"You did say all this was off the record didn't you?"

Sheridan nodded.

"Why? Is there something you haven't told me?"

Tim went a little red. Jo squeezed his hand, encouraging him to continue. He had told her, she knew there was nothing incriminating in what he was to say.

"Well I took his bag to Fieldy that night, left it with him, and that night as I returned home, I could tell something was wrong at home. I sneaked round the back and saw Nancy being held by two men in the house. I had already seen the two men in a silver Ford down the street. I had a double puncture you see."

"Are you telling me that the two men didn't burst in after Church?"

Tim nodded, and continues. "I called him on Joanne's mobile. Asked him what the hell was happening, and what and whom was he hiding from. Anyway he came straight round and well you know the rest. He shot one man, knocked out the other, disappeared for a few minutes to presumably see off the two men in the car, then came back, tied us up for our own protection, you know to keep us out of it, then well just vanished. This is all weird."

Sheridan was shaking his head. "I appreciate you telling me all this, Tim. Trouble is, is that it poses more questions than it answers."

"How?"

Joanne stood and poured them all drinks.

"Thank you miss. No, what I mean, is, obviously Church, or whatever his name really is, was obviously being hunted by these men, and well, with a tiny bit of help from you, he managed to avoid capture.

Now, if he is the serial killer he has been painted to be, then why has so much trouble been taken to fake his death- and worse, to sacrifice somebody in his place- and effectively let him off."

"Assuming he has been let off?"

"What do you mean Tim."

"Well, perhaps, whoever he is, whoever has covered for him now has him, and he's floating face down in some river somewhere."

Sheridan shrugged. He looked up. "His bag!"

"Yes?"

"Where is it?"

Tim shook his head. "He didn't have it with him at the time, and didn't take it with him. Me and Fieldy had a look in it. There were some clothes, money, envelopes with old newspapers in them, nothing of great significance. It's still..."

"..at Fields?"

"Yes."

"Right then, let's go and get it. You are game aren't you Tim? I want this to be strictly between us."

Tim nodded and looked at Joanne.

"I would like it cleared as well. Like I said all along, none of this makes sense to me."

All three arrived at Fieldy's around eight thirty. He was just about to go out.

"Hey, Tim? Jo-jo. How's it hanging? Hey, plod."

Sheridan took charge.

"Mr Field? I need to take possession of a bag belonging to Mr Church in connection with.."
"Hey, sure man. No problem. Come in, it's behind the settee there. Take it. Drink?"

He twisted his neck and smiled at Joanne. The inspector looked behind the sofa

"What does it look like?"

Fieldy gave a shrug of exasperation.

"Come out." He pushed past the inspector and pulled the sofa out slightly, revealing books, a box of letters, some old shoes and an empty wine bottle. There was no rucksack.

"Odd. I could swear.." He then spent the next ten minutes untidying his flat in search of the object. It was nowhere to be seen.

"Look. I know it was there. I saw it a couple of days ago. I dropped a fag down here and had to shift it to find the hot ash- didn't want to burn the place down."

"Are you sure Mr Field?"

Fieldy looked him up and down and shook his head.

"Course. I may be an alcky, but I'm not stupid. It was here Thursday, definitely."

"Nothing else gone missing since then?"

He shrugged. "Nothing I've noticed."

Sheridan nodded slowly.

"Interesting that. Very interesting."

Tim blushed slightly. It was nearly Christmas day, Nick said he would be back then. It was the only thing he hadn't told Sheridan. It now seemed likely he was here.

Nick watched Tim, a handsome young woman and an older man emerge from Fieldy's flat. Interesting that, the older man had a familiar look. He guessed that he and the woman were police. He wondered what Tim was doing with them and melted into the shadows as they climbed into a red car and drove away. He lit a cigarette and pulled his coat close to him in the biting December cold. He thought on to his contract. He would fulfil it, in time, when Tim was no longer in a position to control the pain, when he would beg for merciful release. He would see to it that he ended his life quickly and painlessly. In his London apartment he had some natural herbal extracts from the mountains of Peru, which, if administered correctly, would stimulate a heart attack and be undetectable to any post mortem investigation. Cropwell had taught him that. He would retrieve them at the appropriate moment. He thought about Cropwell, considered his own position once more. He had already decided what to do, but it was a reluctant step for him to take.

Trouble was, it was a dangerous step. He would take it after taking care of Tim. That would be a few months away yet, but he needed to speak to his friend.

If he tackled Cropwell now, he might no longer be in a position to release his friend from pain. It was a kindness he was determined to undertake.

As for Cropwell, he had decided that he had offered the olive branch by setting up a patsy for him. He was not being looked for by the police any more, and it was clear Cropwell wanted him to come out. Well, in his own time. He would plan it all, very carefully. It would be the most difficult assignment he had ever had to undertake. He would plan it meticulously. First thing, he would need to locate him. That would be interesting. The last time they had spoken face to face was in Italy, at a NATO base. He had a number to ring in case of emergency contacted, but he knew that would involve a tortuous re-routing to avoid detection. He knew he was once based in Catterick, but doubted he would be there. But, he had his plan. Christmas Eve would be the ideal time to start it.

The next day, he dialled Whitehall. He had a once private number, he could not be sure it was current.

"May I speak to Major Cropwell."

"We have no Major Cropwell here."

"Forgive me, it is a short while since I spoke to him. He said to contact him on this number."

"Please hold."

He waited and heard the clicking of the connection. No doubt a trace was on him. He was in Birmingham, using a payphone. He was not worried.

"Hello. Who is calling?"

"I'm trying to contact Major Cropwell."

"Who is calling please?"

"Tell him it is Marcellus."

"Hold the line."

The line went dead then he heard the number connecting "Who is this?"

"Ah, good morning. This is Marcellus O'Riordan, I'm just calling to wish my old friend Major Cropwell a merry Christmas."

"I am afraid we do not have any major of that name here. What did you say your name was?"

"Never mind. Merry Christmas."

He replaced his receiver and switched off his tape recorder. He took it back to his hotel in Burton, and unpacked his latest acquisition, a sophisticated tape deck with the latest in filters, bass cuts, and frequency modulators. He would play with it over the holiday period.

"We managed to trace it to a payphone at Birmingham New Street station sir."

"Who was it, do you think?"

Felton shrugged his shoulders. He had worked for the major for years, and knew his ways perfectly.

"Difficult to say sir. He had the private line number, but that hasn't been current for eighteen months."

"Someone before then?"

Felton nodded.

"And he gave the name Marcellus O'Riordan? How did he get through with that name?"

"He said at first it was just Marcellus."

"Ah. Clever man. Now, Marcellus. Who knew about that?"

Felton was quiet. It was difficult to say. Marcellus was a secret code name from five years ago. A vital part in the wheels of mystery and intrigue.

"There could only be nine or so people who would know the name sir."

Cropwell bristled his eyebrows.

"So how did he get through, he's been long dead."

"The line sir. Always kept open for certain information, particularly information regarding him at the time. When your name and Marcellus were mentioned in the same breath, he was put through. Hoax do you think?"

Cropwell fell silent. "Who knew from the list who knew Marcellus, who knew the private line?"

"I can check sir."

"Do it quickly. And, Felton, have the line totally disconnected will you? Make sure there is no way in eh?"

Felton went to the office in the front of the majors. He accessed the computer searching for the information the major required. Cropwell watched him, and smiled. He wrote a name down on a piece of paper and waited for his ADC to return.

"Two names only sir."

The major held up the piece of paper with the name on. Felton looked at and nodded.

"Yes sir, and Butler. Curcic and Butler."

CHAPTER 23

"Christmas surprises."

Sheridan drove into the secure parking of the station. It was Christmas Eve and he was returning to duty after his break. He locked his car and walked to the security box to wish Tony Gould a merry Christmas. Gould let him in as he recognised the man outside.

They shook hands. "Just popped in to wish you a merry Christmas Tony."

"Same to you George..hang on."

A car pulled up and he checked the pass before letting him in, making a note of the number plate and time as he did. "How long you been doing that Tony?"

"Three months now George. A right pain in the arse too. Everyone, checked in, checked out. Wrighty's bright idea."

Sheridan cocked his head to one side. "Do you still have the records?"

"Sure. In that cabinet over there. Why?"

"Just indulge an old man his few pleasures Tony will you?"

Gould laughed. "Here."

He passed a glass with a tot of rum in. "Cheers."

Sheridan checked the date on a calendar. Twentieth. November. He found the log and checked down the list. It was a Sunday, so was shorter than usual. There. 9.03, number DK 56 BB Booked to the name of Cropwell. He made a note, and shut the log putting it away.

"Found what you wanted?"

Sheridan shook his head. "You know me, Tony, always chasing shadows. Anyway, have you got a mint? Wrighty doesn't take too kindly to turning up to work pissed."

"He doesn't take kindly to much "

The station at six o'clock on Christmas Eve was a strange mixture of festive spirit, and apprehension. It should have been a time of joy, a time of goodwill, a time of pleasure. Alcohol and drugs had dispelled such feelings in some, and there were more due. The duty sergeant was struggling with a foul-mouthed woman wearing jeans, a short top, black spiky hair and several pins pierced through ears, lip, nose, and tongue. She was screaming obscenities at him and so Sheridan gave him a hand and bundled her into the cell which Sergeant Wilkins slammed shut behind her.

"Thanks George. Hey, there's a nice festive touch, her name's Holly."

"Hardly a cracker eh? Looks like we're in for a fun night eh Wilko?"

Sheridan glanced at his desk. He would work through the tray later. Tonight would be different to normal. There would be a stream of Holly's throughout the night. He would assist the uniformed branch that night, unless something serious cropped up. First, he would just check something out. He walked through to IT, and saw Maureen Perkins.

"Merry Christmas Maureen. Here all night?"

"'Til ten George. Then off home. Terry's tucking the kids in, but I daresay they'll still be up when I get in. "

"Can you trace this number for me?"

"Sure George." She looked at the number and began tapping the letters into the computer.

"Army "

After a few moments the trace came up.

"Here. Registered to an army fire tender, based at Chillwell, Nottingham."

George leaned forward, examined the screen and the number on the paper.

"What, a green goddess. Are you sure?"

She rechecked. "Positive."

"Jot it down for me, Maureen eh?"

She pushed a button and the screen-printed out by her side.

"Here. Merry Christmas."

He folded it up and put it in his pocket, turned to go, then turned back.

"Maureen could you trace a surname in the army?"

She furrowed her brow. "Possible. Why?"

"Oh, just a case I'm on. Hit and run. I have a name, but no rank."

She smiled at him.

"I'll give it a go. What's the name? It may take some time."

"Cropwell."

She entered the name.

"This could take some time, like I said."

"That's OK. Do your best. I'll pop in before you go."

"George. Bring the mistletoe."

He smiled and walked on. There were loud voices from the front desk, more festive cheer, no doubt.

Nick casually walked down the darkened streets which led to Priory Close. He pulled his coat close to his throat. It was foggy and freezing, but he had some reconnaissance to complete before tomorrow. He had left his hire car some way away, not that it could possibly recognised, but he had to be extra careful now.

It was eleven thirty. Some revellers could be heard rendering discordant versions of popular carols, interrupted by loud laughter. Suddenly he felt alone. He had never felt that way before, and he stood in shadow whilst he smoked a rolled up cigarette.

His Christmases before had largely been spent in the army, usually on tour somewhere, so they had the mixture of duty roster and an excellent meal. Usually in groups of a dozen or so often with Cropwell in attendance. Laughter, like the type he was hearing now, was only ever a small feature of such celebrations, and certainly never from the major. He exhaled the billowing clouds into the nights' mist, and thought on. Since then he had usually spent this time in company, at a bar, a small insignificant cog in a wheel rolling on to celebration. He was never totally immersed in the crowd, but usually found some casual companion and attached himself, albeit temporarily to a small social circle.

But he was alone now. He had, he reasoned always been alone before, but in company. Now he was alone on his own. It was not the most pleasant experience. He stubbed out his cigarette and smiled somewhat grimly. What would be nice would be to turn back the clock, not be the quarry in some grotesque hunt, and spend a riotous time in the company of Simon, Fieldy and Tim. He had felt most comfortable then.

He walked on and slipped to the rear of Tim's house. Lights were on, and he pressed close to the rear windows to see what was happening inside. He was a little surprised to say the least. Inside he could see Nancy, a couple of empty bottles of wine on the coffee table and by her side on the settee a man.

Large and well-muscled with a mane of long blonde hair who was now busily engaged in kissing Nancy with some passion. Nick stood half a pace back. Nancy? Who was this? Where was Tim? He wondered what to do next, and looked back in. For a few minutes he played the part of voyeur. He watched the man unfasten her blouse, fondle and kiss Nancy's erect nipples and then pull down her pants. He watched no more. Although he could normally find some erotic thrill from such events, this was Nancy.

Being unfaithful to Tim.

It rested uneasily with him, gave him no thrill. He slipped over the fence at the bottom of the garden and stood flat against the fence. The same fence a month previously which he had climbed to meet his hunters.

What now? Where was Tim? He said he would return on Christmas day. That he would. Perhaps Tim was out with Fieldy on some serious binge, out partying till late. While the cat was away, Nancy, the cat, was definitely playing. Mind, it was midnight already. She was certainly cutting it fine. Tim was likely to stagger home at any time. This was confusing. He went back to his hotel, armed only with a bottle of scotch to comfort him.

George Sheridan had been busy all night. There was a steady flow of over-the -top revellers, drunk and disorderlies, common assaults, and muggings.

Another day in paradise.

He had not managed to see Maureen before she left, but she had left him a note to say that she had put a list in his tray for him to look over. It was two thirty before things settled down. Still some flotsam of society was washed to the sanctuary of the station, but he managed to get a break. Against all regulations he made coffee for the front line troops and heavily laced it with brandy.

He sat and ate a microwaved meat pie for his supper, in the sparsely occupied canteen. He passed casual remarks with the others and left for the privacy of his own office to catch up on the paperwork which would have accumulated over the few days he had taken off. He picked up a brown envelope first. It was from Maureen. There was a hand written note attached to a computer print out.

'Merry Xmas, George. Got the list, after some nifty footwork and an old friend! Anyway 32 names. Hope it is of use. Best wishes. M.'

He smiled and looked up and down the list. He frowned. He hadn't seen the man himself and tried to recall the description Jenkins had given him. Mid-forties, moustache. Officer certainly. Oh yes, and in a large armoured Rover.

"Green Goddess indeed."

He took a pencil and began crossing names off the list. Of the 32, two were women. Unless he was a very talented drag artiste, they were a safe bet. Next he crossed out those in the ranks. Sergeants and below. Sixteen of them. Already the list was halved. He lit a cigar and contemplated, talking to himself in the process.

"Right, Sherry old lad. What have we here?" The list Maureen had produced was comprehensive. Apart from the surnames, full Christian names and rank, was the date of birth and attachment. So for example he found a corporal Piers Cropwell attached to REME. Now aged twenty. He decided that the age range of thirty five and below would be his next cut off. That was much more dramatic. He was left with only three names. He wrote them on a separate sheet.

1.   Major Paul Henry Cropwell. Age 37. Attachment Artillery.

2.   Colonel Benjamin Cantrell Cropwell. 41. Marines.

3.   Major Goram Stefan Cropwell. 44. Administration.

He scratched his head. For someone to have the super jumping through hoops, he would expect the man to be of a senior rank. He would start with Benjamin Cantrell. Marines. But not now. The world closed down over Christmas. He would have to do his digging in a couple of day's time.

At ten o'clock Christmas morning Nick parked two streets away from the Oakes residence. He couldn't get the picture of Nancy's' seduction out of his mind. He shook it out of his head, and proceeded toward the house. Christmas day was freezing and misty. A certain dullness muffled reality. He noted Nancy's car, but no others. No sign of Tim's. Perhaps he had managed to get it in the garage. He sidled up and peered through the crack in the garage door. There was no sign of another car, and Nick slipped around the back to the position he had taken up by the French windows the previous night. No one was yet up. He prised open the door and entered the room. Inside were the remains of Nancy's seduction. Bra, and pants were strewn across the rug, along with a mans pair of jeans and some spotted boxers. One thing was sure, she wasn't expecting to be disturbed. That in itself troubled Nick even more. She was evidently still in bed with her lover. He looked around, searching out clues regarding Tim. He scanned the Christmas cards. Some were addressed to Nancy and Tim, some just to Nancy. He guessed they had split up. He could ask her, but she might give him away. Fieldy was the best bet. He silently made his exit, and made his way to the home of John Field. He knocked on the door. Within a few seconds the door was opened by a bedraggled looking Fieldy. Christmas celebrations were evidently heavier that usual. Nick didn't know what to expect from the man.

"Oh, hello Nick. Merry whatsits. Come in. Drink?"

Nick shook hands and took the offer of a drink, electing coffee. He looked around the flat as John clanked and banged about in the kitchen off. It was as usual, reasonably tidy. Fieldy had his own routine, his own list of priorities and agenda. The flat he kept manageable, was ruthless when it came to hoarding junk, as a result, for a forty something single man, with a drink problem, the flat was surprisingly clean and orderly.

"Here, Nick. Where've you been then? You look different."

He accepted the drink and sat down. He hadn't reckoned on spinning a yarn, and didn't feel he needed to. When he had asked for sanctuary at Fieldy's he had been granted it without question or condition. He needed not to be over cautious in his company.

"I suppose I've been on the run."

Fieldy looked at him and stretched his neck in his customary manner.

"You know, for a dead man, you look fairly healthy."

"Oh yes. As they say. Reports of my death were a little premature."

Fieldy nodded. "Are you some kind of spy?"

"Spy? No. Not a spy. I just have, well let's say a certain value to people due to my profession. Some people would rather I keep my talents hidden."

"You mean they want to kill you?"

"Well that's true enough. Look, Fieldy, if you don't mind I'd rather not give the whole story, just yet. But I will."

"Fair enough. None of my business. Mind you, your er premature death hasn't exactly convinced everybody you know."

"Oh? Who?"

Fieldy took a sip of his wine, licked his lips and put down the glass, and lit a cigarette. He blew out the smoke and rubbed the stubble on his chin. Nick noticed for the first time the complete absence of Christmas cards. Excess baggage, no doubt.

"Well, old Tim doesn't believe it all you know, and there's this copper."

Nick nodded.

"Small, plumpish, grey, balding? Has a slim young woman with him?"

Fieldy smiled then allowed it to develop into a full laugh.

"Part right Sherlock. Yes, that's the plod. The girl, well, she's no policeman."

"Oh. And who is she?"

"Tim's bit of stuff."

"What?"

Fieldy smiled again. "Yes, my friend, it seems that you're not the only one to be full of surprises."

"When did this all happen?"

"I guess it was just starting at the time you went on your shooting spree. I guess you were a little pre-occupied."

Nick drank his coffee. That certainly explained Nancy away.

"Where is he now?"

"Tim? Here, I've got his new address."

He gave him Tim's new home.

"This fancy bit? Who is she? "

"Joanne somebody from work. She's his boss."

"Screwing his boss eh?"

Nick nodded.

 "Fieldy. I'm going to nip over and see him. What are you doing later?"

"Me? Going to the club. Getting pissed. Mind you, I'm on best behaviour today. Going for lunch with mummy and daddy. That should be fun, I'm a great disappointment to them you know."

Nick nodded, and stood.

"Look Are you in tonight? or still out?"

Fieldy made a point of looking like he was thinking.

"Well chap. I'll do my duty, once a year isn't too bad. Probably be back home around seven. Most of the pubs are shut tonight. I shan't go out. Pop round for a drink if you fancy. You can tell me what you've been up to."

They shook hands and Nick made his way down the steps, first surveying all around him. Christmas day was stuttering into life. Children were riding their new bikes. Dads were starting the walk to the pub with their own fathers. An annual pilgrimage. Nick drove over to where Tim was staying, suddenly feeling nervous about the meeting.

He rechecked the address twice and entered the small courtyard which was in front of the address given. He recognised Tim's car. That made him feel more comfortable. He straightened his jacket and walked down the short path and rang the doorbell. He held a bottle of boxed brandy in his left hand. The door opened and in front of him an attractive woman stood. He recognised her from the day before, leaving Fieldy's flat. She must be Joanne. She was as attractive as Fieldy had told him. She raised her eyebrows.

"You must be Joanne. Merry Christmas. Is Tim in?"

She frowned slightly, and kept the door on the chain.

"Who shall I say it is?"

"Nick."

"Nick? I have heard of you. Hang on."

She disappeared for a moment and he heard voices off then saw Tim, slimmer, more drawn than before, and sporting an apron. He wrung his hands on a cloth, evidently preparing lunch. He look surprised at seeing Nick, and pulled the chain away.

"Nick! Bloody hell."

"Merry Christmas Tim. I said I would see you today."

"Yes you did. Bloody hell. Look come in, come in."

He showed his friend in, and took his jacket along with the proffered bottle. Tim turned to Joanne, then his friend and shook his hand, then hugged him.

"Thank God you're alive. They told me you were dead. Joanne.

Look, this is Nick. Nick this is.."

Nick took a step forward and then planted a kiss on her outstretched hand.

"You're a surprise. A very pleasant surprise."

"Thank you er Nick. She glanced at Tim.

" Would you er care to have lunch with us? If you have no plans that is. We've decided to shun tradition, we've made our calls this morning and we're having curry."

He smiled. Looked at Tim and nodded.

"That would be perfect. Thank you."

She fixed them all drinks and they passed the usual bland comments regarding the cold weather, how different Nick looked, how much weight Tim had lost, all the usual things. Tim looked closely at Nick.

"I suppose you will tell me exactly what you were up to the last time we met?"

"I suppose I will."

CHAPTER 24

'The whole truth, and nothing but..'

Over lunch they chatted. Nick was anxious to find out the state of Tim's health, and get the story behind how he and Joanne had got together.

"It all developed so quickly. Right at the time when you went AWOL, was the time we were getting together. I was going to tell you about Nancy and me, but well events took a rapid turn. Just who were those guys, and why did you shoot them?"

Nick eased back in his chair. He had always intended to tell Tim the story, to relate what he did for a living. There was a bond between them, a similarity of doom awaited them both. Nick could offer a way out for Tim, an end, when it was necessary, to ease his pain. He hadn't yet decided whether or not to reveal the victim of his latest contract. First, there was a tale to tell.

"Before I start. Answer me one thing."

"Go ahead."

"The policeman you were with the other day. Who is he, why was he with you?"

"Easy. He, like me doesn't- didn't- believe you were dead. You know the story in the papers about you hanging yourself. Inspector Sheridan is seriously into a conspiracy theory. He's not on the case, officially, but is still digging- against his bosses orders."

"Is he sound?"

"Sound? I don't understand."

"Never mind. It could be useful for me to have someone like him on my side. I need certain information. Anyway, we can talk about him later. It's Christmas. A time of stories. Here's mine, if you're willing?

They both nodded.

" Basically I joined the army from school, having been shipped out of Mostar by my uncle. He took me with him because, being fairly bright from a young age, my family thought my prospects would be greatly enhanced by an English education- hence uncle Milo's intervention. Well, I wasn't quite as bright as they had imagined, I don't suppose, but nonetheless got three good 'A' levels and joined the army who sponsored me through university. You see I liked the active life. Shooting, hunting, sport, and the rest. I thought the army would suit me admirably. Uncle Milo agreed. Anyway, to cut a long, tedious story very short, I graduated in Accountancy and joined the audit team, but still excelled at the soldiering bit. I was recruited to join a special unit after seeing active service in the Falklands. I did some good undercover work, which by necessity could receive no headlines."

Joanne was puzzled.

"What do you mean?"

Nick shrugged.

"It was war. Even an accountant had to do his duty. No, what happened was that there was a traitor in my unit. I caught him passing information by short wave giving out positions and plans. He saw me, watching him and, well I had to kill him to save myself. Next thing, or rather the next day we were pinned down by a group of about twelve Argies. We were isolated from the rest- just three of us, and the dead captain. It was a nasty old fight but, I discovered a real talent for killing. I shot four dead, stabbed two others and the rest fled. The whole incident was a little embarrassing to the army, a traitor in the time of war and all that, but I was approached to join an undercover team, which I accepted, and the whole story was covered.

I didn't mind. I loved the thrill of the whole incident, and twice more during the conflict I went behind enemy lines with specific orders to kill such a colonel, or other. It was exciting, thrilling even, and when the war finished, I was a little disillusioned. Shall we say that accountancy lost some of its appeal after that?

The head of the undercover team asked me to stay on with him after the war. He was ostensibly a major in Admin. But I later learned his rank was much, much higher. The rank of major gave him the anonymity he needed to operate with. Like I said it is a long story.

Anyway, over the next ten years or so I became a hit man, an assassin, call it what you will. My job was to go deep into enemy territory and take out a specific target."

"Enemy territory? What enemy territory? Apart from the Falklands conflict we have had no wars, have no enemies" Tim asked. Nick cocked his head to one side.

"We, the country has many enemies. Countries work against our best interests, put the lives of our citizens at risk. You ask what enemy territories? Well there were many. The old soviet bloc was rife with enemies, Iran, Iraq.

More recently my own homeland, regimes in South America whose ambition is to supply the western world with endless quantities of drugs to ensnare our young people. Believe me, there are many such enemies about."

"But, but take out? You mean murder people don't you?"

He looked at Tim's paramour. She seemed a little aghast at what he was saying. He smiled poured more brandy and continued.

"Murder, kill, take out. It all amounts to the same thing. You see, we're all going to die. The only certainty in life. Tim and I know that better than most don't we? Some people earn the right for a quick end, by hastening others to unwished-for deaths. I'm an accountant by training; I merely balance the books.

I have no conscience about what I did. To establish some kind of order, to influence the outcome of events, yes and to save lives, then it was sometimes necessary to take one life to spare ten."

"But you have no right to judge. To play God."

"Joanne, I know what you are saying. I have held the same conversation with myself many times. But when you have seen these places, when you have witnessed first hand, the reality behind the scenes, then you start to think differently. The suffering, the misery, and the sheer brutality these people inflict on others- why usually their own countrymen- then well I do not sit in judgement- I just deliver the judgements. The evidence is so overwhelming, that they are guilty as charged. All I did was to hasten the judicial process. I do not act as God. They will have to answer to him directly. As will I"

"Is that why they were after you? Foreign agents or something?"

"No Tim. Well not that I am aware. I'll come to that in a minute. Anyway, a few years ago the unit I was in was disbanded. Not the done thing, politically to have a squad of paid assassins in the pay of the British army. At that point my Major introduced me to the free market side of the business. I took on paid contracts to either shoot, strangle or consign to death in a manner which appeared natural or accidental. In actual fact about 85% of my contracts are the latter two."

"You mean people pay you to kill others, and to make it appear as an accident? Why?"

"Who can tell an individuals motivation? Business? Kill a competitor, leave the field wide open to become rich. Get rid of a troublesome wife, a jealous ex-lover, knock off your uncle to inherit his wealth. I don't know.

All I did know was that I could do it easily. I dismissed the inequity of it , after all I am due an untimely end, as are you. I didn't ask for it. It mattered little to me whether they had warranted it or not. They probably had earned it in some way. I certainly hadn't. Besides, it was thrilling. Yes thrilling. The hunt. In and out, do the job, take the money, move on. Like I told you before Tim, the money then becomes an object of repayment. I have amassed quite a stash I can tell you. It is a particularly well-paid profession. Anyway, over the years I considered all the people who had influenced my life in some way. People who had acted kindly toward me, people who hadn't. Yes, Joanne, in a way I became a judge. I judged their actions weighed up their good and bad, considered both innocence and guilt. You see the one thing that money brings is power. The power to influence lives. People who have acted with good intentions will receive suitable benefits from my estate, either in cash, land, business opportunities, operations, whatever is appropriate. Those who have acted badly shall receive equally weighted retribution. You know the kid who knocked you off your bike when you were young and laughed? Well he'll not find it funny when he wakes up to find his doors and windows bricked up. The business partner who ripped you off- here's one for you Tim- won't find it so amusing when you have sold the same goods as he sells for a fraction of the price. What matters if you lose money on each one? It's payback time. But then there's the priest who stayed up all night with your dying father, alone, cold, no one to thank him for his actions. How will he feel when he receives a cheque so that he can build the new hospice he needs for the dying. It's both revenge and retribution.

We all have certain talents. Mine, unfortunately is for killing.

I use it to the best of my ability."

There was a silence. Joanne was disturbed by all this. Tim less so. He had heard part of the argument before, but didn't then know what Nick's real profession was. He lit two cigarettes and passed one to Jo.

"Nick. So these people you shot. Who were they? Why the story of your death."

"That, my friend is the puzzle. I honestly don't know. I'll tell you my suspicions. Firstly, I am sure that they know- knew- of my job. That is certain. I also know that they were once some part of the army, or military. Whether they're on our side is uncertain, but I knew one of them personally. For reason or reasons unknown they were sent to kill me. To take me out and either prevent me from undertaking a contract, or to hide the fact that one of my victims was actually under contract any way."

"I don't understand" Joanne poured more brandy. Nick lit a roll up

"Let me put it this way. If I had recently killed someone, who the person who had set up the job, wanted to make sure no one ever found out it was a hired killing.."

"Then he'd kill you to stop you from talking."

"Exactly."

"Why then, not just hire another hit man to kill you?" Joanne was getting the hang of this now.

"That is the curious bit. To me, if that was what I wanted to do, would be what I would do. Hit the hit man. These jokers were official. Undercover agents, not private in any way. All the equipment was standard issue. I think that some one wanted me out of the way to cover something up which had been done in the name of officialdom."

"By the government?" Jo was shocked.

"Well someone in the government, or official department at any rate."

Tim shook his head. "But Nick, why then should they fake your death? Even Sheridan has worked that out."

"I think that someone acted on his own initiative by sending this squad after me, and now it failed so badly, are trying to either flush me out or lull me into a false sense of security." "Any ideas who? Or what they're trying to cover?"

"Not a one Tim. Not a one. The trail which led them to me has always been a closely guarded secret. To get to me via that route would implicate Cropwell, my Major. Trouble is, inept squads of agents aren't his scene. He'd have sent a single, top man after me. I think, or rather suspect that the false story is his idea, to try and tell me everything is OK now, he is in control. I don't know."

Joanne was leaning forward both hands holding her head. She was slightly red with the effects of the heat and the drink, but her mind sparkled clarity. He could see why Tim had taken to her. "Have you any way of finding out? Of contacting this major chappie?"

"Well, I'm currently trying to track him down. I hope in the next couple of days to have a phone number. I need to turn that into an address."

"Then what? Kill him?"

Nick laughed. "You know, I haven't thought that far ahead yet. I need to make contact. Knowing him as I do, he'll probably want me back in the fold again. What I need is some access to inside information."

"Sheridan?"

"I don't know Tim. Trouble is, once a copper, and all that. They tend to have a tremendous sense of duty and loyalty. His natural instincts may make it impossible for him to do anything other than want to bring me to justice."

Tim offered around some cigars Anthony had sent him for Christmas. He blew tight rings out.

"Mind you Nick. The heat would really be on then wouldn't it? I mean, a cover up exposed by faking your death. The pooh would certainly hit the whirly thing then wouldn't it?"

Nick smiled. "Certainly would."

Joanne decided that coffee might be in order.

"What next then?" He shrugged and stood up, helping to clear the table.

"I don't know. A lot depends on you two."

Jo stopped as the water began its journey through the coffee grounds.

"On us? What do you mean?"

"Well I have never told anyone what I do. Never told my life story before. Do you have the same sense of duty as Sheridan?"

"If we say yes, will you kill us?"

"Joanne. Don't be daft. I can disappear quickly and easily. You are friends, even though I have not known you for that long. You are in no danger from me, or anyone else. You could expose quite a bit by talking to an inquisitive reporter."

"Is that the way then? Blow it wide?"

"No Tim. At least I don't think so. I need to get to Cropwell. He is the key."

"We'll help if we can."

Nick put his hand on Tim's shoulder. "There's more."

Tim raised his eyebrows.

"You. When it's your time, I could ease your pain."

He noticed a tear in Joanne's eye. They had spoken on this subject before. Tim had a morbid fear of undue suffering. Couldn't take his own life. He had already asked the doctor.

"I offer my services, Tim. I have knowledge of certain drugs which will not be detectable, will act instantly. You'll feel nothing."

Tim looked at his lover. They embraced as tears cascaded down Joanne's pale cheeks. She bit her lip and the coffee gurgled. She nodded quickly. Twice. He kissed her and nodded back, then turned to his friend and held out his left hand which Nick took.

"Thanks Nick. It solves a problem."

He kissed Joanne on the cheek again and offered her his handkerchief, and released her.

"Now that's sorted, I suggest we all get seriously pissed. Nick.

You can stay the night. We have a spare room."

More and more alcohol was progressively consumed. It was like a great reunion, and a catharsis all at once. Tim watched Nick from time to time, noticed him relaxing, watched as his rapid security scans diminished and failed. He smiled to himself, that was good. He was relaxing. Despite knowing that he was a killer, murderer, assassin, no single word seemed adequate, there was still a bond between them. He smiled again as Joanne stumbled as she returned from the bathroom. She flicked back her hair and giggled. Alcohol had taken her.

She slumped in her chair and held her finger up, slightly slurring as she spoke.

"Now then Nicky baby. Just how many people have you killed?"

Nick drained his glass, and laughed as she tried to fill it once more, spilling more than she managed to get in the tumbler.

"I haven't a bloody clue. Dozens."

"Dozens? Bloody hell Nick. Are we safe?"

Tim held her hand, but it was OK she burst into laughter once more.

"As for me, I could murder another drink!"

Nick tried to pour her one but slipped to his knees. "It's no good. I've had it."

He slumped forward, drink having won that particular battle. Tim looked at Joanne, she was in no state to help. He told her to stay where she was and managed to get a semi-conscious Nick to his feet and steered him to the spare room and lay him on the bed, covering him with a duvet. He slipped his shoes off and left him to it.

Joanne draped herself over him when he returned, planting over zealous kisses on him, a potent erotic mixture of scent, natural musk and the juniper from the gin she had nearly drowned herself in.

"Come on, Jo. Bed."

"Oh yes please. Just take me."

He smiled at her. She would be asleep before her head hit the pillow.

"I'm glad about Nick getting pissed."

"Glad? About someone getting unconscious. Why?"

"It shows me one thing. He is relaxed with us. Off his guard..

It's good."

Joanne put her hand down the front of his trousers. He pulled her away.

"Come on then lover. Let's get you to bed."

Nancy looked at her French doors, and the marks on the outside. Someone had evidently tried to break in. She thought nervously about what Richard had said, suddenly she felt vulnerable, and alone. Rick had left to have lunch with his parents, and had asked her to join him. In truth they had fallen out over the subject, she felt she was too old to be taken to see mummy. He just said if they were to be together, then she had a duty. She lost her temper and told him to go away in no uncertain terms. Somehow, now she had him, she no longer really wanted him. Perhaps it was just the excitement of the illicitness of their affaire which was the real turn on. Even last night, a special romantic ordeal. Ordeal? Even that should not have been a chore, but so seemed. She had had to get drunk to see her through the night. They had argued and he had left in a huff. Well, good riddance. Now, well she was alone. Richard and Sally had gone away suddenly, to Austria for the holiday. Anthony was in Southampton, and well even Tim was lost to her now. She had called her mother and wished her a happy Christmas, but felt she should have been invited there for the day. She would have hated it, but felt miffed that she had been left alone for that day, of all days.

Her lunch consisted of a chicken breast grilled with some salad.

It was not the happiest of times.

She thought about Tim, and his cancer, and felt genuinely sorry for him. But then, she had her own future to consider. She wondered if she was in any danger, the door indicated that it was a possibility.

Her future was about as exciting as the day. She still wondered if she could not stop the contract, she could at least warn Tim.

She knew she could do nothing. If she admitted she had arranged

to have her husband killed, there was a very good chance of him

exacting his final revenge by telling the police about her. In

the event, she would be arrested, and not receive a penny from

the insurance company. Her lips must remain, by necessity sealed

CHAPTER 25

'Connection and search.'

"If, by any chance, you happen to find my head somewhere, could you please swap it for this one? It doesn't fit properly and hurts like hell."

Tim looked across to his friend and smiled. Joanne was in a similar state. She had been sick, and then fallen into a deep, undisturbable snoring sleep by his side. He had not fared so badly, despite the drink he slept lightly, in spite of the anodyne effects of the alcohol, he suffered pain. Now, well, apart from fatigue, the pain had subsided, and he felt reasonable.

"Greasy eggs and bacon you two?"

Nick just about managed to raise an eyebrow, and it was still sufficient to reveal disgust. He lit a cigarette, took two drags and stubbed it out, and utilised his hands to hold his head again. Joanne was about the same. She had taken a judicious swig from the orange juice carton, and then taken rapidly to the lavatory to recycle the juice, and returned, determined on only water.

As for Tim? He was starving. He made bacon butties, but he alone ate them. He looked at the less than pristine Nick before him. "What now then Nick? You can stay here just as long as you like you know? No hassle from us, eh Jo?"

She managed to indicate her agreement, but no more. "I think, if I may I'll spend another day here, then return to my studies."

"What studies?" Joanne managed her first words of the day.

"Chasing Cropwell."

"Oh, yes, of course. Will you kill him?" It seemed a harsh question. Perhaps it was. Perhaps everything he did was harsh. But life was hard, it was hard on both Nick and Tim, and all Nicks victims. He felt no urge to justify, or rejustify his actions. But her tone was disquieting.

"No. Not Cropwell. Only in self defence."

"Why did you say you thought he was after you again? Sorry Nick, it got a bit vague last night."

"Why? Only suspected it. You know the people sent after me only occurred after two of his contracts were fulfilled. I have examined them fully and can find no connection."

"Which contracts? Who did you murder?"

"Jo?"

"No, it's alright Tim. Honesty is the thing between us. Friends and all that. It is not something I am used to. But, it is fine. I told you didn't I?"

She shook her head. Despite all the excessive drinking she could remember everything perfectly clearly. But then she always did.

"Well." Nick furrowed his brow and winced with pain. "The timescale worked out that the two November hits seemed to precede the, er, the unwarranted attention."

He looked at them both, sipped some tea and continued.

"Lord Tarrant was the first.."

"Bloody shit?"

"Sorry?"

Jo looked at Nick then Tim.

"I remember it. Old man, died, left all his estate to some nephew, rising politician. Gave it up straightway, took the money and the hundreds."

"Hundreds?" Nick was puzzled.

"Yes. Chiltern Hundreds. It's what MP's take when they resign."

"Oh."

"You mean that was no accident?"

He shook his head.

"I'll spare you the details, but no. It was no accident."

"How would that compromise you Nick?"

"I have no idea."

There was a brief silence, and Nick tried some cold bacon. It was barely acceptable. He continued.

"Anyway other one was a chap named Taylor. It had to look like suicide. Put another bloke in the frame who was screwing his wife."

Joanne screwed her eyes tight, trying desperately to conjure up some deeply hidden thought.

"Knighton. Jeremy Knighton."

"Yes?" Nick said slowly.

"He was implicated in the scandal. Found a cufflink of his nearby, but had a cast iron alibi."

"How do you know all this?"

"Our Jo has a keen interest in politics."

"Politics?"

Tim looked at Nick. Joanne interrupted the thought waves between them.

"Yes, politics. Knighton? Cabinet reshuffle and all that? He was in line for Defence, had to back out and return to the backbenches. For a while. He'll return. Too good a man for that. Probably get Health or something."

"I didn't realise he was a politician. Anyway..."

"Actually, Nick, if you're looking for a connection there is an obvious one."

He slanted his head sideways, attention tight, headache receding.

"Well. It's a bit convoluted I know, but Knighton should have had Defence in the recent reshuffle, but next in line was Jeremy Arran-Harris. You know, Lord Tarrant's nephew. But, well, once he knew he had the inheritance he legged it, and who can blame him. Instead it eventually went to Andrews. Don't you remember? There was a delay for a few days until the reshuffle was finally resolved."

Nick had a problem in focussing his thoughts, but they clarified as Tim verbalised them.

"So basically, the post of minister for Defence would have gone to Knighton, but he was implicated in a messy suicide by his lovers husband, and his successor didn't take up the post because he had just inherited fabulous wealth?"

Joanne nodded. Tim continued.

"Both events which our friend here precipitated?"

She nodded again. Nick was now focussed.

"So now Andrews has the post?"

She nodded.

"Tell me, Joanne, you seem to know quite a bit about politics?"

She once more nodded. He continued.

"Doves and hawks?"

She nodded again. He sipped more tea, his mouth felt very dry.

"The man who was shuffled out?"

"Courtney-Masters? Dove. Big soft white dove. Held the post for six years."

"Knighton?"

"Dove."

"Jeremy Arran-Harris?"

"Dove-ish."

"Andrews?"

"Hawk. Very."

"Shit."

"Doveshit or hawkshit?"

Nick stared absently at her. It had sunk in. The link. The reason for the hunt.

Sheridan spent a lonely Christmas, away from everyone, alone and unwanted. It didn't disturb him unduly, it gave him time to think. Sometimes it was about the past, and the future, but largely it was about the case which had troubled him more than any other he could remember. His thoughts drifted towards Mrs Theobald, and he wondered what kind of Christmas she and her children and grandchild would have. If nothing else they all deserved better, deserved justice. He made himself a promise not to let her down.

Back in his hotel room the next morning Nick felt better, head clear now, his resolve renewed, direction assured. He would seek out Cropwell and have a private word with him. It would have to be so. He needed reassurances, personal ones directly from the major as to his future safety and security. He worked through most of the day, enhancing the recorded pulses from the relayed telephone call. He had been surprised just how easy it was to get through, but the Marcellus connection would have opened doors better than a key. He eventually had it. It was a Hampshire number he found the dialling code by painstakingly looking down the lists in front of him. He would have to do something similar with the much larger local directory. He yawned and stretched. He could do with the inside knowledge which a police or army computer would get him the information he needed instantly. Despite Tim and Joanne's suggestion he could not consider enlisting the Inspectors help. He would be too interested in bringing Nick to justice, and opening up something of a Pandora's box in the process. But then, that was his fall back position.

He visited Jo and Tim the next day.

"Look, I'll be away for a few days."

Joanne looked at him curiously. The initial warmth between them seemed to have cooled somewhat.

"Got another 'job'?"

"No."

"Tell me, Nick, do you get a fix from what you do? You know withdrawal symptoms?"

"Joanne? "

"No, Tim, it's OK. I know that it isn't exactly that easy to embrace a multiple killer is it? But then again the greatest heroes of the world have been killers haven't they? Alexander the Great, Richard the Lionheart, Napoleon, Wellington, Nelson. Did not Churchill order life taking on quite a huge scale? Do not doctors make decisions regarding life or death on a daily basis? But I am not here to justify my actions. Just to tell you I'll be away for a few days."

Tim looked at Joanne, wondered why the sudden burst of opprobrium came from.

"OK? Nick. When will you be back?"

"I'll let you know."

"Don't forget we'll be in Jamaica from the 29th, until the 5th."

"Ah yes. Well, I'll see you when you get back. Have a good holiday, both."

Joanne managed a smile.

"Happy New Year."

"Why were you so off hand with Nick just then? I thought you liked him?"

Tim was puzzled. Joanne lit a cigarette and swept back her hair. She paced the floor, as she often did when she was weighing her thoughts.

"In a way I do. I enjoyed the day he spent with us. A pleasant man, I can see why you like him so much."

"But?"

"But. Well, I can't get by the fact that beneath his gloss of good humour and the rest, there lurks a killer. Someone who takes life, yes a murderer. It's just wrong."

"Murderer? That's a bit strong isn't it?"

"Is it? What else would you call it? A shuffler-off of mortal coiler?"

"I thought I was the one who did sarcasm."

"You are."

"This is troubling you isn't it?"

She managed a smile and shook her head. "Yes, and no. I know we all got a bit emotional the other day when he said he would ease your pain, as it were, but, well you said that Bob Jeffries would do the same. I feel better with that option".

He nodded slowly, recalling the conversation with Bob. He had called it the 'double effect'. He would administer a painkiller to take away the agony at such a high level that it would take his life. It was ethically in order for him so to do, there was no compromising anyone's morals, or breaking of any laws- technically.

"There is still time to talk that particular one through. In the meantime we have a holiday to enjoy."

It was New Years eve when he arrived in town. A pleasant Hampshire setting, skirted by barracks and yet retaining some character of its own. He dialled the number locally this time.

"Hello. May I speak to the OC?"

"Please state the exact name of whom you wish to speak." He thought quickly, remembering his strategy, In all the time he recalled that Cropwell always had the same ADC. Felton. Weasily little man.

"Look, could you put me through to Felton. Captain I believe."

There was a brief pause.

"Hello. Felton here."

"Ah Felton. I need to get a message to you in person. Hand delivered today. I need to know your whereabouts around seven this evening. Sorry to interrupt on New Years and all."

"Who is speaking? What is the nature of the message?" Nick sweated a little. He knew that he could blow it all here. He trusted his instinct and lowered his voice.

"Andrews. I am his personal messenger."

"Name of?"

"Jameson."

"Hold a moment."

Nick sweated more. He knew that Felton would be checking, possibly even tracing the call. He looked at his watch, he would have to cut it in less than a minute.

"What did you say the nature of the message was?"

"I didn't. Eyes only. It's boxed."

"OK. Meet me at the officers' mess in Green Camp at seven. I will need to verify your pass then."

"Fine. Will I be able to clear security?"

"I shall arrange it."

The receiver went dead. He exhaled sharply and quickly left the call box. So far so good. He knew at least that Felton was there. Where he was, was a good chance of Cropwell being there. He recalled the New Years he had spent under Cropwell. Yes, Felton had always been there. Trouble was, he would recognise him, but Nick smiled to himself, and returned to his car. He had decided to first get in, then lay in wait.

"Interesting call that sir."

"Oh?"

"Yes. Direct call, asked for me by name, said he had a special message from Andrews which needed to get to me tonight."

Cropwell looked up, and removed his glasses. He raised his eyebrows.

"Direct? Not through Gordon?"

"No sir. That was the odd thing. Anyway, he said the message was boxed, and his name was Jameson."

"Does it check out?"

"Can't tell sir. Staff records for the department show a Jameson, well two, but nothing else. No special clearance."

"What do you think?"

Felton frowned.

"In other circumstances I would not bat an eyelid. Any decent civil servant would be trusted with a sealed box. In fact the less they know the better. That is not the issue."

"Andrews?"

"Exactly. I wonder why he would make direct contact?"

"Did he ask for me?"

Felton shook his head.

"No sir. Asked for me by name."

Cropwell shrugged.

"Maybe it's kosher. Line normally runs from Gordon to you. Maybe Gordon is away?"

"Yes sir. Anyway said I'd meet him at the officers' mess tonight at seven. Just before the do."

"Fine, Felton. Take the usual precautions will you? I should be inside by then, but I may hang back just to get a view. Try to get Gordon will you? See if he is aware."

Felton left Cropwell's office and returned ten minutes later.

"No reply anywhere sir."

"Probably away then"

CHAPTER 26

'New Years Eve.'

He stalked the perimeter fence as if circling an injured prey, assessing weaknesses, eyeing up opportunity and planning the final assault. It was all relatively familiar fare. No complex surveillance, pressure pads, photoelectric beams or such to negotiate, not like a really secure area such as the armoury would have. There was a straightforward tall fence, overhung barbed wire outcrop. Gravel path regularly patrolled by guards with dogs. They varied the routine- good practise- but gave a window of a minimum of seven minutes before the patrol passed again, sometimes stretching to seventeen. He would rely on the seven.

In the car he had the dress uniform of a lieutenant, and quickly pulled it on in a lay-by someway from the barracks. He donned a light overall and drove back to the weak spot on the fence perimeter, a corner, just obscured from a sentry post by an outhouse. That would be perfect for him to get out. Flat roof, fence and over. Getting in was less simple. Nick donned his chain mail gloves so that he could grab the barbs with impunity, and checking around for one last time he took a short run through the foggy nights chill and leaped high grabbing the top rail with both hands. Unhitching a roll of thick foam bedding he rolled it down the sloping side of the fence and in a rapid movement swung over and rolled down onto the gravel path below. Squatted momentarily to make sure he was not seen then jumped and pulled the bedding down after him. It was ripped, but would serve for the outward journey, should he need it. He quickly rolled it back tight, and shinned the drainpipe to the outbuilding laying it in the guttering. It would survive until morning undetected.

The gravel swept smooth, he then placed the body of a dead rabbit next to the fence. Any inquisitive dogs would be side-tracked by it, or more importantly, their handlers would be. He slipped off his overall and neatly tossed it on the roof with the bedding, then silently moved back and right to make an entrance from somewhere near the junior officers' clubroom. He checked the time. It was six thirty, all was going to plan. He had still kept the Trevor Jemsom looks, and now the moustache had grown bushier. If any one recognised him, he would be very unlucky.

The entrance to the mess was manned, if that were the right word, by two officers who took in the mess invitations, he did not worry about that, but hung back just out of sight, but not hidden from the entrance. Early arrivals were few, but he knew well Cropwell's preferences in such matters. In early, survey the place, sit at a quiet table in the bar, upstairs room if one was available, and make occasional forays into the throng to give a word to his underlings. It was only ever duty for him. Fourteen long, cold minutes passed before he espied his quarry. He looked exactly as he usually did. Moustache a little bushier, and flecked with grey, but otherwise unaffected by the years. He looked constantly round him, saw a figure in the shadows, but ignored it when he saw the tobacco smoke billow out, someone enjoying a crafty smoke, probably on duty. He was waved through and Nick saw him take a left through the main mess hall door. He stubbed out his smoke and moved quickly to the rear of the hall and slipped in through the outside kitchen door, slipping past the sacks of rice and flour into a red tiled short corridor which had a store cupboard off right and which led to staff toilets then to an outside corridor which served the patio area, then having unbolted the doors slipped into the back of the hall.

He was next to the stage, and the hall was in darkness as the lights and sound were being given their last test before firing up and turning the hall into a disco. The dining area was the other side of the stage and was being filled with a buffet of gargantuan proportions. He wandered casually over to the bar area nodding to a fellow officer as he did so. A young soldier carrying a tray approached him.

"May I get you a drink sir? Waiter only tonight."

"Thank you. I'll take a large G&T."

"50p sir."

Nick smiled to himself. So they were having a subsidised bash were they? There would be some serious headaches in the morning. Then he recalled his own from Christmas day. He tossed a £1 coin on the squaddies tray.

"Better get yourself one as well laddie."

"Thank you sir."

No doubt it would be the first of many. Nick waited only around a minute until his drink arrived and he used the time well. Inside the main door, to his right, was a cloakroom and toilets. Directly to his left the main lounge, and just past the lavatorial area a double door through which Cropwell had probably passed, unless he was desperate for the loo. He checked his geography again, just to be sure, and casually strolled across, and waited in good view of the doors. It was now 7.20. Felton would be tired of waiting by now, and would be in any time, probably having left instructions for him to be found should 'Jameson' turn up. He was a patient man and at 7.35 he entered the room and slipped through the double doors. Nick felt smug that he was closing in quickly on his quarry.

"Don't I know you?"

Nick jumped, felt the colour rush to his cheek, and gulped slightly on his drink.

"Sorry?" He looked at the tall brute of a man before him.

Lieutenant Colonel. Nick knew him, his name was Samway-Jones.

Affectionately known as crusher by his men.

Nick saluted.

"Sorry sir. Not had the pleasure. I am Costigan.

Recently transferred from Two Para."

"Know Butler then?"

"Did sir."

"Did?"

"Yes sir. He took to Civvy Street last year. Or was it the year before?"

He knew that much at least. Butler had at one time been one of Cropwell's men. Moved to the paras, then last heard he had demobbed.

"Ah yes, of course. But you are familiar. Costigan eh? It will come to me. Anyway enjoy the bash. Catch you later."

"Thank you sir."

He sipped his drink and looked quickly around and saw Felton re-emerge into the main hall and over to the main bar area. It was perhaps the one night of the year he didn't stay with Cropwell all the time.

Nick made his move, and walked to the toilet area. The place was fast filling with officers, wives and girlfriends, draped in their finest. He slipped through the double doors and took the carpeted stairs two at a time before halting at the top. Three doors confronted him.

The first a single door, he tried gently. It was locked. Probably a service door, or cupboard. Opposite it to his right a swinging door which he eased to and gently cracked open. Beyond was a small bar area and a few deserted tables. A barman and waiter were talking casually, awaiting the rush. He eased it shut. In front of him stood double doors, which he peered through onto a balcony area, which he hadn't spotted from the main hall. There were maybe twenty tables all unoccupied. By the balcony edge, looking over stood two men with their backs to him. One was his man. He quickly checked behind and around him and silently entered the area. He was unarmed, save for a one shot plastic disposable gun, which was sewn into the lining of his sleeve. He had decided against open warfare.

Slowly, casually he walked over to the two men and stood by the majors' side. He stopped talking to the other man and casually spoke over his shoulder without looking. "Hello sergeant. I wondered when you'd find me."

"Waiter. The same for me and. G&T for my friend. Excuse me Johnny, an old pal is here to see me."

It was all seamless as Nick was steered over to a table in the corner, facing the door, as ever, and sitting in front of his old CO.

"How are you sergeant? Still in one piece I see."

"Indeed I am Major, although not through the lack of trying, from certain quarters."

Cropwell nodded.

"Tell me, how did you get here to me? Were you the Jameson chap?"

Nick nodded, and Cropwell gave an unexpected laugh.

"Poor old Felton. He's having kittens. Thinks some secret ministerial box is stuck in traffic, or scattered over the countryside following some car crash. Ha."

He nodded again and smiled.

"So you made the connection then sergeant."

"Andrews?"

Cropwell nodded.

"Yes, but..."

"But you don't know where you fit in do you?"

"I don't know about fit in. Just want to know why, and how safe I am."

The major sipped his drink, and lit a cigar, glancing up in unison with Nick as the doors opened to admit four or five people.

"Look, we can't really talk here. It will be packed soon. Have my assurances that you are safe with me, and we can go to my quarters for a private chat. Is that OK?"

Nick looked at his one time mentor and considered. Ruthless yes. Devious? Definitely. But he had never given Nick cause to doubt his word, even the Priory Close pursuers were not really his method. It was just the trail that led them to Nick which was suspect. He nodded.

Cropwell lifted the cover from his watch face and tapped the glass twice.

"Look, chances are we'll see in the New Year. I'll just relieve the bar of a bottle. Do you like single malt?"

"Fine."

"Laphroaig? Have you got a bottle John?" He asked the bar man.

"There's some in store. I'll be a minute."

The barman disappeared in search of his quest, and Nick looked around him in his usual circumspect manner. Cropwell put on a false smile as they waited. The thought crossed Nick's mind whether

'Laphroaig' was a code word for 'Send in the troops.'

After five minutes the bar man returned with the bottle.

"Here we are Major. Shall I put it on your mess bill?"

"Please. See you later."

Cropwell lived in single quarters within the compound. It was an apartment within a two-storey block, which comprised suitable secure quarters for certain, special, officers. It was a short walk from the mess hall, and the night was closing a sharp frost in on them, and their breath billowed out in front of them as they walked. They did not speak and Nick kept his attention on full alert. They reached his billet, and the major swiped his security pass to allow them into the foyer and they then took a short corridor to his apartment.

"Here we are sergeant. We won't be disturbed here."

He unlocked the door and entered first, showing pointing Nick into the lounge whilst he hung up his coat. The instant Nick was through the door he was jumped on by three soldiers, all in dress uniform. He almost managed to twist and wriggle free but the sheer size and weight of his assailants was too great.

"Easy men."

The major warned, and Nick relaxed a little, and allowed them to search him. The single shot gun was a collapsed plastic tube along his sleeve, which went undetected. The bullet was disguised behind his cap badge. They checked his shoes, inner thighs, buttock cleavage and belt for concealed weapons. They found nothing. Felton reported the fact to Cropwell in a hushed tone.

"Completely unarmed. Not even a knife."

Cropwell nodded, and with a short nod of the head the other three moved from Nick and out of the door. Felton followed them. Before he left he nodded to the major and then closed the door after him. Cropwell indicated that Nick should sit in the armchair opposite. He sat down and poured them each a measure of the malt.

"Sorry about that sergeant. Had to be sure."

Nick was unperturbed. "I would have been surprised if you hadn't."

He offered Nick a cigarette and sipped his drink, as he eyed his protégé. He had a glint in his eye, the twinkle of a scheme.

"So you realised then that you were being chased did you?"

Nick gave a sarcastic laugh.

"A bit difficult not to. I mean, teams of armed men, screeching tyres and the like gave me just the inkling that all was not quite well."

Cropwell allowed himself a smile.

"Ah, but who eh?"

"Well, as it happens, I recognised one of them. Elliott. Used to be one of your men. I suspected your hand in it?"

"Elliott eh?"

He nodded sagely to himself.

"Yes, could well be. He transferred to Butlers crew, about a year ago."

"Butler? Colonel Butler? I thought he was one of your men as well."

"He was. You know, the same time you were in the side. Took the short trip to Intelligence for a while, About a year ago I lost touch, but he's heading up an undercover team now. Still does this business, you will probably have had some commissions from him. Anyway, you suspected me? Still do, no doubt."

"Yes, and no. Although the trail pointed at you, you know via Elliott, the line of communication was yours, the method wasn't."

"Glad to hear it. But how?"

"Well, if you had wanted me taken out, I don't think it would have been letter bombs, and squads of hit men. I think you would have sent your best man after me."

The major laughed out loud.

"Funny. You are the best man. I have told you often."

"Yes, thanks. But you know what I mean, don't you?"

"Yes. It was a clumsy attempt at concealment."

Nick nodded and sipped his drink.

"I suppose the Taylor and Tarrant contracts were the ones which needed the concealment."

Cropwell nodded, but didn't speak. He needed to know exactly how Nick had made the connection.

"Well, I then after quite a while managed to find out that those two untimely ends had opened the door for Andrews to take over, and get a leg up the ladder of promotion. Silly thing is, if I hadn't been chased, I would never had made the connection."

Cropwell shook his head, and drained his glass.

"I knew it all the time."

Nick eyed him, but continued.

"Was I right to assume that the 'other' Nick Curcic was your way of telling me that the dogs were called off?"

"It was certainly my idea. Let me say sergeant, that the dogs were never loosed by me. It was done by amateurs, who don't understand the subtleties of our skills."

"How do you mean?"

"Well. You know my views don't you? I recall having the conversation with you before. The one where we on a strictly controlled basis, subtly influence policies and actions by the strategic removal of key personnel. As you said, the Taylor and Tarrant contracts illustrate

it ideally. The trouble is, is that, it being a refined process, means it has to be used sparingly. Taking people out on a large scale, debases it, and begins to border on genocide. As I said to you before, a team of four, like you, with skills and attitude to match would enable us to exert great influence on pan-European affaires for decades. Trouble is, some others are a bungling shower, with the wrong perspective and attitude."

"How do you mean?"

"Well, you, for a start. They didn't know you, and became paranoid in wanting total control that they decided to eliminate you, to cover their tracks. Trouble was, because they didn't know you, they underestimated you, and the thing blew up in their faces, so that it soon hit the headlines. I hope that my actions have prevented it from becoming common knowledge. I am not totally convinced."

Nick cracked his knuckles and looked at the major.

"Who, exactly, are they?"

"They, my dear fellow are Andrews and his flunkey, Gordon. They took my concept on, and have used it to gain some power, part of that is the re-establishment of my old unit- my pay off if you like. Trouble is, as I said, they do not understand the complexities of it. I believe that they have greater plans to wrest even more power and control. I understand that they have Butler, as their 'enforcer'. What you told me about Elliott confirms that. By the way, did Elliott shape up? I always thought he was pretty good."

Nick smiled.

"Not good enough, I'm afraid. He's dead."

The major smiled and poured more drinks, and there was a silence between them for a couple of minutes. Nick at least felt fairly sure that the major had not been involved in his chase, that what he had told him was the truth. He had never lied to him before. He had no need to now. After all, he reasoned. If he had wanted Nick dead, he would be dead by now.

"Sergeant - sorry I must find some different form of address for you now..."

"Nick. Call me Nick."

"Fine. Nick it is. Right well, I am of a mind to wrest control back from the bungling crew who have temporarily got control. I would enlist your skills to do this."

Nick smiled to himself. He wasn't sure whether he was ready to come back in from the cold just yet. To do Cropwell's dirty work for him. He guessed what he wanted, he needed Nicks skill to take out Andrews, this Gordon possibly Butler. Trouble was, they were high profile men. Powerful men. No doubt they too had reciprocal plans concerning Cropwell. They had tried once before with Nick, they could try again. He would need thinking time. Cropwell raised his glass to his former pupil.

"Happy New Year"

CHAPTER 27

'Butler for hire.'

"It's absolutely bloody freezing!"

"Are you trying to tell me, darling, that you prefer the West Indies to dear old blighty?"

Joanne leaned forward and kissed him as he fiddled with the door lock, the frost nipping keenly at his fingers. She jumped up and down.

"Hurry up!"

At last they were in the car, cold and breathing clouds of icy breath into the atmosphere as the engine reluctantly stumbled into life, and they headed home.

The holiday had been glorious, a precious set of memories to hug as the days grew bleaker, as the winter of Tim's illness took its icy grasp.

They arrived home at last, and pushed wide the door past the small mound of late Christmas cards, bills and assorted mail. Amongst that was a hand delivered letter which was from George Sheridan, asking them to call him.

He came over the next day.

"Happy New Year, to both of you. Did you enjoy your holiday?"

"Fantastic, thanks inspector. How may we be of help?"

Sheridan smiled and eased himself into the armchair indicated.

"Well, it's more of a courtesy call really. A progress report. You see, I have no one else to share my ideas with. I hope you don't mind?"

Joanne did. Since they had last met, and talked over the whole issue regarding Nick, she had met him, been drawn into the web of intrigue which covered him. She felt like an accomplice, and was sure she must have been blushing, but hoped it didn't show. Sheridan continued.

"Well, I have managed to get quite a bit of a lead on who may be involved in the cover up, if my theory is correct. Trouble is, the stone wall of officialdom is thwarting me. With my usual lines of inquiry closed, I hope there may be the smallest of shreds of a clue from you which might help."

Tim sipped a coffee. He had to be careful. He had seen Nick, knew the truth, but was unsure whether Sheridan ought to be involved any more. He and Joanne had spoken whilst on holiday about it, and the matter still lay unresolved between them. Tim agreed with Nick. Once a copper, always a copper. Anything he found out about Nick he would invariably use against him in a court to bring what was, as Joanne had pointed out to him, a killer.

He sighed a little, and nodded as if giving assent to the inspector.

"Well, I think there is a military connection."

"Nick was in the army, after all."

"Yes, Tim, probably a connection there. Anyway, I have a name, but nothing else. No rank or attachment." He looked up at them both and repeated the name.

"Cropwell."

"Major." Joanne blurted out.

Sheridan looked at her, his head cocked quizzically to one side.

"Major? How did you know that?"

If she suspected a full colour before, she was now certain. She shot a glance to Tim.

"Didn't you er..."

Tim nodded. "Yes, er yes I did. I, er I remember Nick saying his old boss was a major. Major Cropwell."

Sheridan narrowed his eyes at them both. He did not voice his concern and painted a smile on his face.

"Ah yes thank you. That could well be a help. I don't suppose you remember the outfit do you?"

Joanne stayed silent. She had done enough damage. Tim furrowed his brow.

"I don't know. He was an accountant. Probably some administration posting I shouldn't wonder. "

Sheridan nodded and made small talk for a few minutes before excusing himself, and wished them a goodnight. He walked to his car and sat in it a few minutes. They were acting very suspiciously. He felt sure that they were concealing something. Probably been in contact with Church. It was a pity that he couldn't mount a surveillance operation on them, see if he turned up. But at least he had been spared some frustration, at least he knew which of the three Cropwell's he was looking for. Problem was, he didn't know how to find him.

Nancy was still struggling with her conscience. She wanted to stop her contract. Wanted to let Tim live his few months out in peace, and yet knew she would jeopardise everything she was entitled to. She had arranged to meet with Richard and Sally, she would talk it over with them.

The atmosphere was cool with regard to Richard, but he excused himself, having to catch up with his business matters which had been neglected due to his quick holiday. As he left them he called to Sally.

"Don't forget I have a visitor popping over around ten."

She nodded. Nancy looked at her.

"Sorry, Sally. Am I in the way?"

"No, no, Nancy. Not at all. Some old pal of his. In the area for the night. He said he'd pop in for a quick reunion. Leave us to it. How's Ricky?"

"Ricky is no more. Packed it in with him. He was getting too clingy, stifling me. Now I'm free I am enjoying my own space. There are plenty more fish in the sea."

Sally gave her a glass of wine and lounged opposite her.

"Interesting. Still having second thoughts about you know what?"

She nodded.

 "Trouble is. I don't think I can stop it."

Sally didn't answer. She and Richard had had words on the subject whilst on holiday. She gulped nervously. Richards's visitor was to be Tom Butler. The contract arranger. She allowed Nancy to continue.

"I can't tell anyone, can't warn Tim, because if I do, I'll be compromising my, er, 'inheritance'. What do you think?"

"Me? You're best rid, as you had already decided. I don't think his illness really changes anything, and besides.."

 she hesitated a moment then continued. "..besides, you might actually be doing him a favour."

"A favour? How do you work that out?"

"Well, you will be stopping his suffering. Stopping him dying in agony. The 'hit' will be quick and unexpected. It would probably be what he would want."

Nancy nodded slowly. That made sense. It was the vindication she needed.

"Sally. You're right. What have I been worrying about all these past weeks. You're dead right. Thanks Sally. You're a pal."

They talked on some more, slipped back into their usual round of gossip, who was with who, which man was most likely to fall under Nancy's spell. They temporarily forgot the cause of their mutual angst.

The doorbell rang and Sally made to answer it but Richard was there first. He smiled and pulled the partition doors close to. Nancy raised an eyebrow.

"Just some silly business associate."

Richard straightened his tie, and smoothed back his hair. Old habits died hard. His old friend, Tom Butler and he had graduated from Sandhurst together and had been in the same regiment. Richard had made it to Captain, but Butler had always been the most ambitious in their class. He was married to the army or had been, and was latterly Lieutenant Colonel. Despite their old friendship, Butler had been a demanding commanding officer. Tough, determined and ruthless. Richard had assumed he was out of the army now, but was wrong. He opened the door. Standing in front of him was Tom Butler. He was tall, gangling almost, and carried a well-lined face on top of square shoulders. A large mole blemished his top lip, and he had a broad grin, which showed, off his gold tooth. His balding pate reflected the amber streetlights. He wore a thick sweater, smart trousers and held a recently removed checked cap. Behind him was his car, one man inside one man peering up the path to Richards's house.

"Sir." Was all Richard could manage.

Butler seemed remarkably friendly.

"Richard! Nice to see you old boy."

He shook hands.

"No need for all the 'sir' business. That's past now. Don't forget our old friendship eh?"
"Come in, er Tom. Come in."

They entered the house and Richard led him into his study. He temporarily left him in there whilst he nipped into the living room retrieving a bottle of scotch and two tumblers. He smiled at the girls but said nothing. Inside the study he poured them drinks and raised glasses.

"Cheers. The regiment." Richard offered.

"No. The future. Cheerio."

They sat down in the small room. It held two comfortable leather chairs, a computer at a desk along with a small filing cabinet, telephone, fax machine and a small stack of assorted papers. Richard ran his own business these days, importing and exporting various goods via a small fleet of lorries. It was doing very well.

"Business good Richard?"

"Great thanks, er Tom. Keeping busy."

"Good. I'm pleased for you. Always were well organised. If there is anything I can do?"

Richard frowned a little then managed a smile. He thought his business now involved hiring assassins. He wondered how he could help. Butler noted the frown and laughed.

"Don't worry Richard. My main business isn't the 'agency' you know. That's just a sideline."

"Oh? What is your main job then?"

Butler studied the light through the cut crystal of his tumbler and sniffed appreciatively of the malt. He declined the offer of another.

"Actually, Richard, what I am going to tell you means that I must remind you of your commitment to the Official Secrets Act."

"Of course. You don't need to ask."

"I do, actually. Anyway, I know you are trustworthy. Anyway. I never left the army."

Richard was puzzled. Only a few months ago he had attended the reunion of his old regiment. It was now disbanded, testament to economies of government purse tightening and an increasingly more stable world. All those there were now civilians. Apparently. "Yes, I know the old regiment has gone, but I took a special assignment. Very hush-hush, so forgive me if I can't fill you in on the details, but suffice it to say that it involves national security."

Richard nodded. He understood what the words 'national security' meant. They meant 'keep your nose out'. He poured himself another drink. Butler leaned forward in his seat and looked directly at his friend. He had the natural air of authority vested in him. "Anyway, to cut to the chase. The reason I am here concerns my sideline."

"Sideline?"

"Don't be coy Dickie. The 'agency'."

He waited for Richard to allow acknowledgement to be given.

"The recent contract you asked me to arrange."

"Oh that."

Richard felt apprehensive. He knew that there was some friction regarding Nancy wishing to cancel it. So much friction that they had taken to Austria for some sanctuary. He feared what Butler was about to say.

"First, the matter regarding the cancellation. Does the client realise that it is impossible?"

"She accepts that, reluctantly."

He didn't think it prudent to say that she was sitting in the next room sipping wine.

"Good. The reason for that is that, well, the contract is set with a particular operative who shall we say has gone a little off the rails."

"In what way?"

"That bit is the Official secrets part. The man in question is working for, well let's just say a foreign country with ambitions on some of our former colonies."

Richard gave a knowing nod, but had no idea what Butler was talking about. "How does that fit in with..."

"Ah yes. Coincidence. He is a gun for hire, who happens to be embroiled in your back yard."

"How do you know this?"

"Which part don't you understand?"

"Well all of it."

"If you keep quiet, I shall explain." The old authority silenced Richard.

"This operative has been recently found to be a traitor, so naturally we are keen to trace him. Trouble is, he has gone to ground. There's the coincidence if you like. As you know, I have been acting as a go-between for the agency, and he was one of the operatives of that scheme. Anyway, although he has gone to ground he has confirmed that he has accepted one particular contract which is not yet fulfilled and has a date for completion in less than two weeks."

"Ah. The contract I asked you to arrange?"

"Exactly."

"So what do you want me to do?"

Butler stood and placed his glass on the desk and paced the room, arms behind his back.

"First, I need to know more about the target. Who he is, where he lives, works, his movements etc, so that I can put surveillance on him, catch out our rogue spy. Then, the person who set the contract, I'll need some background on her."

Richard shook his head. "Why?"

"Because, my friend, there is a danger of this thing going wrong. If needs be, she may have to be silenced, but so far it is only a possibility."

Richard nodded. He had half suspected that that would be the outcome of Nancy wanting to cancel the hit. He knew Butler of old, there was no way that he would let a mere woman get in his way. Despite this, he felt slightly relieved. Butler had come to him for help, so he knew that he must be in the clear. Safe. He valued his own neck much more than he could ever value Nancy's. He nodded to his old CO.

"Anything I can do. I'll do it."

"Good man. I knew you would. You'll be doing us all a great service."

Butler left a couple of minutes later with some details concerning both Tim and Nancy. He didn't have Tim's new address, but would find it the next day and call Butler with it. In the car Butler sat in the back seat. From the shadow a square jaw jutted, and a hand brushed back a mop of sandy hair.

"Well?"

"Like taking candy from a baby."

"Does he suspect anything?"

Butler smiled as the car drew away from Richards's house. He looked at Gordon.

"As I said to you before. This is like manna from heaven. A chance to properly take Curcic out. And, as I said, once Curcic is out, so is Cropwell. He has no one near him, but then, neither do we. No, my friend, once Curcic is eliminated we can consider what to do about Cropwell."

Gordon frowned.

"I really don't see why one man is so critical to all this."

Butler sighed.

"Curcic, as I have told you before is the best. You know what he did in Nottingham, in Burton. You know he has met with Cropwell. It won't be long before Cropwell twigs. And Marcellus. Don't forget Marcellus."

Gordon nodded, acceptance back with him.

"How could I?"

CHAPTER 28

'Shoot out at Linden Grove.'

Tim concealed much from Joanne, regarding his illness. His pain was getting worse, and sometimes it was too much effort to continue. Even in Jamaica he had found it very difficult to hide his distress from her. He had consumed quite a few tablets, despite his natural resistance to them and had obtained more powerful drugs from Bob Jeffries. Bob accompanied to the hospital for a follow up, not that there was any different news concerning his condition, but Bob was both a friend and concerned doctor. The cancer was spreading quickly, but that was not news, and results from liver tests were not encouraging. "What's my ETDA, then doc?"

Bob raised his eyebrows as he broke off from his consultation with the registrar.

"ETDA? I don't understand?"

Tim managed a smile. "Estimated time of death arrival."

Bob couldn't return the smile.

"A little sooner than we thought, but not by that much."

"How long?"

"Like I said.."

"Come on Bob. No shit. It's too late for that. How much longer have I got left."

"Well you know we can't set a clock on it, don't you? But two months. Three tops."

"Shit and bollocks." He delivered the words in a straight, unaccentuated voice. Somehow that made it sound more shocking. He shrugged his shoulders, slipped his jacket on.

"Oh well. Can't be helped. It'll soon pass."

He looked straight back at Bob. Their eyes locked and asked questions of their friendship. Tim smiled again, verbalising his thoughts.

 "No. Not yet. I'll let you know when. I'd better have a word with Joanne."

He could say no more, save to mumble his thanks to the registrar and bit his lip as he trudged away with Bob Jeffries by his side.

George Sheridan was true to Nick's estimation. Once a copper, always a copper, and a damn good one at that. His suspicions had been aroused by his little talk to Tim and Joanne. He suspected they had seen Nick recently, in which case, knowing Tim's condition he would probably see him again. Since he could not enlist the usual methods of surveillance, he did what he could on his own. He reasoned that since Tim and Joanne were still working during the day the most likely time for Nick to revisit them was in the evening. Chances are they wouldn't go out, but stay in for a talk, or a meal. They knew him and his car, so he sited himself a fair distance from Joanne's home, but still kept a clear view on proceedings, when he could, and always called it a day around one o'clock.

What he saw was a surprise.

It was bitterly cold sitting in his car in the sub-zero temperatures of January. He had done it before, on many occasions, but always with support. It was lonely, cold and dispiriting on his own, save for what he witnessed. Some way closer to Joanne's, alternating between different nights were two cars with two, sometimes three men inside. The cars were a red Cavalier, and a white Cortina. Both old enough to be easily missed in the street. Sheridan didn't. He looked at the men, just normal, everyday looking men, blending nicely into the neighbourhood.

"Right then Sherry my boy. We seem to have some professionals staking out Miss Woodward's place do we? I wonder who they may be? Ha. You're not so daft are you Sherry? Seem to be on the right lines after all."

He cracked the window seal to relieve some stuffiness from the cigar smoke filled car and watched and waited. He watched and waited the next night too, and the next and the next, but to no avail.

Meanwhile he had made one concession to seeking help on this 'hobby' of his. Maureen was enlisted to chase up Major Cropwell and his whereabouts. Trouble was, any direct enquiry would have raised the flag of suspicion in Cropwell's wide web. So using Maureen's army friend, and her husbands cousins brothers cleaners aunts sister-in-law, or whatever the particular informal line of communication was, he set about tracking the elusive major. It would have been easier to find Lord Lucan riding Shergar, but often gossip bears more fruit than factual information. He took Maureen for a drink after work, since she said she had some information for him. He had to break off from his vigil, and felt a little guilty at so doing.

Maureen was nice. He had known her for years, knew her husband well and they had always enjoyed harmless verbal flirtation with one another. He brought the drinks over to a quiet table in the corner of the lounge bar at the Golden Hind. "Here you are gorgeous."

"Cheers George."

They sipped their drinks and made small talk for a couple of minutes before George steered the talk to the point of their liaison.

"You said you had found something out about my mysterious major?"

"Mysterious! You can say that again. He's almost invisible- officially."

"And unofficially?"

"Well, from what I can gather, and all this is off the record,"

George nodded.

"that our major is very very hush-hush. He seems to have the ear of Generals, and politicians."

"A Major?"

"Well. Personally I think that his rank is a lot higher than that, but keeps the major title because it gives him a sort of anonymity."

"Blimey Maureen. You're turning into a regular Sherlock aren't you?"

"Thanks Georgie, but anyway, the major spent some time on overseas tours, Middle East, Bosnia, Falklands etc, always right in the thick of things. Exactly what he does, I don't know. Right now he is in Bordon, in Hampshire. Apparently he's quite aloof, snotty. Never passes the time of day with anyone, often slips away for a few days unannounced. But that's all."

He leaned over and planted a big kiss on her forehead.

"That's all! Bloody brilliant. More than I could have hoped for."

"George? What is so important about this major? Why is everything so hush-hush about him? Why are you keeping this such a secret?"

He leaned forward conspiratorially. He didn't like lying to her, but felt he had to, to protect her from unwanted enquirers.

"Like I said before. I suspect he is responsible for a hit and run. Trouble is, because he is so well important, I think there's a cover-up to protect him. Call me old fashioned, Maureen, but I don't think it's right. Once I have the necessary evidence, I shall nail him. What you have told me tonight will help me get it. More wine?"

Richard and Sally were on their own. Both their guests had gone.

"Was that who I think it was?" she asked.

"And who do you think it was?"

"Come on Richard. Don't play games. It was Butler wasn't it?"

He nodded. She had never met him.

"What did he say?"

"Say? Nothing. Well nothing which need concern you."

"Don't be so damn condescending."

"Look, Sally. Everything's fine. There's no bother regarding this contract thing with Nancy, he's assured me of that. He just needed a word about some business contacts of mine. He's spreading his wings on the continent and wanted my help to aid him. We were close at one time you know. He always trusted me."

"And do you trust him?"

"Doesn't enter into it."

Nancy opened her mail. In it the bank statement. She was well overdrawn, and she quickly scanned the credits and debits. There was no salary payment for Tim.

"Bastard! He's screwed me. Right."

She pulled on her coat and grabbed her car keys. It was seven in the evening, so he should be home. She would sort it out with him right now.

It was a frosty slippery night and she drove her car to Joanne's house, shut the door behind her and stormed up the path and hammered on the door. From a white Cortina opposite, two men noted her arrival and photographed her. From further back George Sheridan saw them see her. Behind him, well to the left, a small figure in a large coat rolled a cigarette and lit it. He leaned against his own car and noted the white Cortina. He would drive to the rear of Joanne's house and find a way over the back wall.

He walked the half mile or so to the street to the back of Joanne's home, fading in and out of shadows with accomplished ease, no footfall giving away his approach. In the roads side one man in a red Cavalier nudged the other awake as he caught a glimpse of the scurrying figure. Nick looked over and wondered about the car, but saw only one man; he was wearing a jacket and tie. Probably a salesman about to make a call, He hurried on, slipped down a darkened driveway and quickly and effortlessly skipped over the wall at the bottom of the garden and over into the small enclosed courtyard which served as Joanne's private sanctum.

The man in the car spoke into his radio.

"Suspect entering by rear. Repeat rear. Over."

There was a moments pause before the reply came back.

"Follow and observe only. Repeat observe only. Switch to private."

The men nodded to one another and put their earpieces in, checked their weapons and made silent pursuit. The white car likewise checked their weapons but remained in the car.

Nancy pushed past Joanne without a word and strode straight over to Tim shaking the bank statement at him.

"Bastard! I knew you'd do this!"

Tim felt the pain in his side, his stomach and back. Felt the band of agony tighten across his forehead. He was in no mood for a raging Nancy, he had had enough years of that. "Nancy. Shut up! I haven't a clue what you're talking about."

"This, you bastard. You said you'd pay your way, pay the bills, but you haven't. Your salary hasn't gone in. I suppose it's her idea is it?"

Joanne was now at Tim's side, and Tim managed a smile, then shook his head.

"Nancy, if you'll calm down, I'll explain. Obviously, there's been a cock up at the bank. Look, rather than we still operate the same joint account, I thought it better if you kept our old one, save transferring al the standing orders etc, whilst I had an account of my own, into which my money goes, and from where the sum we agreed would be transferred to your- or rather our old joint account. Don't you see? Obviously the money hasn't managed the electronic journey from my account to yours. Look, if you don't believe me.."

He stood slowly up and crossed to the small bureau, retrieving a letter from the bank. It was confirmation from them outlining exactly what he had just told her. She read it and put it down, stammering and reddening slightly.

"Oh, er.." She couldn't quite manage a 'sorry'.

"Here, have a drink. The coffees fresh."

She nodded and took the drink, and sat down at the table with them, she started a faint form of apology, but Tim halted her. There was little point in hearing an insincere justification for her actions, but they were spared by a gentle tapping on the French windows.

"Who the hell..?"

Tim walked over to the curtained doors and smiled. He managed the correct guess, pulling back the drapes and seeing the small dark figure of Nick looking behind him. Tim unlocked the door and let his friend in. Nick smiled as he saw Joanne, and widened it as he saw Nancy. Nancy did not return the smile. Her jaw dropped, as if she had seen a ghost, but to her she had. As far as Nancy knew Nick was dead.

"Hi Nancy. How are you? You're probably the last person I expected to see here."

"You.. you can say that twice. What about you? I thought.."

He smiled again. "Sorry to disappoint you."

George was out of his car now and popped the last piece of sandwich into his mouth, and wondered what Tim's ex was doing there, but his attention shifted very quickly as three cars swept into the street in front of Joanne's' house. The men from the Cortina jumped out and spoke to those emerging from the new cars. Men climbed from them, checked weapons, automatic weapons, rifles, serious stuff.

George gulped down the bread and radioed in.

"Gamma One Seven. Look quick. This is Sheridan."

The radio crackled back.

"Come in, I can hear.."

"Cut the crap. Just send armed response teams to Linden Grove and NOW. This is bloody serious."

"Inspector? Could you repeat that please?"

"Gamma one bloody seven- come on, you know it's me. Sheridan. Armed response team to Linden Grove. Now. There's something heavy going on. Have you got it?"

"Confirmed gamma one.."

He chucked the microphone back into the car and hurried down into the fray, pulling his warrant card out for full view.

Inside the house, the four had just started to talk when the heavy thud at the front door sent the wooden portal tearing from its' hinges. As Tim, Nancy and Joanne looked round, Nick sprang into action, leaping back from the chair he was sitting on and pulling a small pistol from behind his back and thrust himself into the corner next to the French window. He shouted out to the others.

"DOWN, DOWN, DOWN, DOWN!"

The instruction seemed plain enough.

As two men piled through the front door he pulled three shots from his weapon. The first man fell, head bleeding, and the second was spun round and to the floor as the bullet ripped through his shoulder. The third shot embedded in the wall by the door side.

The muzzle of a gun pointed through the door and fired into the room. Nick repeated his command, and Tim and Jo were already on the floor under the table. Nancy stood petrified. A sound was heard outside, and Nick crouched slightly, twisted to his left with his gun against the curtain and fired twice. The sound of the retort and breaking glass was echoed by a cry of pain. Two more shots entered via the front door loosening the plaster above Nick's head. Tim jumped up to pull Nancy down as she still stood motionless as more shots were fired. Tim and Nancy hit the ground with a heavy thud.

Nick was pleased she was out of the way. He shot the lights out with two more bullets, loosed another toward the door and ran quickly to the stairs and up, changing the clip in his pistol as he did. He heard more shots fire into the living room and cursed to himself as he ran into the rear bedroom, slipped open the roof light and pulled himself onto the roof. Below he could see three men, crouching to the rear of the garden. They didn't look up and he skipped lightly over the four rooftops which formed the mews where Jo lived. In the distance he could hear the wail of a police siren. He eased himself over the edge of the roof, and using the drainpipe as a steady, half fell, half dropped to the ground, and ran full speed away and into the night.

Sheridan joined the fray as he called out 'Police'. He was stopped by two armed men, who held him at bay. At the house doorway he could hear a voice calling out.

"Give yourself up Curcic. There are too many to escape. Throw out your gun."

Under the table, Nancy was sobbing. Tim rolled from on top of her and was breathing heavily. Joanne reached her hand out to hold him and she felt a wet, sticky patch on Tim's' shirt. From the faint glow of light from the kitchen she could see it was blood.

"Tim? Tim! Are you all right?"

He felt across and held her hand, and laughed out loud.

"Bloody silly point in my life to get all heroic don't you think?"

She leant over him and kissed him.

"Tim?"

She turned her head to the door. It had been a couple of minutes since Nick had dashed off, leaving Tim bleeding.. She heard the messages being shouted through her shattered door.

"Stop! He's gone. There's a man injured in here. Stop."

As Sheridan was arguing with his guards the sirens and lights of the cavalry screeched into the square. Butler raised his eyes to the sky.

"Great. The old bill. Just what we need."

He turned to his henchmen.

"OK boys, let them to it."

He walked over to Sheridan.

"I suppose you called these in did you?"

Sheridan was defiant. It was Butler and his type who had caused the mayhem in November. He didn't know him, but resented him. Butler signalled for his men to free him. George shook his shoulders.

"Yes, it was me. You lot are bloody maniacs. What do you think you're doing? This isn't twenties bloody Chicago you know."

Butler shook his head.

"You really don't know what you're interfering with do you?"

The armed police were now in a semi-circle around them and more cars arrived. Sheridan recognised Inspector Mawkes, tall, Kevlar jacketed and megaphone in hand.

"Put down your weapons."

Butler nodded to his men who did what they were told, and Butler returned to his car where he sat with the door open, as armed uniformed police buzzed around in a carefully orchestrated manner gaining access to the front door. Joanne called out again.

"Please. Can you get help? There's a wounded man in here. Please!"

Mawkes was at the door, Sheridan close behind him. The megaphone called out again.

"Lay down your weapons and come out."

Joanne screamed out.

"There's nobody here, save us. Please he's injured. Help!"

Sheridan pushed past Mawkes.

"Miss Woodward? Is that you? Are you alone?"

"Yes, yes inspector. Please get help."

George entered the room and switched on the main lights, Nick having shot out the table lamps. He went over to Tim and saw the pool of blood he was in. He coughed. Frothy rose wine coloured fluid came from his mouth as he did. George saw Joanne's worry squeeze her eyes wide. Noted Nancy hugging her knees, and paying no attention. He called out to the others.

"Ambulance! NOW"

CHAPTER 29

'Marcellus.'

Nick soon reached his car and sped away. He had to reach Cropwell and quick. He knew from his talk with the major that he had anticipated matters correctly. Butler was the man in the ascendancy, and as such saw Nick as the Majors' right arm, and one which needed amputation quickly. He would doubtlessly move on Cropwell next, if he hadn't already.

He headed south. Took the A444, picked up the M42 and M6 before he felt he could stop. He called the private number Cropwell had given him and recognised Felton's sharp tone at the other end.

"It's Curcic. I need to speak to Cropwell, urgently."

There was a seconds delay and he recognised the majors' voice.

"Yes?"

He quickly related scant details of the trap into which he had barely escaped. He thought onto Tim and the women. Sincerely hoped they were OK, and felt guilty at abandoning them.

"Right Nick. It is as I suspected. Get down here pronto. My quarters. They'll not move against me here. How long will you be?"

"About two hours."

"See you then."

The street and small square at Linden Grove was still buzzing an hour after the initial charge. Butler and his men had kept quiet, refusing to speak, until the chief constable and an army colonel arrived, and they spoke to Butler in private. Sheridan was fuming because he was not allowed near. Superintendent Wright had scolded him on doing 'private' work, and not keeping him informed, but his pomposity was deflated somewhat by the chiefs arrival. Butler and his men left with a police escort and the chief came over to Wright.

"Who raised the alarm on this little escapade?"

The super was only too pleased to point the finger at Sheridan.

"Ah Inspector Sheridan isn't it?"

Sherry was surprised he was recognised, but murmured his assent.

"Good. Then tell me all about it."

He looked down his nose at the superintendent. "We won't be needing you, Wright."

They sat in the Chiefs car, in private, and Sheridan related in totally his tale. Told of his suspicions over the Nottingham killings, the apparent cover up regarding Priory Close and the alleged death of Curcic. The fact that he had reappeared this very night in close pursuit by Butler and his men gave George the conviction that his theory was correct. He told of the mysterious major Cropwell and the impenetrable wall of secrecy surrounding him. The chief listened with great interest, neither butting in, nor questioning his inspector as he told his story.

"And the superintendent told you to drop your investigations did he?"

"Yes sir."

There was a pause. Sheridan spoke again. "Sir?"

"Yes inspector."

"Who, exactly were those men? Obviously army."

"Indeed. Top secret bunch- oh, this is strictly between us, for the moment- seem to be run by a well-respected Colonel. Butler. You saw him. Anyway, not quite got it all yet, but I got the call from the Home Office to meet up with the army to sort this out. Mitchell, who I arrived with, has the task of sorting Butler out, in conjunction with me. Inspector, this lot stinks."

Sheridan nodded.

"My feelings all along sir."

"Why didn't you come to me before with this?"

George felt himself blush.

"Quite frankly sir, with all the doors being slammed in my face, I felt I didn't trust anyone anywhere. I had to rely on myself, on my own instincts."

"Well done inspector. I think we ought to meet tomorrow at say noon. I should have a clearer picture by then. I'll be at the station. By the way."

"Sir?"

"Any word on the civilian casualty or this Curcic man?"

"Mr Oakes died on the way to the hospital sir, and no news regarding Curcic. Slipperiest man I've ever known, to escape that lot."

"Damn. Pity about Oakes."

"Yes sir. Nice man. Knew him quite well in the end. Helped a lot."

"OK. Thank you inspector, we'll speak tomorrow. Wright can clear this lot up. You get off to your bed."

George headed for the hospital. It had been two hours since Tim was taken away. He knew Nancy had gone home, or at least to her friends, but he wasn't aware where Joanne was. He guessed correctly. She was sitting, staring in a corridor just off the main entrance. A cold cup of tea was by her side, and she bit her lips, tears no longer flowing. She looked up as the inspector sat next to her.

"I'm sorry Miss Woodward. Really sorry."

The tears started again. She caught her breath. It was difficult to talk openly. Her feelings swamped normal functionality.

"It's so unfair. We had so little time anyway. Now...there are no new memories for me to cherish in later life. I only have a few short months worth. They are not enough. Not nearly enough."

She started to sob, and he put his arm around her feeling some of her emotion for himself. He was not predisposed to such moments, but amidst the trail of bodies surrounding this whole case, Tim's death was a genuine tragedy. He was such a gentleman. He felt one tear trickle down his own cheek.

After a while he stroked Joanne's hair.

"We ought to get you home. Have you any relatives around here?"

She shook her head.

"Look. Best stay away from the house for tonight. Let the boys tidy and gather what they want. I'll arrange for a hotel for the night. I can pop and see you for breakfast if you like, and have a WPC stay over."

She nodded. Not that she could or would sleep, but she couldn't return to the house that night, and that was a fact. She allowed Sheridan to make the necessary arrangements.

Nick showed his new pass at the gate of the camp, and after a short telephone call, the sentries allowed him through. He drove around the compound, past the mess hall to where the majors quarters were. He rang the bell and the major himself showed him in.

"Not followed were you?"

"No. No chance."

Nick looked around the apartment, half expecting to see Felton, but they were alone. The major was talking to him.

"How did they find you at the house? A tail?"

"No. They must have had the house covered. I was only inside less than five minutes when the shooting started. They took me unawares- a rare feat I can tell you."

"Important they didn't get you, though. You said you thought you heard sirens?"

"Yes. Pretty sure about that. The police were very quickly on the scene."

Cropwell frowned.

"I don't understand why, mind you it would make life interesting for them. Was it Butler?"
"Couldn't say. I just concentrated on escape."

"You were very lucky sergeant. Do you think they let you go?"

Nick cocked his head to one side, then shook it slowly.

"No. They were too over-confident. Believed that the element of surprise and numbers was enough. I suppose, because of the illegality of their exercise, they didn't have the time and organisation, which a police operation would have enlisted. They'd have blocked off the surrounding roads, had searchlights and helicopters. Done properly I'd have never escaped."

The Major paced the floor. He had had some thinking time since Nick's phone call, and had considered his own position. If he had guessed correctly, then he surmised that Gordon and Andrews had decided to use Cropwell's plan for their own means, using Butler as their instrument.

Trouble was, they didn't have Cropwell's contacts, his intelligence, nor his forethought. At the moment the latter was failing him. He wondered what the repercussions would be from the Linden Grove incident. He was still unsure. On the one hand it could serve to scupper Butler certainly, and possibly Gordon. The trouble was, he couldn't be sure whether he would be in the clear. The fact that the police had been on the scene so quickly concerned him and his position most. It was a possibility that they were also trying to home in on Nick. He shook his head.

Certainly there would be no open move against Cropwell himself, Nick was a different matter. But the two were inextricably linked. Well since Marcellus.

It was three a.m. when the telephone rang. It disturbed Nick who was asleep in the majors' office on a bunk bed. He waited at the majors' door, but could hear no news, but then the call was short. The major put on his dressing gown and opened the door and saw Nick.

"Ah, sergeant. I should get dressed. We have guests on the way.

About five minutes. OK?"

"Who is it?"

"Don't worry. Friends, with information for us"

They both dressed and a few minutes later the bell rang and Cropwell allowed four men in, all uniformed. Nick was a little apprehensive but the major showed him the settee, and they sat down. He turned to Nick.

"I need your gun, Nick. Sorry, but we must yield to these men here. Don't worry, you'll be quite safe, I have their word."

Nick tensed and wondered what to do. He summed up the position quickly. If he pulled his gun, he could maybe take two out, but would soon be overpowered. He considered taking the major as a hostage, but relented. He would have to go along with Cropwell's suggestion. He pulled out his gun, saw the tenseness in the other men's faces and smiled to himself. He dropped the clip from the weapon and handed it, handle first to the major.

"Thank you. Now, I'm sorry, but your reputation precedes you. You must wear these bracelets I'm afraid. Sorry old boy."

Nick allowed the handcuffs to be placed around his wrists and shook his head. Was he being betrayed by Cropwell? Although he had been handed over to his new captors, he still didn't feel like it. The major said he was doing it for his, for both their protection, and he had little choice other than to believe him. He was not happy.

The major stood.

"Now, sergeant. I must entrust your safe keeping to these gentlemen. I have a journey to make and a meeting to attend. I shall see you tomorrow. Do not worry I will return. Do you trust me?"

"It seems I have little choice."

The next morning saw a lot of coming and going at the Curzon Street police station. The Chief Constable had taken over and saw a succession of army personnel, grey suits and media. He was late for his appointment with Sheridan, and around three he called him into Wrights office, which he now commandeered. In the room were three other men, one the army Colonel whom Sheridan had seen the previous night and two other men wearing suits. He was not introduced by name, but the chief smiled warmly at Sheridan and indicated for him to sit.

"If you'll just wait a moment, only there is one more person coming."

The wait was brief, and the door opened to allow in the dark green uniformed figure of an army major, six feet in height, greying black hair and pencil moustache. He nodded toward the colonel and the other men and sat down without speaking. Sheridan guessed it was Cropwell. The Chief cleared his throat and began.

"Now, I thought it appropriate to gather us all together to sort out this business once and for all. I need not say it, but I will. Everything which is said in this room is highly confidential. It is a time for reckoning and for making decisions. Too many people have, from what I've seen and heard, been doing their own thing for far too long. It must all be pulled together. I have the authority from Downing Street to see to it.

Now. First a time for stories. Colonel?"

Colonel Mitchell, white haired, immaculate and clearly spoken nodded and began.

"We seem to have a bit of a hornets nest here, particularly regarding the man Curcic. The understanding of the operation is complex, but also involves Cropwell here, and Colonel Butler."

He glanced to the other two silent men.

"The politics will be taken care of?"

The dark haired one of the two nodded.

"Good. Well it appears that Butler and his men are a clandestine unit set up to 'enforce' certain political beliefs and influence decision making by a series of appropriately timed killings. You know, take out the leader and the followers cave in. That is the reasoning. The trouble is, the ethics of gangland have no place here, in a modern society. Besides which..."

Cropwell interrupted.

"... besides which Butler is like a bull in a china shop. I'll tell you about him. I'll tell you the whole story. The ethics of the gangland you called it? Not quite Colonel, not quite. We're both professional career soldiers, and have seen enough death to last several lifetimes. But we've been lucky. Before us, millions were killed in world wars. Millions of men called up to fight for king and country. It's hard enough for professionals like ourselves to be killed, but when innocent men are slaughtered wholesale, well it is a position to which we must never return.

Trouble is. We need peace. We need to control our enemies, to stop them becoming too powerful and threatening, but without spilling the blood of our countrymen. The answer is in, what you call the ethics of the gangland. You summed it up neatly, Colonel, but I would add more. In order to preserve the peace, which we all crave, someone has to man the watchtower. Someone has to be on permanent guard. That task is one I have dedicated myself to. I do not seek justification for my actions, just the security of the knowledge that by a selective cull of enemies, by a careful weeding out of thorny unwanted growths, that I have sacrificed a few lives to save the many. It is a point, which may cause great debate.

Suffice it to say that I have had the debate many, many times with myself over the years, but it is one, which I feel quite conscience free about. I only wish that the philosophy was more widely accepted, but I also appreciate that it must. Repeat must be kept under very firm control. It is this lack of control that brings us all here today.

The philosophy has been usurped. Used for political self-advancement, and thus brought into disrepute. In its' purest form, the philosophy works. The philosophy which I practised until five years ago."

Sheridan looked at the man.

"You mean you went abroad and killed, or had killed our enemies?

Is that where Curcic fits in?"

Cropwell nodded.

"Indeed. I had three men only who I used. Three quite brilliant individuals in their own field. You see, you need a specific type of man for this job. That is where Butler went totally wrong. He recruited top class soldiers. All excellent fighting men, men with whom I personally would be very very glad to serve with- in the field. The type needed for my type of work were different. They needed a certain detachment. Definitely not team men. Needed to be totally self sufficient, and independently motivated. Let me tell you about Curcic, Inspector. He is the best I ever worked with.

His skills are prodigious- but you have seen that for yourself last evening."

"He was also prodigious as you say, in Priory Close and Nottingham wasn't he?"

The major nodded.

"Again, Butler sent in the army, against a guerrilla. Bungling and inappropriate. The thing about Curcic is his independence and motivation, which set him head and shoulders above the rest.

You see he is a dying man. He has an incurable, hereditary condition, which limits his life. I guess he has no more than five years left to live. In a way, that is the key to his success. On the one hand, his impending doom gives him a kind of recklessness, and on the other, the limited time he has available means that time is precious to him. The result? A complex, and highly efficient man who can kill efficiently and with total detachment. In the right hands, a totally invaluable weapon."

Sheridan was shaking his head.

"Tell that to Mrs Theobald."

The Major looked at him and shrugged slightly.

"Mr Theobald was murdered by your beloved Curcic fleeing from capture following the Priory Close shoot-out. What was he? A casualty of some so-called war? Not good enough."

"No it isn't. The one thing I can say about that, and I'm not defending the man, is that it followed Butler's heavy-handed approach. I organised Nicks' fake death to defuse the situation. Otherwise there would be a trail of bodies up and down the country. When cornered, my man finds a way. A way which you find unpalatable Inspector, but a way nonetheless. Anyway, my point is this. Curcic is a machine. A tool perfectly honed to do a specific job. It is he who is now hunted. Butler, the Colonel now have tried. That is good. Let them do what they are best at- old fashioned cavalry charge and all that. Leave the thinking to others. As for Andrews and Gordon? Well in a way I am the guilty party.

Following Marcellus my unit was disbanded, and in the intervening few years, I saw my previous painstaking web of influence start to fall apart. I stayed it for as long as possible by influencing certain events by timely intervention, but without the military network, it was beginning to fail. I managed to enlist Gordon and Andrews, to reinstate my programme by giving them what they wanted- power. I managed, via Curcic, to ensure that Andrews succeeded to the ministry, then, well you know the rest. Tried to set it up for themselves for their own purposes."

The grey suits looked at one another and the Chief Constable looked in their direction.

"Take it from us sir. They will be out of power within hours.

Official announcements may take a little longer."

Sheridan shook his head.

"This needs a court case. Make a show of it. Justice being seen to be done and all that."

Cropwell smiled and the Colonel spoke up.

"Sorry, inspector can't be done. You see a court case would ruin the country- politically."

"Why?"

Mitchell looked at the grey suits who nodded their assent.

"Well it's all due to the so-called 'Marcellus' case."

"Marcellus? I heard you mention him before. What, or who is that exactly?"

Mitchell stood up, then sat down again.

"Only nine people know the truth. You will be the tenth. The Chief here thought it important for you to know, rather than let your laudable zeal for justice ruin us all. Major?"

Cropwell nodded.

"Do you remember about six years ago, during the Yugoslav civil war, the fuss regarding the Presidents son."

Sheridan screwed his eyes up, and nodded slowly.

"If we go back a couple of years before that, there was the real problem in the states when Tom Kitchens youngest boy insisted on field work. He was damn good. Became one of my operatives. Kitchen was unimpressed that he was working for a Brit unit and there was a lot of friction then between the two governments. Mark was strong willed and he wouldn't give up his chosen career which the president ultimately had to accept."

"Wasn't he killed in a helicopter crash?"

"So the story goes. In actuality his helicopter crashed behind enemy lines. An umpteenth secret mission. He had talent. Curic's talents.

His crew were killed and he was the only survivor. He was captured and interrogated, but they didn't know his true identity. Imagine the immense political bargaining chip they would have if they knew they had the son of the President of the United States in their possession? Trouble was, one of his captors suspected it. There was no way we could get him out and so.."

"..so you killed him. Curcic killed him."

Cropwell nodded.

"Trouble is, to this day, all the world thinks he died in a helicopter crash. The President thinks he died in a helicopter crash."

"So if they knew that we had had him killed, then we would be in very deep shit wouldn't we?"

"Indeed. You see now the grave importance of it all."

Grey suit one spoke.

"Marcellus- the code given to him- must remain a total and complete secret."

"What about Curcic. Does he know?"

Cropwell shook his head.

"All he knew was that he was an undercover agent with top secret information which must remain hidden."

"So what do we do with Curcic- should we ever find him?"

The Chief spoke.

"We have him, or rather the Major here has him. That is one question which needs an answer. The others need sworn agreement too. This is what I suggest.

First, another shooting incident so close to the Priory Close one has already proved to be irresistible to the media- hardly a surprise- and so I think it only proper that we give them a large slice of the truth."

"The truth?" Grey suit one was red.

"Yes, the truth. The most important thing in all this is for Marcellus to stay hidden. To that end, we sacrifice Andrews, Gordon and Butler, all power crazed who believe they could control things by murder squads. They know nothing regarding Marcellus and can go to court for justice."

"How does that explain away Curcic?"

"Counter espionage agent acting undercover to thwart their plans.

He knew too much, they tried to get him, but failed- twice."

"But what exactly happens to Curcic? I am still very disturbed about Theobald, and now Tim Oakes is dead. What happens to Curcic?"

The colonel spoke next.

" He goes. Exiled back to Bosnia, to his family, initially and officially at least. He's got only a few years left, anyway. His loyalty to Cropwell will endure. The major will see to that, and of course Cropwell here fades away into early retirement. Despite his best motives, I'm afraid it is a policy which must be sacrificed. Sorry Major."

Cropwell smiled. "I knew what was coming. Suppose fishing is my future now."

Sheridan nodded slowly. He was still a little troubled but knew the score. Close down all 'killing' operations, that was good. Curcic exiled, he would have preferred a court case, but had to be practical about it. The stakes were so high. He nodded.

"What about those involved with Curcic? Tim Oakes and company.

They may know something."

The Chief spoke. "The court case with Butler and the story about undercover agent should clear it. Tell them- in confidence- he is to be exiled. I'll let you sort out the exact form inspector. Anything else? Anyone?"

They all individually nodded and the Chief closed the meeting.

"Thank you gentlemen. There will be a press conference in one

hour. Colonel? Gentlemen. Major. Thank you."

CHAPTER 30

'Hitting home.'

The Inspector was subdued for the rest of the day. The whole mess had been cleared up and his private suspicions vindicated, yet he still felt ill at ease. No doubt it revolved around Tim, and his sad end. He had arranged to visit Joanne at home later that day. When he arrived it seemed appropriate that those closest to the mystery were all assembled there.

Joanne and Nancy were both there, locked in mutual grief, but for different reasons. Joanne had lost her true love, Nancy felt she had caused it, and despite her wishing Tim out of her life, this was the worse possible way for her. In a way it was his revenge. She had the money and the guilt, it was an unhappy price to pay. Anthony had driven up and consoled his mother, and a distraught looking John Field sat staring into empty space. The shallowness of his life revealed to him in its' full glory. Sheridan sat down and told them the story.

"We have Curcic at last. I know you knew him, but he was, after all a killer. He is being deported under diplomatic immunity. I'm afraid it is not entirely to my satisfaction, but.."

"It wasn't Nicks' fault. Those others killed Tim."

"I know. But there were others. Anyway, I understand that Curcic is writing to you. It was his very specific request. Those who raided last night are in custody and will be tried in due course."

"What about Andrews?" Joanne's face was red and she looked exhausted.

Sheridan raised his eyebrows. She evidently knew more than he suspected.

"What do you know about him?"

"Only that we reckoned that was why Nick was being so tirelessly hunted. We knew he was a hit man you know."

Anthony and Nancy shot her a bewildered glance. Nancy felt dizzy.

Joanne continued.

"We knew about him, worked out that he had caused Andrews to get his political office. Couldn't halt it mind."

Sheridan nodded. "Yes, you were right. He and his agent, Gordon, along with Butler were all implicated."

Richard and Sally were now feeling decidedly uncomfortable.

"They will all be brought to book. No doubt the whole sordid mess will be revealed in court. Have no fear about that. That is it really, save for me to offer my condolences to you all."

He walked away from Joanne's house, left her life in pieces, but she was young enough and still had time to find new happiness, but not for a while. Anthony? Well he would never forget, but would survive. Fieldy would slide back into his own personal pool of murk and alcohol, it would make little difference to him- or would it? As for Nancy, and Richard and Sally, they would get what they deserved. A year of mental torment never quite knowing whether they would be exposed in court would fray their tempers and gnaw at their nerves. After that? Well guilt would trouble them for ever, but Sheridan didn't know that, nor ever would. As for George Sheridan, he was forever a changed man. His instinct hadn't failed him, and yet the huge wheels of international wheeling and dealing were an anathema to him. It was wrong, there was no natural justice there, all covering up, secret deals and legalised killing, it was all wrong. Funny thing was he could see Cropwell's point.

Funny thing was he could admire Curcic's skill. He loathed the end product. Despised the pain inflicted on the likes of the Theobald's, and Timothy Oakes.

The army transporter slowly climbed into the evening sky, and Nicolai Curcic looked down at the grey countryside below them. There were so many things he had wanted to do. So many things he wanted to say, and started already to miss the promise of normality which his friendship with Tim. But that was gone now. All he had left was his motivation which had served him so long. Pay back time beckoned for those in his history. It seemed so trivial now, but was all he had left.

A friendship lost hurt him more than any nerve degeneration. He felt in his inside pocket at the long letter he had written to Joanne. It said everything. It exposed the core of his soul, for once revealed weakness within him. He smiled, and put the letter back.

Old habits died hard with him.

THE END

HITTING HOME

by

ROBERT WILKINSON

Made in the USA
Charleston, SC
26 July 2015